ABEL

―――――

A SABINE VALLEY NOVEL

KATEE ROBERT

TRINKETS AND TALES

ALSO BY KATEE ROBERT

Sabine Valley

Abel

Broderick

Wicked Villains

Book 1: Desperate Measures

Book 2: Learn My Lesson

Book 3: A Worthy Opponent

Book 4: The Beast

Book 5: The Sea Witch

Book 6: Queen Takes Rose

A Touch of Taboo

Book 1: Your Dad Will Do

Book 2: Gifting Me To His Best Friend

The Island of Ys

Book 1: His Forbidden Desire

Book 2: Her Rival's Touch

Book 3: His Tormented Heart

Book 4: Her Vengeful Embrace

The Thalanian Dynasty Series (MMF)

Book 1: Theirs for the Night

Book 2: Forever Theirs

Book 3: Theirs Ever After

The Kings Series
Book 1: The Last King

Book 2: The Fearless King

The Hidden Sins Series
Book 1: The Devil's Daughter

Book 2: The Hunting Grounds

Book 3: The Surviving Girls

The Make Me Series
Book 1: Make Me Want

Book 2: Make Me Crave

Book 3: Make Me Yours

Book 4: Make Me Need

The O'Malley Series
Book 1: The Marriage Contract

Book 2: The Wedding Pact

Book 3: An Indecent Proposal

Book 4: Forbidden Promises

Book 5: Undercover Attraction

Book 6: The Bastard's Bargain

The Hot in Hollywood Series
Book 1: Ties that Bind

Book 2: Animal Attraction

The Foolproof Love Series

Book 1: A Foolproof Love

Book 2: Fool Me Once

Book 3: A Fool for You

Out of Uniform Series

Book 1: In Bed with Mr. Wrong

Book 1.5: His to Keep

Book 2: Falling for His Best Friend

Book 3: His Lover to Protect

Book 3.5: His to Take

Serve Series

Book 1: Mistaken by Fate

Book 2: Betting on Fate

Book 3: Protecting Fate

Come Undone Series

Book 1: Wrong Bed, Right Guy

Book 2: Chasing Mrs. Right

Book 3: Two Wrongs, One Right

Book 3.5: Seducing Mr. Right

Other Books

Seducing the Bridesmaid

Meeting His Match

Prom Queen

To Sierra Simone

1

ABEL

We time our arrival perfectly. The feast is more than halfway over. The early fights—the ones people froth at the mouth for—have come and gone. By the low sound of voices in conversation, people have begun to eat and enjoy themselves, relishing the fact that it's one of the few nights a year when Sabine Valley's three factions can mingle without repercussions.

We're about to ruin their night.

We're about to ruin their whole fucking life.

I glance back at my brothers. They have their emotions locked down tightly. This *will* go our way, but it's impossible to ignore the fact that last time we were in Sabine Valley, we were running for our lives. Eight years later, and it's time to settle the score. "You with me?"

One by one, they nod.

"As soon as the ceremony is over, we retreat to the warehouse. The handfasting has to be consummated tonight, but don't force them or do anything that will jeopardize the next year." I don't expect it to be an issue—even my brothers and I have lines—but it still needs to be said. "Got it?"

Another round of nods.

I turn without another word and lead them across the rooftops to the edge of the grounds. From this vantage point, I can see everything. The deep curve of the natural amphitheater marking the middle of the island in the center of the city. The three factions have mingled a little, but the lines are still remarkably clear. Each of the leaders has a dais at the edge of the amphitheater, creating three points of a large triangle.

In the center of the amphitheater, two fighters are in the middle of combat. From the look of them, they're an Amazon and a Mystic. The Amazon is a Latina who's a good six inches taller and moves with the deadly efficiency her faction is known for. The Mystic is a thin, Black man with flowing robes who looks like a stiff wind will blow him over.

"Mystic will take it," Cohen murmurs at my side.

"When they're finished, we go in. Don't let anyone stop you." As long as we can get down there and issue an official challenge, there's not a damn thing any of the factions can do except meet it. The laws of the feast days are there for a reason. To ignore them is to invite ruin. That shit *should* have been enough to keep peace, but the rules didn't help my father when these fuckers slit his throat, they didn't help our people who burned alive in the house they should have been safe in, and they sure as hell didn't help me and my brothers when we were forced to flee for our lives.

Now I'm going to make them choke on their goddamned laws.

As we watch, the Mystic catches the Amazon's punch in his robe, twisting the fabric to trap her. He delivers a brutal jab to her throat and bears her to the ground, punching her in the face once, twice, a third time. Her hand slaps the ground twice. Just like that, the fight is over.

The Herald steps forward. She's an ancient Korean woman with her long, white hair pulled back in a high knot at the top of her head. "Gerald wins. The Amazons will allot him the agreed amount."

A cheer goes up from the wedge of the amphitheater that's mostly Mystics. They're easy to pick out because they dress like they just stepped out of a fantasy novel. Robes in a variety of colors; hair designed in towering spirals and peaks and stuffed with trinkets and ribbons. They're also smart as hell and like to use others' perceptions of them to their advantage. They're not as strong and fierce as the Amazons, not as brutal as the Raider faction, but there's a reason they've held their wedge of the city since its inception. They are not to be underestimated.

"Now," I murmur.

One by one, we drop off the low roof to the street. I pause long enough to ensure all seven of us are on the ground and then lead the way through the crowd. It doesn't take long for people to start noticing us. Seven men in dark clothing with murder in their eyes. Even if they don't recognize who we are, they begin to part, pushing each other to make way for us.

We reach the lip of the amphitheater and start down the stairs. One of the Herald's guards moves to stop us from entering the sand, but she holds up a hand, and he shifts back. This woman has been Herald since I was a child, a neutral party that oversees all the feasts and calls no faction home. She surveys me and finally nods. "Have you come to challenge?"

It's obvious to everyone present that it's exactly why I'm here, but Sabine Valley is nothing without its ridiculous rituals. I can't ignore them if I want this to work. "Yes, Herald."

Her dark eyes flick over my face and those of my brothers' behind me. "What grievance have you brought to us, Abel Paine?"

"My brothers and I were wronged by the leaders of the factions present." The space naturally amplifies my voice, but even if it didn't, everyone would hear me. They've all gone silent. "Seven fights for the seven lives they've ruined."

She studies me for a long moment. The Herald has never stopped someone from engaging in ritual combat during Lammas, but she still has the authority to do it. "Who will be fighting?"

"I will."

"You'll stand in proxy for your brothers?"

"Yes, Herald." Things aren't traditionally done this way, but that's going to work in my favor tonight. Those fools will look at me and think that there's no way I can possibly win seven fights. They'll happily wager the things they can least afford to lose on that assumption. And then I'm going to shove their failure down their throats and make them choke on it.

The Herald tilts her head to the side. "And the stakes?"

"For every fight I win, one of my brothers chooses a Bride as restitution."

Her eyes widen ever so slightly. "A high price."

"So was exile."

At that, she nods and turns slowly to meet each of the faction leaders' gazes in turn. I've avoided looking at them until now, but I can't avoid it any longer. First up is Aisling, queen of the Amazons. She's a fierce bitch and looks every inch of it—a lean white woman with hard, green eyes and pale blond hair braided back from her face. I once watched her gut a man and walk away without so much as a hitch in her stride.

She sent her warriors to set my childhood home on fire the night my father died.

Now to Ciar, the Mystic's leader. He's a grizzled white man with a cloud of gray hair who looks like someone boiled him down, papery skin stretched tight over muscles and tendons. He likes to pretend the gods speak through him and uses it to rule his people with an iron fist. He's also got thirteen wives at last count and dozens of children.

It was his order that provided the drugs that sent our household to sleep, killing dozens in the fire.

And finally the person I've both dreaded and craved seeing. I stand there and stare up at the man who was once my friend. Eli Walsh. He's filled out since I saw him last, a white guy with long-ish blond hair swept to the side and black frame glasses. He always was too attractive, and now he looks fucking flawless. Someone who didn't know better would assume he's as useless as he's pretty, and he likes to play up those perceptions. In truth, he's nearly as deadly as I am.

His father slit my father's throat and would have killed every single one of my brothers if I didn't take them and run for our lives.

All while Eli stood by and did nothing.

He's taken our future, our territory, *everything.*

The Herald raises her hands. "The stakes are fair. Send your warriors."

I turn to my brothers. Six faces that I know as well as my own, and none of them look happy. They've locked their shit down, and they trust me to take care of this. I pull my shirt over my head and toss it to Broderick. "Wait on the stairs." If something goes wrong, he'll get the rest of them out.

He shakes his head, a small smile pulling at his mouth. "Never could resist a chance to take off your shirt."

"They want a show. I'm going to give it to them."

"Uh-huh." He nudges Gabriel, our youngest brother, with his shoulder. "Let's give him room to work." He gives me a long look. "Don't die."

"Please. As if these assholes could kill me." Technically, fights on Lammas *can* go to the death without repercussions, but that's not on the agenda tonight. If I slaughter my way through seven of their best people, it will turn the city against me. We're back, and we're here to stay, which means playing this clean. Even if it's only obeying the spirit of the feast, rather than the explicit rules.

The faction leaders spend ten minutes communicating, and then seven people move out onto the sand. I study them the same way they're studying me. Three women—all Amazons—and four men. Two of Eli's people. Two Mystics. I only recognize two of them. This should be interesting.

The first steps forward. It's one of Eli's people, a Latino man built like a prize fighter. He's light on his feet as he approaches me. I roll my shoulders and take a slow breath.

Eight years of exile. Eight years of fighting and scraping and clawing for survival in a world that wants nothing more than to eliminate me and my brothers.

It ends tonight.

The Herald lifts her hand. "Begin."

My opponent rushes me. He's even faster than I expected, and he moves like he knows what he's doing. I hold perfectly still as he closes the distance between us. He takes that as my being unprepared and strikes with an uppercut that would take off my head if it landed.

I shift back just enough that he misses. He sank too much into that punch, and it leaves him wide open. I hammer a brutal punch into his ribs. Something cracks beneath my fist, and he stumbles. I don't give him time to recover. I kick his knee, dislocating it, and then punch him in the face.

He hits the ground and doesn't get up.

One of the Herald's people comes over and crouches next to him. She presses two fingers to his neck. "He's alive."

The Herald nods. "Abel wins the first match. The prize?"

I glance at Gabriel. My youngest brother is pale and looks vaguely sick, but he steps forward and lifts his chin. "I claim Fallon of the Mystics as my Bride." Ciar's heir.

A murmur goes through the crowd in a wave. I hold my breath as I wait to see what they'll do. Ciar looks like he wants to kill us, but he finally waves a hand, and a gorgeous redhead steps forward. She comes down the stairs quickly, moving with a grace that screams combat training. Her face shows nothing as she crosses to stand next to Gabriel.

One down, six to go.

The factions sent their best. I'm better. I defeat them one by one. I'm not showy, choosing to conserve energy instead of being entertaining. One by one, my brothers claim their Brides. Sons and daughters, siblings, loved ones of the people responsible for our father's death, for our exile.

Until there's only one opponent left.

He's a giant of a man, a huge white guy who has six inches on me and probably outweighs me by fifty pounds. I turn my head and spit blood—the last Amazon got in a couple good hits—and motion. "Let's get this over with."

The crowd doesn't cheer, doesn't speak, doesn't seem to breathe. Guess I am being entertaining, after all.

The giant lumbers toward me. Too slow. This is their final fighter? I almost laugh at the absurdity of it. This time, I don't wait for him to reach me. I rush forward and hit my knees, driving my fist up into his balls with everything I have. He makes a high-pitched whistling sound and topples, curling in on himself like a dead bug.

I climb to my feet and look down. He's too busy clutching his balls to tap out, but it's clear he's not getting up anytime soon.

The Herald raises her eyebrows. "Abel wins the final match. The prize?"

Here it is. The thing I've been waiting for. I turn and find Eli. He's leaning forward, his elbows propped on his knees. His expression is smooth and free of worry, but that shit doesn't fool me. Eli's always been the best liar I've ever known. He managed to convince me that we were friends, that we'd always have each other's backs. I won't be fooled again.

I give him a bloody grin. *Got you, fucker.* "I choose Harlow Byrne."

Eli's woman.

2

My breath rushes out in a gasp. For the past thirty minutes, we've watched Abel Paine decimate the best Sabine Valley has to offer. And now he's looking at *me* like he wants to devour me whole. My head goes fuzzy, and I start to push to my feet.

Eli grabs my arm without looking over. "No."

I stare at his fingers wrapped around my forearm. "Take your hand off me." There was time when we were always touching, where we couldn't get enough of each other. When I was younger and more foolish and honestly believed that Eli saw *me* rather than the fantasy of the helpless princess he expects me to be. Five years later, and that hope is ash on my tongue. Five years later, and our love has started to feel a whole lot like hate.

"Let me go," I say quietly. We work *so hard* to prevent the rest of the faction from seeing the cracks in our relationship. We have a stable faction, but we both know all too well that both Amazons and Mystics will pounce on any perceived weakness. If they realized that Eli and I are hardly the solid unit we pretend in public, there's a decent chance they'd attempt to use it against the faction somehow. Eli's done as much to them in the past, after all.

Eli's never slipped in public with me, not once. He's slipping right now. There's not a damn thing he can do to change this. He has to let me go, and I have to walk away. Something releases in my chest at the realization.

Finally—*finally*—this is over.

"No," he repeats. He still hasn't looked at me. He's too busy staring down at Abel. A man who used to be his best friend. An enemy that is obviously determined to hurt him. To hurt all of us.

But denying the Herald is unthinkable. Eli agreed, just like the other faction leaders, and neither Aisling nor Ciar balked as their daughters and wives and brothers and sons descended to stand next to the Paine brother who called their name. Eli *can't* keep me.

Being a Bride means cutting off all previous ties, at least for the year of handfasting required. It's an old-fashioned way of creating alliances, of ensuring a year's worth of peace between Bride's people and whoever won them. It's highly ironic that the Paine brothers are using it as a punishment, but I can't deny it's a brilliant move. With one fell swoop, they've ensured they're untouchable for an entire year—and they've all but declared that they won't be moving against the three factions in the process.

I clear my throat. "You gave your word, Eli."

He finally looks at me. I search his handsome face, looking for some sign of the man I fell in love with all those years ago. He gives me nothing. Nothing but the carefree mask he wears at all times. The only indication that he's affected at all is the intensity of his hazel eyes. "No."

He can't just say *no* and make it so.

"Yes," I snarl. "It's over. You lost. Let me go."

Let me go.

Just fucking let me go, *please.*

I don't want to be a Bride, especially to a Paine, especially to Abel Paine. Of course I don't; I remember his father all too well, and the man staring up at me is a carbon copy of that monster. But he won't kill me, won't do anything to permanently damage me, and I can survive anything else for a year. And then? Then I'll be free in truth.

But first Eli has to release me.

The Herald's voice reaches us. "Is there a problem, Eli Walsh?"

If he balks when the rest of the faction leaders didn't, the entirety of Sabine Valley will come down on his head. Our people will pay the price. I look at Eli, but he has a stubborn set to his jaw that I don't like. He's still trying to find a way to protect me, despite the fact that I don't need his protection. *I* will keep my word, even if he is considering breaking his.

Fine.

I'll do it myself.

I jerk my hand from his and start down the stairs. I can feel the eyes of everyone in the amphitheater on me, but none of them burns as hot as Abel Paine. He waits in the center of the sand, shirtless and covered in sweat. His lip is bloodied, and he'll have a constellation of bruises on his body tomorrow, but he's still standing with the casual arrogance he displayed from the moment he appeared.

He's handsome in an ancient warrior kind of way. He's a white guy with short dark hair and a close-cropped beard that seems to highlight his strong jaw, rather than conceal it. Broad shoulders and a thick chest. He's built like a tank. Nothing extra, every inch of him contributing to his power.

He doesn't smile as I cross the sand to stand next to him,

doesn't gloat or grin or talk shit. He simply nods as if this was the expected outcome from the start.

That's scarier than anything he's done so far.

He holds a hand out to me. It's broad and just as bloodied as he is, the evidence of his violence there on his knuckles.

I very much do not want to do this. But living in this place means adhering to its rules, and I'm no oathbreaker. *It's just a year. Twelve short months. It's nothing. Becoming his Bride will protect my people, and that's all that matters, all I've ever wanted.* I take a slow breath and lift my hand.

"Stop."

Eli's voice sounds behind me, too close. I spin to find him on the sand with us. He stalks to us and looks at the Herald. "One more."

She thins her lips. "You're not obeying the letter of the law."

"One more, Herald." He glares at Abel. "If I win, Harlow doesn't become his Bride."

Shock slaps me in the face. If we're the only faction without a Bride linked to the Paine brothers, then it will be open season on our people. What is Eli *doing?* "No."

The Herald considers him and turns to Abel. "This is unprecedented."

"I accept, Herald." He grins, his teeth bloody. "But if I win, Eli becomes my Bride, too, and the Raider faction returns to its rightful leaders—me and my brothers."

Eli doesn't hesitate. "I agree."

I spin to him. "What the hell are you doing? You can't." If Eli loses, that means his territory—*our* territory—becomes Abel's. At least as Brides, those things are separate. He's not simply bargaining for our lives. He's bargaining our people's, too. "Eli, no."

"It's too late." He takes his glasses off and hands them to me. "It's done."

"You fool," I whisper. I never thought he'd go to such lengths to preserve the fantasy that I need protecting. But then, of course he will. Eli insists on seeing that woman instead of the one in front of him. It's why our relationship has devolved to smoking ruins of the love we once had.

He gives me a quick grin. "He's already fought seven people. I can take him." The way he speaks is so relaxed, as if we're about to go out to lunch instead of enter a fight that will decide the future of our faction. It's a lie, just like everything Eli presents the public is a lie.

There was a time when he didn't use it to try to lie to me. Gods, I am so angry, I'm shaking. "If you do this, I'll never forgive you."

He flinches, the tiniest of reactions. "You can hate me later, when I've saved you from this."

I close my eyes and strive to push back the panic and rage coursing through me, strong enough to have me weaving on my feet. "You have to win." There's no other option, not one our people can live with.

"I will."

I open my eyes as he crosses the sand to Abel. The Herald raises her hand. "Begin."

In every fight except the last, Abel has waited for his opponent to make the first move. He's taken them down with a handful of strikes, ending the fights almost as soon as they began. But his opponents always started it.

Not this time.

The word is barely out of the Herald's mouth when he's on Eli. They meet in a spray of sand and the heavy impact of fist meeting flesh. They're nearly the same height, but Abel is built thicker than Eli. For all that, I think Eli might be faster. It's hard to tell when they're moving so quickly.

For a moment, just a moment, I think Eli might have a chance. He's stronger than he appears—deadlier, too. Not just anyone can hold our faction together, and he's done it since his father died five years ago. He intentionally leads people to underestimate him.

He lands a punch that snaps back Abel's head and sends the other man staggering a few steps away. Hope wars with fear, and I press my hands to my chest, trying to school my expression.

But when Eli moves to finish Abel off, the other man grabs his wrist and yanks him forward. They hit the ground with a dull thud that makes my body hurt in sympathy. Then they're off again, first Eli on top, and then Abel, and then Eli again. Fists fly. Blood flows. They beat each other with a brutality that leaves me breathless. This is nothing like the cold efficiency with which Abel took down his other opponents. No, he goes after Eli like he wants him dead.

Stop.

I clamp my lips shut to keep the word inside. No one can stop a fight during Lammas, not once it starts. We must simply stand by and witness.

Abel pulls some move that lands him on top again, and this time, he uses his legs to pin Eli's arms to his sides. He delivers punishing blow after punishing blow, snapping Eli's head to one side and then the other.

Eli goes limp.

I look at the Herald, but she watches Abel beat Eli and doesn't call the fight. Abel shows no signs of slowing down.

He's going to kill Eli.

I don't stop to think. I simply react. The sand gives beneath my feet as I sprint to them. I throw myself at Abel's back and wrap my arms around him. Not fighting. Not hurting. Not doing anything that would make me another opponent to battle. "Stop." I cling to him as his blows slow. "Please stop. You've won."

Finally, a small eternity later, he sits back and exhales roughly. He ignores me clinging to his back and looks at the Herald. She lifts her brows and raises her voice. "Abel wins. Eli will be his Bride alongside Harlow. The Raider faction returns to the Paine brothers."

Around the amphitheater, the crowd begins to seethe and move. Everyone is talking over each other, and it creates a din that makes this situation even more unreal.

Abel reaches up with bloody hands and easily breaks my hold on him. He doesn't hurt me. He simply removes me from his back and rises to his feet. Without looking at me, he motions to the Herald. "We'll hold the ceremony now."

The ceremony.

It's been a long time since anyone has claimed a Bride as a prize during Lammas. It's an old tradition, dating back to the beginning of Sabine Valley. If a Bride is won, they renounce all former personal ties and handfast with the victor for a year and a day. At the end of that, the term is finished, and they can go their separate ways, but for the duration, they might as well be married. Not even marriage to another person is enough to stop the handfasting from happening. Either they annul their marriage or return to it once the handfasting is done, but for that year, the only partner they claim is whoever won them.

I look at the Brides, and my breath catches in my throat. The Paine brothers have chosen well if they want to make a statement. The Amazon heir. The Mystic heir. The Amazon queen's youngest brother, and her daughter. The Mystic leader's newest wife, and his son. Me. And now Eli, and by way of him, our entire faction.

All three factions are well represented, ensuring a forced peace for a year and a day, more than long enough for someone savvy to put down roots and a plan to strike their enemies down once the deadline has passed.

The Herald nods. "Of course."

Abel hauls Eli to his feet and clamps a big hand on the back of his neck. Eli's weaving, and his gorgeous face is a mess. He looks half a second from passing out. I take a step toward him, but Abel plants a hand on my neck, too and turns all three of us to face the Herald.

The ritual passes in a blur. I think I'm in shock. This went from a mundane Lammas festival to a nightmare in less than an hour. The Herald's people move forward in front of each couple and wind their hands with ribbon, reciting words that sound like a buzz in my ears. I stare down at my hands bound to Eli and Abel's, at theirs bound to each other. I was *so close* to something resembling freedom. One small step, one year away.

Now, I'm in even deeper than I was before. Eli won't be able to do anything but fight Abel. It's his nature. They'll be so busy going for each other's throats that neither will consider the people who need protection the most—the members of our faction.

Once the ceremony is finished, Abel turns us and leads our fucked-up little procession out of the amphitheater and through the streets to a trio of trucks waiting for us. He shoves Eli up into the bed of the first one, but when I move to follow, he tightens his grip on the back of my neck. "You're up front with me."

Two of his brothers climb behind the wheels of the other trucks, and the rest of them and their Brides pile into the beds. No one says a single damn word. Are they feeling this same shock that I am? Surely at least Monroe, the Amazon heir, will fight this?

But then, she follows the same laws I do.

Abel opens the driver's door and gives me a light push. "Up."

"If Eli bleeds out—"

"He's made of tougher stuff than that. A little beating isn't enough to kill that bastard." His tone goes even harder. "In the truck, Harlow."

I reluctantly climb up and scoot over to make room for him. It's not enough. Even though Abel isn't a giant by any definition, he fills the limited space until I'm choking on his presence with every inhale. I want nothing more than to curl in on myself, but I won't give him the satisfaction of seeing my fear. Instead, I sit straight and stare out the windshield as he turns on the truck and pulls away from the curb. I don't ask where we're going. It doesn't matter.

We've lost everything.

"You seem like a good girl who follows the rules." He speaks low enough that I have to strain to hear him, an edge of a growl in his voice. "You know what comes next."

It's not a question, but I answer it all the same. "Consummating the handfasting." It's not required under normal circumstances. Handfasting isn't like marriage. There's no annulment or divorce. If the couple wants to part ways before the end of it, there's no harm, no foul.

Brides are different.

Abel takes the west bridge off the island and into our faction's territory. Of course he would come here. It's his now. The thought makes my stomach lurch. He doesn't speak again for several blocks. "You have a problem with that?"

I blink. Is he really asking my permission *now?* "Would it matter if I did?"

"Answer the question."

I want to say that I'll fight him every step of the way, but I've consented to this. I chose to stay in Sabine Valley. I chose to be in a relationship with Eli, knowing that it would mean adhering even more strongly to the laws because I'd be in the public eye. I chose to walk down into the sand to take Abel's hand.

I look out the window. "I'll do my duty."

"Duty." He snorts. "Uh-huh. And what happens when that man of yours starts spitting fire and trying to fall on a sword to protect you from big, bad me?"

I refuse to look at him, refuse to let him see how sick this situation makes me. Eli should have let me go. He didn't have to like it—*I* don't like it—but when you're the ruler of a faction, sometimes sacrifices have to be made. I was willing to take the hit to protect our people. He should have been willing to do the same.

Instead, once again, he's stepped in to protect me from something I don't need protection from.

I take a breath and force myself to turn to Abel. Even bruised and covered in blood, he's a handsome fucker. Powerful and entrancing, he's got the kind of charisma that makes people sit up and take notice even before he opens his mouth. "I will do my part because I gave my word that I would, but I won't play punching bag or let you harm me. If you try, I'll cut your fucking balls off."

He barks out a laugh. "You'll try, sweetheart."

"Even you have to sleep sometime."

He glances at me, new appreciation lighting his dark eyes. "Guess I do. I have no beef with you, Harlow. You just shacked up with the wrong man, and now you're mine for the next year. Play nice, and I'll play nice back. Try to stick a knife in my back, and I'll cut off your pretty head." He delivers the threat mildly, so mildly that it takes me a moment to register the words.

He's a Paine. He's not bluffing.

3

ELI

I fucked up.

I've spent my entire life learning to control my emotions, to never let them get the best of me, and I threw it away when I could least afford to. Abel brings us to some kind of warehouse. It's got a large room with plenty of space for the trucks and then some, and each wall is lined with four doors. Nothing fancy, but then, they can't have been here long. I have people reporting to me throughout the entire faction, and surely someone would have noticed the Paine brothers returning if they'd been here a while. But then, Abel's managed to acquire a fucking warehouse without me noticing, so I can take nothing for granted.

I am a fucking fool.

I never saw this coming.

I watch the Paine brothers and their Brides climb out of the truck beds. They gather around Abel, and rage makes my vision bleed red at the sight of him holding Harlow by the arm. She doesn't look too freaked out, but she's got one hell of a poker face. She's got to be terrified.

Abel looks at each of his brothers in turn. "Consummate the handfasting tonight. No exceptions. Get it done."

Abel hauls Harlow to stand before the bed of the truck and levels a hard look at me. "Get the fuck up."

My body grumbles in protest as I leverage myself to my feet. My face is one big, throbbing ache. I'm going to have a black eye by the end of the night. At least he didn't break my ribs or do any lasting damage. I suspect that was on purpose, and I hate that he had the control to hold back when I was in a frenzy. Even when I was lost in rage, Abel was delivering punches with pristine focus. Goddamn it.

My vision goes a little blurry when my feet hit the ground, but I stay standing through sheer stubbornness. "You got what you want. Let her go."

"Nah, I won Harlow twice over. I'm going to enjoy the fuck out of her." He leans in, dark eyes mean. "I can't wait to taste her pussy and have her come all over my cock."

I shoot forward, but Abel's ready for me. He grabs my throat and drags me the rest of the way to him until our noses are nearly touching. "I'll tell you what I told her; play nice, and I won't fuck her up."

At our side, Harlow jerks. "That's not what you told me."

"Yeah, well, the principle is the same. Play nice, Eli, or I'm going to take my anger out on this pretty little woman of yours." His grin is just shy of gruesome. "Hell, she's not nearly as sweet as her reputation says. She might even like it."

"You piece of shit."

"Call me karma." He turns and drags us in the opposite direction that his brothers went. I catch sight of half a dozen trucks and cars before we reach a nondescript gray door. Abel gives Harlow a little shove. "Open it."

"Stop manhandling me, asshole." She sounds more

angry than scared, but I don't trust it. I knew when I fell in love with her that having her at my side was the most selfish thing I could do. Being with me puts her in the kind of danger I promised I'd never let touch her again. Still, I rationalized that I could keep her safe from the worst of it.

Joke's on me.

The door leads to a white hallway and a trio of doors identical to the first. Abel points to the one on the far left. "In there."

Harlow stalks to the door and pushes it open. Inside is a bedroom. Brushed concrete floor. Plain white walls. King-sized bed. An open door that shows a small bathroom. That's it.

I stare at the bed. "Abel, you're not a rapist. Leave her out of this."

He laughs. The bastard fucking *laughs*. "I'm going to take a shower. You have five minutes to figure your shit out." He stalks into the bathroom and shuts the door. A few seconds later, a shower starts.

I stagger to Harlow and take her hands. "You have to run."

She stares up at me as if she's never seen me before. We've been together five years, but she looks nearly the same as she did the first time I saw her across the street seven years ago. Pale skin, large, dark eyes, a body that just won't quit. She's taken to dyeing her hair a light red color that's darker at the roots, and it just works for her. I've seen her laughing, crying, angry enough to commit murder.

I've never seen her look at me with disgust.

She yanks her hands out of mine. "You might be an oathbreaker, but I'm not."

Her words sting. How could they not? "I'll find a way out of this."

"Eli, *stop*." She drags her hands through her hair. "It's over. You lost. There is no getting around this or finding some clever loophole or whatever it is that you're trying to come up with in that impressive brain of yours. We *lost*. We are handfasted to Abel Paine. It would have been bad enough if it was just me, but you couldn't leave well enough alone, could you? You had to offer the entire faction up to him on a silver platter."

I stare. "That's not what I did."

"That's exactly what you did. Or did you not hear the prize for winner over the sound of your own ego rushing in your ears?" She sounds so angry, angrier than I've ever heard her. "You fucked up, Eli. You've been fucking up. There is no coming back from this. We're under Paine's control now, and the only thing to do is make the best of it."

"I can't accept that." There has to be a way. I just need to calm down and *think*—something nearly impossible with the way pain bellows through my body with each breath. The stiffness hasn't set in yet, but it will before too long, and then it'll be a small miracle if I can move at all.

Harlow turns away from me. "You don't have a choice."

I don't know why she's pissed at *me*. "All I did was try to protect you."

"At the expense of the people who really need your protection." She still doesn't look at me. "Just...stop. Eli, just stop, okay? Abel isn't bluffing. If you try to double-cross him, he'll make you pay."

By using her.

I slump down into the chair next to the bed. She's right. I've fucked this all up. It doesn't change the reason for my actions. "I've only ever wanted to keep you safe."

"I know." She sounds like it makes her sad.

I've never wanted to make Harlow sad. I only want the

best for her, to keep her as protected as a person can be when they live in Sabine Valley. She's the most important person in my life, and I've failed her. "I'm sorry."

In the bathroom, the shower shuts off. I stare at the door. If I kill Abel—

"Don't. Whatever you're thinking, don't. Even if you somehow incapacitate him, there are six Paine brothers outside this door. They will kill you, Eli. Even if he doesn't, they will." Her breath hitches. "Please stop fighting this. Please just *think* for a minute. You're going to make everything worse."

Just like I did in the amphitheater.

But I couldn't sit there and watch him take my woman. I barely have any memory of following her down the stairs, of challenging him to another fight. The fight itself? Every single missed opportunity is tattooed across my mind. Even with all my training, I was no match for Abel.

I never was, even when we were kids.

I drag my hand over my face and wince when the move reopens a cut on my cheek. I'm a fucking mess. "I won't make things worse for you tonight," I say softly. The knowledge of what comes next clogs my throat and has rage creating an inferno inside me.

The door opens, and Abel appears, a towel wrapped around his waist. He looks... Fuck, he looks good. I hate that he looks good. Now that the blood is cleaned away, I can see the scattering of new scars across his torso, the sign of a life roughly lived.

Where's he been for the last eight years?

My father's men chased the Paine brothers for years after their father's death. I know for a fact that the search continued until my father's death five years ago. They never found a trace of anything. It was as if Abel and his brothers disappeared into thin air.

Abel never was one to let a blow go unanswered, and my family dealt him several on that bloody night eight years ago.

He looks at me now, and there's nothing of the man I used to know. Abel always was harder than his brothers, as befitting the heir to the Raider faction, but he was never cold. Now, it feels like the room temperature drops twenty degrees as he walks in.

He looks like his father. More, he *feels* like his father.

That scares the shit out of me. Bauer Paine was one of the most monstrous people I've ever come across, and the one thing Abel never wanted was to become his father. That the events of that night put him on this path...

I can't afford to feel guilty. I can only deal with the situation at present.

He gives me a long look. "You have two choices, Eli."

As much as I want to wring his neck, I can't help drawing on my public persona. It's a stress response, but it's served me well throughout my life. People underestimate me constantly. Abel won't, but that doesn't matter. Lifelong habits are impossible to break. I laugh. "Let me guess; an easy way and a hard way."

"You got it." Abel doesn't miss a beat, doesn't blink. "You can be a good boy and go take a shower so you don't get blood on the sheets, or you can choose the hard way."

Go take a shower and leave Harlow alone with Abel? Out of the question. "Fuck off."

Abel arches his dark brows. "Figured you'd say that." He nods at Harlow. "Bedside table, top drawer."

For a second, it looks like she'll argue, but she finally

nods and obeys. A few seconds later, she turns around with handcuffs dangling from her finger. "Kinky."

"You have no idea, sweetheart." He motions to me. "Cuff him to the chair. Do a good job of it, or I'm going to have to hurt him. Again."

Harlow thins her lips but doesn't argue. She moves behind the chair I'm sitting on and slaps the cuff around one wrist. I feel her lacing it through the back of the chair, keeping me in place, and then she cuffs the other wrist. I yank on it. I can't help myself. The chair is metal. Even if I wasn't one big ball of pain right now, there's no way I could break free. "Fuck you, Abel."

"Don't put this on me. You chose the hard way." Abel gives me a vicious grin. "I was trying to be *civilized*. You're the one breaking your word and putting everyone you care about in danger. I'm merely the natural consequences in action." He turns to Harlow. "You good?"

She glares. "Good is not the word I'd choose."

"Figured as much." He stalks a slow circle around her, devouring her with his gaze. "You're a sexy little thing, aren't you? Bet you can take a beating."

I tense, and the cuffs rattle against the chair. Harlow looks at me a long moment, and there's something in her dark eyes that I've never seen before. She turns away before I can fully comprehend it, but the image lingers in my mind. Realization washes over me.

Rage.

Not just angry. Not just upset. She's fucking *furious* with me.

And Abel knows it.

4

ABEL

I let myself enjoy the shock on Eli's face for several long moments before I turn my attention entirely on Harlow. She's surprised me several times already. From the information we were able to gather on her, she seems to be a fragile thing in need of protection. Or at least that's how Eli treats her. He has a guard on her at all times when she's outside their compound, and she's never once fought in the amphitheater during Lammas—something unheard of in a ruler or partner of a ruler. All the others have, including Eli.

He keeps her in a glass house, and it was my impression that she liked it. That she needed it.

She's blown that assumption out of the water. I didn't expect her to be so practical. I sure as fuck didn't expect her to push back. I thought she'd faint like the princess in a tower the entire city believes her to be.

She's pretty enough to be a princess. Strong features, a solid body that isn't delicate in any way, lips made to wrap around a cock.

All in good time.

She's wearing a cute little sundress thing, which might make me laugh under other circumstances. It's completely impractical. She knew she wouldn't be fighting tonight.

To test her, I reach out and take her shoulder, sliding my thumb beneath the strap of her dress and her skin. She shivers, but she doesn't flinch away from me. Good. No matter what Eli believes of me, I'm not in the business of forcing sexual partners. Not even tonight.

"I'm taking off your dress now."

"No need to draw it out." Before I can react, she reaches up and tugs the straps off her shoulders, knocking my hand out of the way. She works the thin fabric down her full breasts and wide hips and lets it drop to the floor. It leaves her standing before me in only a pair of blue cotton panties.

For a moment, I simply stare. It feels a little like we're playing a game of chicken, just the two of us. If she thinks she can brazen her way through this, she's got another think coming. I take a step back and drink in the sight of her. I'm aware of Eli going stock-still in the chair to the side of us, but my attention is solely on Harlow.

Fuck, she's sexy. Nice tits, soft stomach, a hint of muscle definition in her legs and arms, pert little ass.

She huffs out a breath. "Stop looking, and let's get this over with."

"You got somewhere to be?"

She glares. "I prefer to rip off bandages all at once, rather than taking my time."

That surprises a rough laugh out of me. "You wound me."

"I'm sure you'll survive."

"Mmm." I close the distance between us, stopping just short of pressing against her, and take her chin. "You going to close your eyes and bear it? Do your duty and get this nasty business over with like a good little martyr?"

She arches a perfectly shaped brow, but I can see the way she shakes a little. "I agreed to consummate the hand-fasting. I didn't agree to enjoy it."

Eli curses, but we both ignore him.

I lean in, shifting until my lips nearly brush her ear. "Oh, you're going to enjoy it."

"Unlikely."

Fuck, but I think I like her. She's got some steel in that spine, and it's appealing in a way I didn't expect. I thought I might have to get creative to bring her around, but this is just another battle. I've been fighting my entire fucking life. Harlow doesn't stand a chance of resisting.

I turn my face and press a slow kiss to her neck. My mouth hurts like a motherfucker, but it's irrelevant. I've experienced worse, and I will again. "You're furious, aren't you, sweetheart? You were going to do the right thing, and then he went and tried to make you break your word. Fucker didn't learn his lesson, either. He'd tell you to knee me in the balls and run right now if he wasn't too busy choking on his own tongue out of pure fury."

"Stop it."

I drag my mouth up her neck. Fuck, her skin is soft. "Take it out on me. I can handle it." I take her hips in a light grip. "Just like I bet you can handle anything I give you."

"You are such a bastard," she whispers.

"Not according to my mother." She's been gone fifteen years, taken by cancer. That loss barely stings anymore. Some days I wonder if it wasn't a blessing that she didn't live long enough to see us lose everything. Other days, I suspect Eli's father never would have made the move he did if she were still among the living. She tempered Bauer Paine in a way I never could, and when she died, he lost what little humanity he had remaining.

Dark thoughts. Not the time or place for those.

I lift my head and look down at her. "You want to lie back and think of England? Go for it." I motion to the bed.

For the first time, Harlow looks a little uncertain. But she finally sets her jaw and nods. "Sure." She skims off her panties, and fuck if my mouth doesn't water at the sight of her ass as she walks to the bed and crawls onto it.

I glance at Eli. He looks like a man staring death in the face. Good. "How many times do you think I can make her come before I finish?"

He flinches. "You're such an asshole."

Guilty, but that's never stopped me from taking what I want. It's not my fault he makes it so fucking easy. The Eli I remember used to have his shit together. He wasn't walking around with an open spot in his armor big enough to drive a truck through. Harlow is a pressure point that he can't seem to help reacting to, and I'm going to take great joy in smashing that button over and over again.

I just didn't expect to enjoy the method of vengeance so much.

I stalk to the nightstand and pull out a string of condoms and toss them onto the bed next to where Harlow has positioned herself. She stares. "We only need to do it once."

"Let's keep our options open." I snag her ankle and tow her around so that she's lying perpendicular on the mattress. The better to maximize Eli's view. "Spread your legs."

"For fuck's sake, Abel, just get over here, and fuck me already."

Eli startles hard enough to rattle his cuffs against the chair. "Jesus, Harlow."

She sits up and glares at him. "Don't you dare judge me right now. *You* did this. You agreed to this. You put us in this position. I'm just following through on it. Sit there, and be silent."

I whistle. "You've pissed her off something fierce, Eli." They're really making this easy on me, but that doesn't mean I'll hesitate to twist the knife every chance I get.

"You." She points at me. "Stop talking, and let's get this over with."

"Yeah, no. I'm not operating on your timeline." I lean down and grab her thighs, using the hold to yank her to the edge of the bed as I go to my knees next to it.

She blinks big, dark eyes at me. "What are you doing?"

"Don't worry about what I'm doing. You were planning on just enduring it, right?" I give her a wicked grin. "Just lie back, and suffer." I push her legs wide and run my hands up her thighs. Her expression is uncertain for the first time since she walked down to join me on the sand. Can't have that. I part her pussy with my thumbs and growl. "You look like my favorite kind of dessert, sweetheart."

"Abel—"

I dip down and drag my tongue over her, cutting off her words. Her thighs shake, and she makes a sound suspiciously like a whimper. I keep her spread as I explore her slowly, but my gaze is on her face. She's staring at me like she's not sure if she wants to kick me in the teeth or dig her fingers into my hair and ride my face to orgasm.

I know which I'd prefer.

I flick her clit with the tip of my tongue. "Problem?"

"What are you doing?" she hisses.

"Don't worry about me." I trace her clit again. "Unless this feels too good? Be a damn shame if it's distracting you from your suffering." I pause, my breath ghosting against her clit with every exhale.

Harlow seems at war with herself. She doesn't want to like this, but there's a fierceness in her that can't help but respond to the challenge. I feel it, too. I don't know what the fuck is going on with her and Eli, but it's not as simple as I thought. There's almost an animosity there on her part, and he seems determined not to see it.

She glances at Eli, and her expression goes flat and angry. It's like a flip is switched; gone is the hesitation, the shock. She digs her hands into my hair. "Fine. Fuck, *fine*. If you're going to do this, do it right." She drags me back to her pussy and lifts her hips to meet me.

I hear Eli cursing, and I grin against her heated flesh. In all the scenarios I ran, this didn't number as a possibility. I couldn't have planned this better if I tried. Even if I didn't want her, I'd still use this as leverage to widen the wedge between them. But I do want her, and that changes things.

Tonight, I've taken everything from Eli.

His territory. His people. His fucking woman.

5

A person shouldn't be able to feel so much rage and still keep moving. I am furious at Eli, furious at his insistence on making things worse, on trying to protect me when I don't need his fucking protection. I love him, I've loved him for years, but he's never *seen* me. After tonight, it couldn't be clearer that it will never change. He doesn't listen to me. He doesn't care about what I want, what I need, that I'm more than capable of holding my own and being a full partner. Full responsibility, full capability of protecting our people.

And Abel?

The man currently fucking me with his tongue as if he can't get enough of my taste?

I fucking *hate* that he seems to enjoy it when I snap back. That, after an hour together, he's offering me something Eli never did. That he sees me. I hate that I like it, even if I can't sit back and allow him to harm our faction in his revenge. My only chance to alter whatever his plans are is to submit to this.

I didn't expect to enjoy it, though.

Abel sucks hard on my clit, and my back bows off the mattress. "*Fuck.*" He does it again, this time wedging two blunt fingers into my pussy. It takes the bastard fifteen seconds to find my G-spot, and then he begins stroking it lightly as he plays with my clit.

He's going to make me come.

I stare blindly at the ceiling as my body coils tighter and tighter. I'm doing my duty. Yes, that's all it is. But as I turn my head and look at Eli, see the furious, tormented look on his face as he watches Abel eat me out, a dark, savage part of me enjoys it. I'm so angry at him. I'll regret this tomorrow, but right now, the chains of control that usually keep me placid and submissive have long since snapped. They snapped the moment Eli served himself and our faction up without a second thought. He's supposed to be better than Bauer Paine. Better than his father, too. He's supposed to be a true leader.

A leader puts our faction first. They protect our people, even if it means sacrifice.

They do not, under any circumstances, throw that all away for single person. Not even if they love them. I catch Eli's gaze and, even now, he's trying to find a way to save me from this. As if I'm nothing more than a victim to be sheltered.

He never did see me as a full partner.

I turn my face away, breaking our eye contact. It couldn't be clearer that he'll never see me for who I truly am. After all this time, I didn't expect it to hurt so much. I let the pain buoy me, embracing it with both arms wide open.

Abel turns his head and nips my thigh, making me jump. His dark eyes drink me in, and he's not faking the lust burning there. His mouth and beard are wet from my desire, and he holds my gaze as he works a third finger into me.

"How does that feel, sweetheart?" A gauntlet thrown at my feet.

I make myself release his hair and stretch my arms over my head. It feels so good, I'm pretty sure my bones are in danger of turning to liquid, but I'll be damned before I admit it. "It's adequate."

"Adequate." His dark eyes flare hotter. He likes this verbal sparring. He likes it a lot. "Guess I'll have to up my game." He dips down, and then his mouth is on my clit again. I didn't realize he was just toying with me until now. Testing me. Figuring out what I like. He puts all that knowledge to good use now. Abel strokes my clit with his tongue slowly, his eyes on my face, his fingers buried deep in my pussy.

It's so intimate. Horribly, unforgivably intimate.

It's everything I can do to hold still and not grab his head and grind my pussy all over his face. I grab fistfuls of the sheets, my breath coming in harsh gasps. Fuck, I'm close.

Tighter and tighter. Hotter and hotter. Higher and higher.

And then he tips me over the edge, and I'm hurtling into an orgasm that draws a cry from my lips. I clamp my thighs around his head, but he yanks his fingers out of me and wedges my legs wide again, devouring my pussy in deep kisses as if he's trying to lick up every bit of my orgasm.

When he finally raises his head, he looks completely feral. "I'm giving you my cock, Harlow."

I pant as I watch him rip open a condom and roll it onto his massive cock. And it is massive. He's wide and thick, and my body clenches at the sight. Abel plants a hand next to my shoulder and leans down to cover me with his body, his gaze on my mouth.

Oh fuck, he's going to kiss me.

Panic flares, and I shove at his chest. He stops immediately. "Second thoughts?"

"No." I want this, even if I don't want to want this, but I can't let him kiss me. I can't lose myself that much when I've already compromised everything. I keep pushing his chest, and he lets me guide him back enough that I can turn over.

Abel gives a harsh laugh. "You're not going to be able to forget that it's *my* cock inside you just because I'm taking you from behind."

I know that. Of course I know that. But it feels less intimate, and it *has* to be less intimate. This man already looks at me like he sees me. I can't let him get closer. I bend down, pressing my face to the bed. "Stop talking, and fuck me already."

He digs his hand into my hair and turns my face in Eli's direction. I could close my eyes, but that's the coward's way out. I stare at Eli as Abel guides his cock to my entrance. He doesn't ask me again if I'm sure. I appreciate that small kindness, just like I appreciate the fact that he doesn't comment on how fucking wet I am. Abel starts working his giant cock into me, and I stare at the man I both love and hate.

And Eli?

I expect the guilt on his bruised face. I expect the anger.

I don't expect the lust.

He watches Abel thrust into me, and there's a heat in his hazel eyes that burns hot enough to set the room aflame. He sits perfectly still as if memorizing this moment. Alarms blare through my head, but I've gone too far to change my mind now. And, truth be told, I don't want to. Things were always going to end between me and Eli. I've known that for longer than I want to admit. I didn't expect them to end like *this*, but life has a way of throwing curveballs.

I expect Abel to drive into me and chase his own pleasure. I really should know better, even after such a short time.

He covers me with his big body, pressing me into the mattress, and snakes his hand around my hip to stroke my clit. He kisses my neck and chuckles when it makes me clench around his cock. But when he speaks, it's all for Eli. "She feels fucking good, Eli. Hot and tight and wet just for me." He thrusts into me in slow, grinding motions that nearly make my eyes cross. I'm pinned between his cock and his hand and, gods, it feels so good, I might die from it.

"Shut up," I grind out.

He doesn't pick up his pace, doesn't do anything but keep fucking me in the direction of another orgasm. Abel lowers his voice, but not enough that Eli won't hear. "Do you scream when you come for him, sweetheart? Do you fuck him mean like you're doing to me?"

Eli's cuffs rattle against his chair as he leans forward. He's got his practiced smile in place, a mask I loathe because he's started using it on me in private and not just when we're in public. The bruising of his face dampens the effect, but only slightly. He laughs, easy and light and completely at odds with the look in his eyes. "Enjoy Harlow's pussy, Abel. I'll be taking her back when this is over, and you'll only have the memories."

Something ugly and dark surges through me. I am not a toy to be fought over like they're jealous children. I expect that from Abel. The only reason he chose me as his Bride was to hurt Eli. I didn't expect it from the man I've been sharing my bed and life with for the last five years.

Abel's dark chuckle teases the damp skin on the back of my neck. "Don't like that, do you? He's a fool if he thinks you belong to him." He grinds into me in that decadently slow motion. "You do what you want, don't you, sweetheart? And right now, you want to come all over my cock." He shifts his hand, adjusting the angle of his fingers against my clit, and then resumes fucking me.

I'm spread out for him, pinned in place by his big body, but I can't help enjoying every moment of it. Regrets will come later, maybe, but right now I am riding on a wave of darkness akin to hate. I let go, free-falling into an orgasm that has me arching back against Abel, trying to take his cock deeper. He hitches my hips higher, giving me exactly what I need, coaxing my orgasm into wave after wave, until I collapse onto the bed in a sweaty mess.

He drags a free hand down my spine as he leverages himself off me. It's a weirdly comforting move, especially the way his touch lingers on my hip for a long moment. He turns away and drags the condom off his cock then tosses it in the trash. "Your turn, Eli. We're back to my original question; easy way or the hard way?"

Eli looks at me for a long moment before he focuses on Abel. "What are my choices?" He still sounds carefree and distant, and it makes me want to slap him.

Abel's expression is strangely neutral. "I fuck your mouth. I fuck your ass. Either way, I'm not going to be gentle, but if you choose mouth and try to bite my cock, I'm going to break your nose."

"There goes that idea." Eli grins, though his eyes remain cold. "My mouth. Make it quick."

Abel moves to stand next to the chair but doesn't bother to uncuff Eli. I don't blame him. I wouldn't either. He grips Eli's blond hair and gives it a tug. "Behave."

"Tonight, I will."

I expect more taunting, more...something. But the air is charged with a tension that goes beyond hatred. Abel holds Eli's gaze as he guides his cock into his mouth. I half expect

Eli to pull something, but he simply sucks the other man down.

I lay there and watch Abel fuck Eli's mouth in short, brutal strokes as he holds the back of his head. It's hot. Really, really hot. Every muscle in Abel's body stands out in restrained violence, right up until the moment he curses and jerks as he comes down Eli's throat. "It's done. You're mine for the year." He glances at me. "You're both mine."

My eyes feel gritty, and my throat is hot, but I muscle down the response. I can't show weakness right now. Not to Eli and certainly not to Abel. I won't give these assholes the satisfaction of knowing that either of them hurt me.

I can't believe it's come to this, but I'm nothing if not resilient.

I'll find my way through.

I always do.

6

ELI

I can still taste Abel on my tongue. Maybe I truly am concussed because I sit there and stare at him as he walks to the dresser and pulls on a pair of jeans. A shirt quickly follows, and then he disappears into the bathroom. When he returns, he's got his boots back on. He tosses a key onto the bed next to Harlow. "Uncuff him, or don't. Your choice. Don't try anything funny."

And then he's gone.

It feels like he sucks all of the air out of the room when he leaves. I don't know what I'm supposed to do, how I'm supposed to feel. I'm pissed, but this is a thousand times more complicated than a simple coup. We have too much history, and it bled into every moment of that interaction.

Once upon a time, Abel was the most important person in my life.

I know all too well how love can turn to hate and fester, especially after what he's experienced, but I didn't expect to feel anything resembling conflicted.

I didn't expect to enjoy the sight of him fucking Harlow, even a little.

I sure as hell didn't expect to like sucking his cock.

I push the confusion away and look at Harlow. "Are you okay?"

"I'm fine." She climbs to her feet and bends over to grab her dress off the floor. She's got beard burn on her thighs, and her skin is still shining from the sweat of their fucking.

She fucked him right in front of me. She came twice. That's not simply submitting to the handfasting consummation. She did it out of spite.

I exhale and slump back against the chair. My whole body aches. My face, my mouth, my shoulders. It's not impeding my ability to breathe, but everything hurts like a motherfucker. "I didn't realize you meant it when you said you'd never forgive me."

"I meant it." The quiet words land between us like bombs. Harlow sinks onto the bed facing me, her expression painfully locked down.

It strikes me that we haven't been alone like this in a very long time. She's taken to sleeping in another room, citing our differing schedules as a reason. I let it go at the time. I thought she just needed some time and space because things had gotten so tense between us. The more I tried to hold her close, the more distant she became. Nothing helped, not gifts, not little surprises, not doing the shit that forged our relationship in the first place. Not even sex.

But the days turned into weeks, and before I knew it, a year had passed and her shit started disappearing from the room we once shared. The room that was only mine now.

And I let it happen. It was easier that way. Easier to ignore the growing distance between us. Easier to keep going through the motions of running our faction and keeping the people I care about safe. Always a delicate dance, and now I've gone and fucked it all up.

I rattle the cuffs. "Are you going to free me?"

"I'm thinking about it." She studies the key in her hand. "I told you to let me go, Eli. You should have just done what I asked."

"I couldn't let Abel hurt you."

She narrows her eyes. "I can handle Abel just fine on my own. Something you'd know if you ever bothered to pay attention. He's a monster, but he's a monster with a code."

"You don't know that." That might have been true with the Abel I knew eight years ago, the one that I was raised practically alongside, but that was before everything in his life went up in flames. This new version of him is harder, colder, crueler. *Like his father.* I can't say I don't deserve everything coming to me—I do—but I don't want Harlow to pay the price of my sins. I witnessed what Bauer Paine did to his enemies; I can't afford to assume Abel won't do the same.

"It took two conversations to figure it out."

"I'll talk to him. Now that it's consummated, he can let you—"

"Eli." She shakes her head. "Stop whatever you're about to say. He's not going to fuck me, pat me on the ass, and send me on my way. He won me, just like he won you, and it couldn't be clearer that he intends to keep the faction even after the year is up. He might not technically need both of us to make that happen, but he's not going to throw away a resource just because it bothers you. If anything, he'll keep me around to needle you with until the very end."

She's got a pretty clear read on the situation, but that doesn't mean she's right. "I'll talk to him," I repeat.

Harlow lets out a bitter laugh. "Sure. Right. Why listen to me? Do you know what's going to happen if you keep pushing Abel?" She holds my gaze, her dark eyes hard. "He's going to take it out on me."

Fear raises its ugly head. I don't want to see her harmed. That's the very last thing I want, the last thing I've always wanted. "I won't let him hurt you."

"Who said anything about hurt?" She drops the key on the bed and stands. "We gave him the perfect method of punishment tonight, didn't we? You hate to see his hands on me, and I'm just angry enough to welcome it. How many times of him fucking me in front of you will it take to get the truth through your thick skull?" She glares. "You've only ever seen me as a prize to keep safe and display when it suits you. Now he's stolen that prize, and he's going to rub your nose in it every chance he gets."

"Don't talk about yourself that way."

"Why not?" I've never heard her sound so cold. "It's the truth, isn't it?" She walks into the bathroom and shuts the door quietly behind her. A few seconds later, the shower turns on.

I let my head drop and curse hard. I fucked that conversation up, just like I seem to fuck up every conversation Harlow and I have had in the last couple years. No matter what I say or how I say it, I cut her with my careless words. The closer I try to hold her, the farther she slips from me.

If this hadn't happened, she would have left me within the year, and I still don't understand *why*.

"You're a fucking fool."

I lift my head. I hadn't heard the door open, but now Abel leans against it, watching me with a cold expression. He was never so icy when I knew him, but I recognize it all the same. It's the same face his father presented the world. "Thought you'd be gone for longer."

"Yeah, well, plans change." He studies the bathroom door. "I thought I'd have to spend some time bringing her around, but she's so angry, she's only too happy to jump on my cock to punish you."

It takes everything I have not to react to that. I give him a slow smirk. "Are we going to talk about Harlow? Or are we going to talk about the fact that you just fucked my mouth and liked it?" He's not the only one, but I'd rather die than admit it.

"A means to an end." He's still watching the bathroom door with a contemplative look on his face. "You know, I thought you'd make it more difficult for me, but you've served your faction up on a silver platter. Your old man must be spinning in his grave."

More like my father might find a way to come back from the afterlife to gut me for the events of tonight. "He's dead. What does he care?"

"Mm-hmm." Abel finally looks at me. He was never soft, but the years away from Sabine Valley have made him look like he's carved from stone. Like he's seen shit and made choices no person should have to make. Because of what my father did to his family. Because of events I helped put into motion.

I search his face for the Abel I used to know, even as I recognize it as a hopeless endeavor. My best friend is gone. The man who's become my enemy is the only one who remains.

"Why not just kill me and be done with it? That's what you really want, right? Your revenge."

"All in good time." He says it so casually. "Where did you find her?"

I don't like how I can't seem to distract him from Harlow. No matter what she thinks, you can't get a good read on a person from two conversations. Even with his absence, I've known Abel Paine the majority of my life. He is not a man to be trifled with, and while the man I used to know wouldn't hurt an innocent, he won't see Harlow as an innocent. She's my woman, my other half in public. As far as he's concerned, she's in this world up to her eyeballs, and he'll treat her accordingly. As a threat. Which means there are no protections in place to keep her safe.

"Answer the question, Eli."

I give him an easy smile. "She's been here all along. She grew up in the faction."

He finally looks at me. "Tomorrow we go back to your place. You will inform your people that I'm now in charge— and of the consequences of trying the same shit they did eight years ago. You caught my father flat-footed. You won't be able to do the same to me."

"Abel—" It's on the tip of my tongue to tell him the truth. I had a part to play that night, but it was never meant to be against *him*. Except intentions don't matter, only actions and consequences do. I might not have wanted any harm to come to Abel and his brothers, but harm came nonetheless. Beyond that, I didn't find them and bring them back. I let their exile stand.

So, yeah, I'm just as much to blame as my father.

"The only words I want to hear out of your traitorous mouth are 'yes, Abel.' You can stuff anything else."

I clench my jaw and have to fight back a wince when the move sends pain splintering through my skull. "Why would I play nice?"

"You're really going to make me spell it out?" He stops in front of me and drops into a crouch, putting us almost at eye level. Despite fighting eight people earlier, he's moving without any stiffness or apparent injury. There are bruises on his face, yes, but they don't seem to bother him in the least. Abel reaches out and taps my chin. "You're so ready to throw yourself at me to distract from her. It'd be cute under different circumstances, especially because she fucking loathes it when you do that, but I don't have time for the bullshit. I will fuck her every time you push back, Eli. And I'm going to make you watch me do it."

I should dig in my heels. My faction comprises one-third of Sabine Valley and thousands of people. My father might have been just another flavor of Bauer Paine, but I've done a lot of work to help our people in the five years since his death. Things are better here now, better than they ever were under Paine rule, even if the territory still holds their name. That should be more important than anything. Even Harlow would say as much.

But...

I can't let her be hurt. I just fucking can't do it. I can be ruthless in every other way but that. She's too important to me to let her pay the price for my sins. I swallow down my rage. "You really are a monster."

"Pot, meet kettle." He doesn't blink. "How many people died in that fire because they were drugged and unable to flee? Don't think too hard, Eli. I can tell you the answer. Forty. Forty fucking people dead because your old man wasn't content with slitting my father's throat in his sleep. It would have been forty-seven if we didn't get out, and you wouldn't have lost a damn bit of sleep over it."

"That's not true." I know better than to argue, but the words slip out all the same. "I cared." I cared so much, I did the unthinkable that night. I just didn't realize how out of control things would get, hadn't possessed the foresight to realize my father's plans would include the other factions.

Intentions don't matter; actions do.

"You can say that, but you didn't do shit to stop it. That's not caring. That's cowardice."

"I'm not a fucking coward. Your father was a rabid dog, and the entire faction suffered because of it. You know it, and I know it. You're just pissed because we took him out before you had a chance to." *Fuck, fuck, fuck.* I didn't mean to say that, either.

"You always did like to spin the truth to suit your purposes. Whatever I planned for my father, I never would have done shit to hurt my brothers or our people, and you damn well know it." He pushes to his feet. "And you've pushed me far enough tonight. Guess it's time to pay Harlow a visit."

True fear clogs my throat, shattering my control. "Abel, wait."

"No, Eli." He turns away. "You don't get to try to call my bluff and then change your mind when it's time to pay the piper. Or when it's time for *Harlow* to pay the piper."

"Wait. Fucking goddamn it, Abel! Wait!"

He ignores me, stalking across the bedroom and wrenching the bathroom door open. A waft of steam escapes, and he gives me a cold look over his shoulder. "Look, she's all ready for me. Nice of her, don't you think?"

"You fucking bastard!"

His dark laugh trails after him as he steps into the bathroom and closes the door. The click of the lock sounds unnaturally loud in my ears. I yank against my cuffs, but they don't give. Of course they don't give.

That doesn't stop me from trying. If I can get to the bed, get to the key...

I try to hop the chair sideways, but my head is still fucked up, and I overcompensate, tipping over. I land on my arm and curse. No matter how hard I struggle, there's not a damn thing I can do.

Once again, Harlow's going to pay the price of my sins.

7

HARLOW

I know who it is the second the bathroom door opens. There's no way Eli could have escaped the cuffs. He's capable, but even he has his limits. I duck my head under the spray, prolonging the moment before I have to turn around and face Abel.

It doesn't help that the bathroom is set up in the most utilitarian way possible. The shower is an open-air one, just like in a gym: a shower head and a drain in the middle of the tiled floor. There's a toilet and a sink and...that's it.

Which means there's nothing between me and Abel.

I turn slowly and slick my hair back. He's leaning against the door, a contemplative expression on his face and heat in his eyes. My body responds even as my mind digs in its heels. I know he can make me feel good, but the price is too high. It was one thing to go through with the consummation, to let my anger slip its leash, but that doesn't mean it's going to be a regular occurrence.

I reach to turn the water off, and he gives a sharp shake of his head. "Leave it on."

I doubt Eli can hear us through the door and across the

room, but obviously Abel wants to ensure it's true. I step away from the water. "Hand me a towel?"

He snags the white towel off the counter and walks to me in the slow stride of a predator on the hunt. It takes everything I have to not take a step back as Abel stops in front of me and wraps the towel around my shoulders. We're too close, and it's all too easy to remember what we were doing last time he had his hands on me. I force myself to hold his gaze. "Let go."

He waits a moment and then slowly releases the towel. I have to grab it to keep it from sliding off my shoulders. I expect him to move back, but he just stands there and watches me dry off. "It's about time you and I had a chat."

"So chat." I focus on getting as much water out of my hair as possible. There's no hair dryer in this room, so I'm going to be a frizzy mess in the morning, but it's the least of my worries right now.

"You liked what we did in there."

It's not quite a question, but I answer honestly all the same. "You served a purpose."

He gives a rough laugh. "And the claws come out."

I should leave it at that, but there's something about Abel that sparks a fierce part of me that rarely sees the light. "Yes, I liked what we did in there. That doesn't mean a damn thing. I'm not going to let you use me to hurt the faction."

"Interesting that you're more worried about the faction than about Eli."

If he meant that to sting, he's talking to the wrong woman. The good of the many has always outweighed the good of a single person in my eyes. "I have my priorities in order. Not everyone does."

"And what will you do to protect the faction, sweetheart? How far will you go?"

I know what he's asking me, and for a moment, I truly consider rolling over and giving him everything. I know better, though. It's not in my nature to give up without a fight, and Abel isn't the type of man to respect anything but strength. But he wants me. He wasn't faking what happened in that bed any more than I was. We might have met in mutual rage at Eli, but the pleasure was real.

Does he realize he's handing me a weapon to fight with? Surely he must.

It doesn't matter. I'll use whatever I have at my disposal.

I drop the towel and close the distance between us. I carefully press my palms to his chest. "Are you asking me if I'll fuck you in order to protect my people?" I run my hands down his chest and hook them into the band of his jeans. "If I'll bargain orgasms for leniency?"

He leans forward, his dark eyes alight with lust. "Well?"

I snort and drop my hands. There's no missing the hard cock pressed against the front of his jeans. Poor thing, he's going to have one hell of a case of blue balls. "No." I lift my chin and meet his gaze. "If I ride your cock again, it will be because I want to. We both know that no sex is good enough to manipulate you into doing what I want."

He gives that dark laugh again, the one that slides along my skin like a rough tongue. "You're not wrong."

"Yeah, I didn't think so." That sort of thing might work on another man, and I'd be more than willing to go there. The safety of thousands is worth more than my pride, my freedom, my life. It won't work with Abel, and so I won't play that game. He likes the challenge I present, and I'm only too happy to step to the line he draws in the sand.

"There's just one question left, then." He catches my hands and presses them back to his chest. "Do you want to ride my cock, Harlow?" Abel takes a step, and this time I can't stop myself from moving back. I don't drop my hands, though. I just stare at him as I let him herd me until my ass presses against the sink.

My heart aches so fucking much. The events of the last couple hours whirl around in my mind and give me no relief. Fear for the future, anger at Eli, frustration over how fucking helpless I feel—it all rattles the chains in my head. The only time I wasn't thinking was when Abel was inside me.

I dig my nails into his chest, just a little. "What did you tell Eli before you walked in here?"

"Who says I told him anything?"

I give him the look that statement deserves. "You might be back here to take the faction, but you're going to get your revenge in the process. Did you tell him that you're going to hurt me?" I lean forward a little. "That you're going to force me?"

"We both know I won't have to."

I snort. "We both know you wouldn't in the first place." *That*, I'm sure of. He might kill me, but he won't cross that line. I'm not sure it's a relief, but it feels like one all the same.

There's that expression on his face, like I've surprised him. Abel plants his hands on the sink on either side of my hips. "You seem to think you know a lot about me."

"Tell me I'm wrong."

"You're not wrong." His gaze drops to my mouth. "You're wasted on him. He's so busy trying to save you, he's suffocating you."

I jolt. Apparently I'm not the only one who got a quick read on my opponent. Still, I'm not about to give Abel anything for free, and I'm certainly not going to let him crawl around inside my head. "I don't know what you're talking about. We're deliriously happy. It's sickening, really."

"Liar." Slowly, giving me plenty of time to react, he shifts his hands from the sink to my hips and then lifts me up to perch on the counter. I don't mean to spread my thighs, but he takes advantage of it, stepping between them. He doesn't press against me, not exactly, but one deep breath could have our chests rubbing together. Abel drops his face to my neck and inhales deeply. "Tonight's full of surprises, isn't it?"

I can't quite catch my breath. "What are you talking about?"

"I figured I'd take you, he'd come after me, and I'd beat him somewhere nice and public and then send him into exile just like my brothers and I suffered. Instead I get two Brides for the price of one, the faction handed over with minimum fuss, and you're no helpless flower in need of a glass cage. You're like me, Harlow. Monster, through and through."

I'm not sure he's wrong, but I'm not about to admit it. "You have a point."

"Yeah." He drags his mouth along my neck, and it takes everything I have not to moan. "I'll offer you a bargain."

It will be nothing good. Abel is too smart, and he's got all the cards. The only thing I have to offer is my body, and I've already taken it off the table, at least on this subject. It seems silly now, with him kissing my neck and me clutching his shirt and fighting not to pull him closer, but I won't change my mind. Sex is sex and has no place in these negotiations. I draw in a ragged breath. "I'm listening."

"Be mine." His thumbs skate up my sides. "We have the year. You know the faction as well as anyone, and you obviously care about the people. Help me take over, help me rule, and I'll keep the bloodshed to a minimum and take your input into any changes I make."

Shock turns my thoughts to static. "What?" Surely this is

a trick, some kind of cruel manipulation. Surely he's not casually offering me the one thing I want more than anything in the world.

The one thing Eli's denied me for the last five years.

But when Abel lifts his head, he looks devastatingly serious. "Be my partner, share my bed, and if you want to leave at the end of the year, I'll set you up with the resources you need to go wherever you want." He gives me a sudden grin. "And if you want to stay, you're more than welcome to do that, too."

"You're out of your mind."

"I've been accused of worse."

"You don't even know me."

He gives me a long look. "Sweetheart, I have a file on you an inch thick."

Of course he does. He put too much planning into this night going his way to *not* have researched everyone involved. It still doesn't change anything. What he's offering isn't exactly too good to be true, but it's definitely in the realm. All I want is to protect my people. If Abel gives me the opportunity to do that, there's no way I'm going to say no. I suspect he knows that. "You're just doing this to hurt Eli."

"I won't lie. Punishing Eli plays into it." He shrugs. "But I could just seduce you, and it would serve the same purpose. You know it as well as I do. This"—he motions between us—"sparks hot enough to burn Sabine Valley to the ground. We'll fight, and then we'll fuck, and it will drive him out of his mind. I don't need to offer you a full partnership to get the perks."

I hate that he's not wrong. Even now, I want him with a borderline frenzy. It's as if he's woken up a part of me that's spent most my life in slumber. I feel *feral* around

Abel. I try to slow down, to think, but it's hard when I'm breathing the same air as him. "I'll do it on one condition."

"You seem to be under the mistaken impression that you have bargaining chips in this situation."

I raise my eyebrows. "Don't I? I'm a valuable resource, and I'm more useful to you if you keep me relatively happy."

His hands tighten on my hips ever so slightly. "Oh, I'll keep you happy."

"Don't kill Eli. Give me your word that you won't—not by your hand or order or brothers."

He searches my face. "You really were going to leave him, weren't you?"

I hate that he sees things so readily after such a short time interacting with us. If Eli was half as perceptive... But it's not his perception that's the issue. It's the rose-tinted glasses he wears whenever he looks in my direction. He has no problem seeing everything *else* clearly. I take a slow breath. "Yes, but that doesn't mean I want him dead." I still love him, even if the feeling is barbed and poisoned after so many years of being shoved into a role too small for my skin. Even if part of me wants to punish him for that pain, I don't want him irreparably harmed.

Abel finally nods. "Deal. I never planned on killing him."

I'm not sure if he's telling the truth or not. It's enough that he agreed. I don't exactly trust his word, but it's better than nothing at this point. "Then yes, I agree."

"Good." He steps back so suddenly, I nearly topple off the counter. Abel pulls his shirt over his head and tosses it at me. "Put this on."

"Excuse me?"

"Come now, Harlow. You know the importance of

appearances. We're leaving, and you're going to be wearing my clothes when we do."

It's tempting to argue, but it's a small enough concession. I shrug and pull it over my head. Abel is bigger through the shoulders and chest than Eli, and the shirt hits me mid-thigh. Not exactly indecent, but it *feels* indecent when every breath gives me a lungful of his dark scent. It feels like he's marking me. I'm not sure if it's a pleasant feeling or not. I pull on my panties again, mostly to give myself an illusion of armor. Something that's mine and not his.

"Come on." He turns off the shower, opens the bathroom door, and stalks out of the room. I glance at myself in the mirror. I look like a mess. My hair is drying, and it's just as frizzy as I expected, and there are red marks on my neck and thighs from Abel's mouth. I shiver. This night has not gone at all like I expected.

I step into the bedroom and stop short. Eli is on his side, having somehow tipped over the chair. Abel grabs the back of the chair and hefts him upright, but Eli ignores the other man. His hazel eyes are on me, and the way he looks at me, he expected to see my half-dead bloody body crawl out of the bathroom. "Are you okay, Harlow?"

I start to cross my arms over my chest but force myself to let them drop to my sides. "I'm fine."

From the expression on his face, he doesn't believe me. "He said he'd punish you…"

I glance over his head at Abel, who's giving me a stone-faced look. I was right. He must have said something before he came into the bathroom to make Eli think that I'd pay the price for whatever conversation they had. What a bastard. I glare. "I'm fine. I'm unharmed."

Eli exhales, but Abel doesn't give him a chance to settle into the knowledge. "For now."

Clearly, he's going to use threats against me to keep Eli in line. I'm not sure how I feel about that. I'm furious at Eli, but eventually my anger will cool. I don't want to torment him.

Abel uncuffs Eli and drags him to his feet. "Let's go."

I snag my shoes off the floor and slip into them. "Where are we going?"

"It's time to claim the faction."

This night's been full of surprises. Primary among them is Harlow. She's a fierce little bitch, and I like her despite myself. There's the added bonus that her at my side will be a constant dagger in Eli's heart for the next year, but she's an asset that I have no intention of wasting.

Neither of them speak as we wait in the main warehouse for my people to gather, including my brothers. I don't expect a fight, not when word would have spread about what happened during the Lammas feast. Eli's people show every evidence of being loyal, but they're also citizens of Sabine Valley. They know the laws. I won him, Harlow, and the entire fucking faction through combat. There's no taking that back. If they try to dig in their heels and fight, they run the risk of the Amazons and Mystics moving to crush them entirely. Better to bide their time and wait to see what my brothers and I will do.

Cohen is the first to arrive, towing Winry—the Amazon queen's youngest daughter—behind him. She looks frazzled and scared but not overly traumatized. Good. She's softer than I expected of one of Aisling's daughters, and I wouldn't have paired her with Cohen if I'd realized it when we decided on Brides. For his part, he looks just as cold and intense as ever.

He glances at Harlow and Eli and raises his brows. "You get it done?"

"Yeah. You?"

He doesn't look at Winry. "Yeah." His tone invites no other questions, which is just as well. I don't need the details of the consummation. Fuck, I don't want them. It's enough that he got it done and didn't maul her.

One by one, my brothers appear. They all give me nods of confirmation. It's been done.

And then Donovan shows up with Ciar's former youngest wife...and another woman. The Mystic's wife is a curvy white woman with curly, dark hair and full lips that look like they've been sucking cock for hours. The other woman is muscular with straight, dark hair and a body that suggests she punches through walls for fun.

I point at her. "Who the fuck is this?"

"Bodyguard." Donovan shrugs. "She showed up as we were getting in the trucks. She's loyal to Mabel, not to Ciar. She got pushy, so I brought her along."

I stare at him. "She was pushy, so you brought her along." Donovan just stares at me, as if he didn't potentially breach our security on a whim. "And you didn't think to mention it?"

"We were all otherwise occupied." He gives me a slow grin. Of all my brothers, he's chosen to deal with the harsh realities of our exile and survival with humor and a determination to take nothing too seriously. Sometimes it's a welcome relief. Sometimes—like now—it makes me want to wring his neck.

I turn to the bodyguard. "You do anything to fuck with us, we won't just kill you. We'll kill her, too." I point at Mabel. "Got it?"

She sets her chin and leans forward on her toes, obviously wanting nothing more than to punch me in the face. "She's my priority. I couldn't give a fuck about the rest of it as long as she's safe."

Yeah, we'll see. I level a dark look at Donovan for complicating my life and jerk my thumb at the trucks. "Load up. We're relocating."

This time, I don't toss Eli in the bed of the truck. I drag him to the passenger seat and shove him in. Harlow, I guide around to the driver's seat. "In the middle."

"Lucky me." She climbs up, giving me a flash of the lower curve of her ass.

She's taken sex off the negotiating table, but not off the list of possibilities. Hell if I don't respect her more for realizing that I'd never let my cock guide me in making policy decisions. And for not denying the obvious; we're attracted to each other, and the sex was hot enough to set the entire warehouse on fire. I'm going to have her in my bed again, and soon, but right now that's not the priority.

I lead our little caravan out of the warehouse. As we leave, several additional trucks join the line—our people who've been keeping watch of the perimeter to ensure no one decided to pull anything underhanded.

After several blocks, I glance at Eli. He's retreated into himself the same way he used to do when we were kids and he came up against a challenge he couldn't immediately find a way around. That impressive brain of his is firing on all cylinders, trying to figure out a way to turn this situation to his advantage.

Despite my best efforts, my gaze drops to his mouth. It's

still all fucked up from our fight, but the memory of him sucking my cock isn't one I'm going to be able to erase from my head anytime soon.

I'd always been attracted to him, but we were friends first, and in our world, true friendship is rare enough that I didn't want to fuck with it by adding sex to the mix. I never bothered to find out if he felt the same; it was too risky to fuck up our dynamic. I trusted him. That was more intimate than any sex could ever be.

Look where that trust got me.

Orphaned and exiled.

It doesn't matter if my father was a monster, that he would have died before the end of that year regardless of whose hand held the blade. We had a plan—for us, for the faction—and Eli threw it all away to grab power for himself. I welcome the anger that surges in response to the memory of that night. The ash on my tongue from the smoke of our childhood home going up in flames. The fear. Fuck, I was so goddamn scared that night. The knowledge that if I fucked up, my brothers might die as a result, had burned away any thought but getting out of the city and getting out fast.

I can never forgive Eli for taking everything from me, for making me fear, for throwing the truth in my face—no matter how strong, how fucking fierce I am, it can all be turned against me in a moment because I trusted the wrong person.

"You will tell your people to stand down."

Eli stares out the windshield. "And if I don't?"

Harlow opens her mouth, but I shut her up with a hard look. This is between me and Eli. "If they try to fight, I will cut them down without hesitation. If they start shooting, they're not going to just hit me and my brothers, Eli. They're going to hit Amazons and Mystics and Harlow."

He clenches his jaw, still not looking at me. "I'll give the order."

"Good boy." Even with that order, his people can't be trusted. Eight years ago, I might have believed otherwise, but most of them were part of the coup. The laws of Sabine Valley won't make them hesitate if they see an opportunity to strike me and mine down. "They'll have an hour to collect their things and get out."

"What?"

"You heard me." I have my own people, ones who have walked through hell and back with me. I might not trust them as intensely as I used to be capable of, but they have no reason to betray me at this point. It's not in their best interest, and *that* I trust.

It takes fifteen minutes to get to Eli and Harlow's headquarters. It's a compound of sorts that stretches an entire city block, tucked safely behind a ten-foot wall with guard posts on each of the corners. Eli's father learned from mine's mistake and tucked the things he cared about behind enough security to make a small army hesitate.

I pull up to the gate and glance at Eli. "Now's a good time to prove that you intend to keep your word. For once."

Eli glares, but by the time he leans out the window, he's got an easy grin on his face. "Hey, George. Open up."

The man standing outside the gate walks up to the car. He's a short and stocky Black man, and he's got his hand set easily on the pistol in a holster at his hip. "Heard you had some trouble during the festival."

Eli shrugs. "You win some, you lose some. You remember Abel." He motions idly in my direction. "He's in charge for the time being."

Damn, he couldn't resist even that little dig, could he? I

keep my expression locked down. George's eyes widen a little, and he looks back at Eli. "Sir—"

"Open the gate. And then let everyone know to meet us in the inner courtyard as soon as possible. That's an order." He says it so casually, but then Eli was always a fan of using honey instead of a knife to get what he wanted. He used to argue that it was better to have people underestimate you than fear you—something I've never agreed with.

Back then, between the two of us, my brutality and his cunning made us damn near unstoppable.

I knew being back in Sabine Valley would have those memories surging, but fuck if it doesn't sting after all these years. We had so much *possibility*. If he'd just been patient, had just been fucking honest with me, we could have pulled off all our plans without so much loss of life.

I've never forgive myself for being unable to see that he was ambitious enough to never want to share the throne. Eight years, and he hasn't changed. He has a perfect partner in Harlow and he keeps her hobbled so he's got the power all to himself.

George finally nods and hustles back to the gate to open it. I drive in slowly, taking in our surroundings as I do. Two rows of short, squat buildings that I suspect are barracks for Eli's people. Past that are a pair of warehouses on either side of the road. Their doors are open, showing civilian vehicles in one and combat vehicles on the other. Interesting.

Next up is the house. It fits in with the rest of the compound, though it's three stories tall and nondescript with small windows on the sides facing the exterior walls. "Expecting a siege?"

"You never know," Eli says softly. "Especially these days."

It will serve nicely. I pull to a stop in front of the house and grab Harlow. "Just in case anyone gets any funny ideas."

I haul her over my lap, and she's the one to exit the truck first. I keep a hand on her hip, not letting her get too far away.

Harlow gives me a sharp look. "A human shield? *Really?*"

"No one will shoot if they might hit the princess of this faction." I look up at the building. Sure enough, there's a sniper on the roof. I give him a cocky wave. "Eli."

Eli takes his time getting out of the truck. I can't tell if he's being difficult or if his injuries are giving him issues, but I choose not to comment on it. He rounds the truck to stand by me as a white woman with a rifle stalks out the front door. Eli holds up a hand. "Call them off, Marie."

"But—"

He shakes his head. "I gave my word. The Herald witnessed."

She blanches but finally nods and yanks a radio off her hip. "Stand down."

Eli sighs. "Get everyone here."

Marie's still glaring daggers at me, but she relays the order. It takes fifteen minutes for everyone to appear. I study the crowd, matching names with faces. Nearly everyone is here. Good enough. "You have an hour to clear out your shit. When you leave, pass the word on. The Paine brothers are back. The Raider faction belongs to us in truth again. You don't fuck with us, we won't fuck with you. Try some shit, and we'll make examples of you." I meet several of their gazes in turn. "You do *not* want to be made an example of."

Silence greets me, but it's got a mutinous quality. They don't seem to give a fuck that if they attack us, they'll undoubtedly take out some important people to the other factions. Violence broils in the air, and I glance at Broderick. We figured we might have to fight our way through those loyal to Eli, but we'd hoped to avoid it. Nothing gets people up in arms like killing a few dozen of their friends and family. We can't afford a civil war within the faction.

Harlow steps forward. She should look ridiculous wearing my shirt, but she just looks sexy as fuck. She glares down at them. "Are you going to dishonor your leader? Are you going to dishonor our faction, your vows? The laws are there for a reason. I don't like this any more than you do, but I will keep my word. Will you do anything else?"

One by one, they drop their gazes and the possibility of violence dispels. I catch Eli looking at her like he's never seen her before, and I have to wonder what the fuck he expected. How can he have this woman in his bed and at his side for five years and not realize what an asset she is? It doesn't make any fucking sense to me, but then Eli stopped making sense to me the moment he betrayed my family.

Harlow stares at them for a long moment. "Don't bring shame on us. Do as you're told."

I glance at Cohen. "You, Ezekiel, and Donovan go with our people to monitor things and start moving our shit in the second it's clear." And then at my brother, Finnegan. "Take Gabriel and find the security shit and change the codes. That takes priority over anything else right now." And finally at Broderick. "Get the Brides gathered up and inside. We'll figure out living arrangements shortly."

Everyone scatters, but I grab Eli's arm before he can follow Broderick and the rest of the Brides into the house. "Not you. You're with me."

Eli hesitates but finally nods. I start walking, and he falls into step next to me as I circle the perimeter of the house and walk along the wall. I wait. He's been stewing since I left him in the bedroom and joined Harlow in the bathroom. It doesn't take long before he boils over. "Let Harlow go."

"She doesn't want to be let go." It's the truth, and I take

great delight in using it as a weapon. "She's exactly where she wants to be."

He stares straight ahead, jaw clenched. "She deserves better than to be used as a whipping boy when you're pissed at me."

"No argument there," I agree easily, just to see what he'll do. "But I like taking out my frustration on that hot little body."

He lunges for me, but I'm expecting it. I grab his arm, using his own momentum to shove him face-first into the wall and pin him there with a hand on the back of his neck. I step closer until I can speak directly in his ear. "She wasn't faking it when she came all over my cock, and you know it. I thought you were smart, Eli. You never used to be the kind of man to let an asset like her go to waste."

"She's not an asset. She's a person."

"Semantics."

Eli curses and tries to shove off the wall, but I use my body to keep him in place. We're as close as lovers now, and it's a fight not to let myself react physically. I laugh in his ear. "You're so determined to protect her from something she doesn't want protection from. No wonder she's ready to jump ship."

"Fuck you."

"Oh, she will. Repeatedly."

Eli goes still. "You never used to be this cruel."

"I don't know why you're surprised. Betrayal has a way of burning out all the good in a person." I take a slow breath, fighting to keep my tone moderate. "You'd throw yourself on a sword for her, wouldn't you? Would you let me fuck you to spare her?"

"Yes," he grinds out.

I lose my battle with control, and my cock goes hard

against his ass. I growl against the back of his neck. "You liked my cock down your throat, didn't you?"

"I'll submit to anything to save her."

"That's not an answer."

He curses again. "It's the only one you'll get."

Yeah, that's not going to work for me. I have eight years of revenge to play out, and letting Eli make noble sacrifices isn't on the list. "Pass. When I fuck you again—and I will—it will be when you get on your knees and ask me nicely. You will say *please*." I ignore his shoving back against me. "And after I make you come, you will thank me for the pleasure."

"Not fucking likely."

I set my teeth to the back of his neck, and Eli's breath shudders. Oh yeah, he feels that inconvenient attraction, too. Well, he can choke on it just like he choked on my cock. "Everything I do to Harlow, she welcomes." I shouldn't offer even that much, but it slips out despite my best intentions.

"Liar."

"Ask her." I shove away from him. "Then again, you don't seem to listen to a single fucking thing she says, so why start now?" I turn back toward the house. There's shit to accomplish, and it's going to be a pain in the ass, but I fully intend to reward myself by seducing Harlow tonight.

She's one hell of a reward, and if it infuriates Eli to know his woman welcomes me between her thighs, all the better.

9

ELI

It's more than a little shocking how seamlessly Abel takes over the compound. Within two hours, my people are gone and his are established in their place. I don't get a chance to see much of the other Brides; Abel sends me to my rooms and leaves me there. I've just showered and pulled on a pair of pants when Harlow walks through the door.

She stops short when she sees me. "Hey."

"Hey." This is what we've come to. As awkward and unsure as strangers.

She shuts the door behind her and tugs at the bottom of the shirt she's wearing. *Abel's* shirt. Impossible to miss that silent message he's determined to send to me; he'll take everything from me.

Harlow. My home. The faction.

"Harlow—"

"You look like shit." She crosses toward the closet. "Let me change, and I'll put some butterfly bandages on the deeper cuts."

I want to ask her if she's okay, but it couldn't be clearer

that she doesn't welcome the question. So, instead, I sit on the bed and wait for her to return. When she comes back in, she's put on a pair of jeans and a black tank top. She's also carrying the first aid kit we keep stashed in the bathroom. I can't remember the last time we've had to use it, not since the first year after I took over for my father. There were some challenges during that time and for a few Lammas after. I took down every one publicly enough that they stopped coming.

Until now.

Harlow sets the first aid kit next to me on the bed and begins setting things out in a neat little row. "How are your ribs?"

"Bruised, but nothing serious. I can breathe just fine."

She nods, not quite meeting my gaze. "This will sting."

I close my eyes as she disinfects the cut on my cheekbone. She's right. It stings like a motherfucker, but not nearly as much as the understanding of just how impassable the chasm between us has become. I wait until she starts on the bandages to speak. "He said he won't touch you if you don't want it."

"I know." She pauses. "Eli, I will do anything to keep our people from feeling the brunt of this. And that includes allying with Abel."

I tense. She's being so damn practical, but I can't help feeling like she's choosing him over me. "You have no reason to trust him."

"I have to try." She shrugs and presses the last bandage to my cheekbone. "Someone has to clean up this mess."

There it is. The truth is that we're in this situation because of me. Because of what my family and the other factions did on that night eight years ago. It doesn't matter that I had no knowledge of my father's plans for Abel and his brothers; the only thing that matters is what was done. "Abel cut down seven of the best people we put down there. All of them are undefeated."

"All of them *were* undefeated." She sits back. "Eli, *why* did you chase me down into the sand?"

"You know why."

She stares at me with dark eyes. Over the years I've seen those eyes go hazy with pleasure, alight with joy, and even darker with sorrow. I've never seen her look like she's disappointed in me. "After all this time, I don't understand how you can be so determined to see me as a damsel in distress. I survived twenty-seven years before we got together, twenty-four of them in a faction ruled by Bauer Paine. If we start comparing scars, *you* grew up more sheltered than I ever could have dreamed of being."

"I know that." I want to take her hands, but I can't stand the thought of her pulling away from me again. "You've suffered enough for several lifetimes. I don't want you to suffer any more if there's anything I can do about it."

Harlow gives a sad little laugh. "That's the thing. There *isn't* anything you can do about it. I could have gone with Abel and worked behind the scenes to ensure that any coup he attempted would fail. Instead, you handed the entire faction over to him without a second thought."

"I wouldn't ask that of you." In that moment, I hadn't thought of anything at all except that I couldn't watch Abel take the woman I loved.

"That's the problem." Harlow pushes to her feet and drags her fingers through her hair. "I can't do this with you. We just keep going round and round. I..." She looks away. "I was going to leave you anyway."

I suspected as much, but there's something about

hearing her say it aloud that shocks the hell out of me. "What?"

"After Lammas. I was already planning on it."

"*Why?* I have tried everything I could think of to make you happy."

"You tried everything." Harlow gives a bitter little laugh and turns away. "The fact that you actually think that after everything we've talked about in the last twelve hours just proves leaving is the right choice. You tried everything *except the one thing I needed from you.* I can't do this. I can't keep letting you bottle me up as if I'm made of something more fragile than glass. You're suffocating me, Eli. You have been for a long time. You don't trust me, you don't *see* me."

Something ugly surges in my chest. "And Abel does."

She spins back to face me. "I never said that."

"You stood at his side and told our people to leave."

"To *save* them, you asshole. You weren't going to do it. Someone had to."

I stalk closer to her. I have been so fucking careful with Harlow. So cognizant of how much she's survived, of how much better she deserves. Her father almost killed her dozens of times over before she finally put a knife in his chest. And then she spent years drifting about the faction, doing whatever it took to survive. She deserves to be protected, to be indulged. I knew shit had gone sideways between us, but I didn't realize it was because she resented that I was trying to do right by her. "So you jump into bed with Abel to punish me."

"No, Eli." Derision drips from each word. "I jumped into bed with Abel because I am his Bride, and it's my duty. You swallowed down his cock for the same fucking reason."

I've been trying really hard not to think about the feeling of Abel's cock in my mouth. Or the way he pinned me to the wall and bit the back of my neck in some sort of twisted mating ritual earlier. I hate the man. My body might not have fully gotten the memo, but I've never been one to let control slip over something as inconvenient as lust.

Or at least I never used to be that guy.

Now, I don't know who I am.

"Are you going to keep fucking him, Harlow?"

She lifts her chin, a sure sign that I'm not going to like the answer. "I haven't decided yet."

"You know what? You're right." I shake my head slowly. "I don't fucking know you. The woman I fell in love with would never consider him."

"Then you fell in love with a fantasy and not a real person." She practically snarls the words.

I don't know who moves first. One second we're glaring at each other from a few inches away. The next her arms are around my neck, and I'm grabbing her ass and hauling her body against mine. For the first time since I met her, I'm not thinking about anything but getting inside her. Not about her pleasure. Not about her past. Not about our future going up in ashes with every word we hurl at each other.

I take her mouth just shy of violently, and she meets me halfway. Her nails dig into my neck and drag down to my shoulders, and I relish the pain. This deserves to hurt. It's goodbye, after all. We might be Abel's Brides, but that's the only thing connecting us right now. That and far too much hurt and resentment.

I shove Harlow back onto the bed and go for the front of her jeans. She lifts her hips to help me yank them down her legs, and then she's hooking the front of my pants and shoving them aside to get at my cock.

A small voice whispers that I should slow down, should make sure she's ready, but I ignore it. It's as if someone else is riding shotgun in my skin. I hook her legs and drag her to the edge of the bed, and then she's guiding my cock into her pussy. I slam into her and curse. Fuck, she feels good. She always feels so goddamn good. Everything else might change, but that won't.

She holds my gaze in a glare as she strokes her clit, chasing her own pleasure even as I pound into her. I growl. "No matter what else is true, you love my cock."

"Cold fucking comfort, Eli."

Her cruelty and anger only drive me on, feeding mine. I drop on top of her and hitch her leg higher to get deeper. I wrap her hair around my free fist and jerk her head to the side. She gives a breathy moan that I feel all the way to my balls. "Is this what you want, baby? You want to be fucked hard by someone who doesn't give a damn about you? Someone who's going to treat you like a dirty little slut and make you come all over his cock?"

She digs her nails into my ass, pulling me closer yet. "No matter how hard you fuck me, it's not going to change the fact that you want *his* cock."

I hate that she's right. That's not what this is about, though. Or at least not entirely. "You might think he sees you, but he's using you just like he's using me. When he's done with you, he's going to drop you in the trash and walk away without looking back."

She moans, and her back bows. "Still a better future... than the one in a gilded cage that you're offering." Harlow cries out as she comes, clenching around my cock hard enough that I lose control. I pound into her, chasing my own pleasure, hating how things have turned out between us even as a dark part of me delights in taking off the gloves. A part of me I never, ever let off the leash. Looks like I don't have a fucking choice right now. It's in the driver's seat, and there's no going back now.

I collapse on top of her and turn my head to find that we're no longer alone. Abel stands in the middle of the room, watching us with an unreadable expression on his face. He catches my gaze and raises his eyebrows. "By all means, don't stop on my account. I was just beginning to enjoy the show."

The man I was twenty-four hours ago would have moved to cover Harlow, to protect her. But she doesn't want my protection. She hates me for even thinking to offer it.

I leverage myself off her, leaving her splayed out and spent. "Enjoy my sloppy seconds, asshole." I stalk to the bathroom and slam the door behind me.

Regret hits me hard enough to buckle my knees. What the fuck am I *doing*? I brace my hands on the sink and let my head drop between my shoulders. This isn't me. This isn't what I do. No matter how pissed I am at Harlow, that doesn't excuse how I just acted.

The urge to go out there and apologize nearly overwhelms me, but I muscle it down. Even if I do, all it will accomplish is making them believe I'm even weaker than they already do. No, backtracking isn't an option.

Come on, you're better than this. Stop reacting and think.

That's just it. I need to think. I've been pure reaction since the moment Abel and the rest of the Paine brothers walked into the amphitheater. I have not successfully run this faction in the five years since my father's death by being impulsive and emotional.

I need a fucking plan, and then I need to put it into motion.

If I'm going to take back everything Abel stole from me, I have to start now. Right this fucking second.

After all this time, I should really be past the point where Eli's able to break my heart. I hate that my throat is tight and my face is on fire as I sit up and strive for some kind of dignity at that dose of humiliation.

For his part, Abel watches me the way I'd watch a cornered animal. Not sure if it's going to collapse or attack. I wish I knew the answer to that question, too. I reach down and snag my jeans off the floor. It takes a few moments to set them right and pull them on, but I don't feel better once it's done. Not when I can hear the water running in the bathroom. No doubt Eli is scrubbing off every bit of evidence of me from his body.

That's what I want, isn't it?

I should be happy that it's over. Or at least relieved.

Except it's not over. For better or worse, we're tied to Abel for the next year. There's no clean break, no escaping this proximity. We're going to be sharing space, digging our fingers into each other's wounds, trampling each other's emotions, for twelve more months. It makes me exhausted just thinking about it.

I smooth my hair back from my face. "Did you need something?"

"This your room?"

I don't know if I'm grateful or irritated that he's going to ignore what just happened. Maybe a little bit of both. "Sometimes. It's mostly Eli's." I'd claimed a room down the hall and spent more and more nights there in the last year. Eli never commented on it, simply taking my half-assed excuse about differing schedules at face value. Not a single fucking word to address the growing distance between us. No, he just kept on moving as if nothing had changed. It felt —it still feels—like further confirmation that he never really wanted *me*. He wanted what I represent.

Someone to save.

Proof that he's not like his father, that he's really a good man.

Joke's on both of us, after all.

Abel looks around the room for a long moment. "Get what you need."

"There's nothing I need here." I've long since moved most of my stuff to the other room. There's just a handful of clothes and books here, but nothing irreplaceable. I give the closed bathroom door one last look and then follow Abel to the door and out into the hall. He motions for me to precede him, and I walk four doors down and open it.

My room started as a spare room, but over the last year, it's acquired a scattering of my knickknacks on the dresser, most of my clothes in the walk-in closet, and all my various makeup and bathroom stuff in the large en suite bathroom. It still doesn't quite feel like *mine* the same way that my bedroom with Eli used to, but it's better than lying next to him every night, listening to him breathe and aching over our shattering relationship.

Abel moves around it, eyeing my bed, sifting his fingers through the container of jewelry on the dresser, disappearing into the closet and then the bathroom. When he returns, he looks just as unreadable as he's been since I met him. "This will do."

I know I need to dig in my heels, to tell him to fuck right off with what he's obviously assuming, but I'm still reeling with how ugly things became with Eli. "You're living on the edge if you think I really won't smother you in your sleep."

"Nah, you're too practical for that." He walks to the narrow window and peers out. We're high enough to see over the wall, and this room has a decent view of the river that separates our faction's territory from the Amazons to the northeast. "Even if you managed to kill me before I snapped your neck, my brothers would tear you to pieces."

I know. It factored into my decision to accept Abel's offer. I have little recourse. The Paine brothers might as well be a hydra. Even if someone manages to kill one, there are six more where he came from, and they'll all howl for the responsible party's blood. The only way would be to kill them all, and if Eli's father and an alliance with both Amazons and Mystics couldn't manage it, I doubt anyone living can.

No, better to work this from the inside and use his obvious attraction to me; anything to benefit my people. Abel isn't the type to let desire cloud his mind, but he's wise enough to realize what an asset I am.

I cross my arms over my chest. "What's next?"

"My people will use today to get settled in. Tomorrow we start patrols out into the faction to let people know who's in charge and see us." He glances at me. "That means you and I will be taking a nice little walk through Old Town. Eli, too, if he can behave himself."

Old Town is a sector that runs seven blocks long and about three blocks wide, filled with shops and bars and restaurants that have been here since Sabine Valley's inception. Or that's how the story goes. Most of the business owners can trace their lineage back at least three or four generations in the same place, and they compromise the backbone of the faction. If they don't get on Abel's side, then he doesn't have a chance in hell of transitioning smoothly into power.

I almost sit on the bed but think better of it at last moment. What happened with Eli is too fresh; I don't trust myself not to do something self-destructive like fuck Abel just to get the memory of Eli's ugly words out of my head.

Enjoy my sloppy seconds.

He'll be lucky if *I* don't sink a knife between his ribs the next time I see him, the bastard.

"Harlow." From the tone of Abel's voice, he's said my name more than once.

"Sorry, I'm listening now."

He doesn't move from the window, but somehow he seems closer. "Did you know that Eli and I were friends when we were kids? All the way up through our teens and most of our twenties until all that shit went down eight years ago."

I knew that, but only because people like to gossip about the Paines when they think no one is listening. Eli never talked about Abel. Not once in all the time we've been together. I should have recognized that as a red flag, but I had stars in my eyes for too long after we started dating. "Do you have a point for this little walk down memory lane?"

His dark eyes flare, and his lips curve in something resembling a smile before he shuts it down. "My point, sweetheart, is that Eli was never the kid who'd come at a problem head-on. I wanted something, I'd go after it with everything I had, no matter what stood in my way. Eli likes to flank the situation and attack it from the side. He always has."

"I'm aware of how Eli works." This isn't making me feel any better, but then why would Abel want me to feel better? I might not have been in any kind of power when his father was killed, but I've been fucking the man who was for five years. Surely he blames me, at least by proxy.

Abel slowly crosses to me. "I got used to losing. You can't win them all, and I learned something valuable every time I lost. It made me better, sharper, hungrier." He stops in front of me. "Eli never lost. Not once he set his mind on something. He's too damn good, spent too much time playing out scenarios in that big brain of his. He never makes a move unless he can be sure he'll end up victorious."

It's the truth. Eli's hesitance to act quickly might have driven me up the wall more times than I can count, but when he finally *did* make a move, it usually led to victory. "And?"

"And he just lost you. Fuck, he just realized that he lost you even before I came on the scene, all on his own failure. It's going to fuck him up for a while, and he's going to strike out at the cause during that time. At you."

I stare up at him. "Are you trying to make me feel better or worse?"

"Neither. I'm stating a fact. You should have run the second you realized you didn't want to be with him anymore. Now you're stuck here in the bed you made, and it's going to be messy as hell." He shrugs. "That going to be a problem?"

Of course it's going to be a problem. No matter how much I'd like to avoid Eli, the truth is that it's impossible. At least for any extended period of time. Every time we end up in the same room, it's going to be more of the same. Ugly words and uglier actions. "I have it under control."

"Do you? Because you were coming all over his cock twenty minutes ago."

I lift my chin. "Do you find that threatening, Abel? Even when he's being an asshole, he makes me feel so fucking good when he's inside me." I know I'm tugging a tiger by the tail, but I can't seem to help myself. I hurt. I hurt so fucking much, I can barely breathe past it, and Abel's standing here, solid and unbreakable. He can take whatever poison I need to purge; I'm sure of it.

"What you do with him has nothing to do with us. Keep fucking him, for all I care." He leans down until his breath ghosts over my lips. "But don't pretend you weren't still aching even after he was through with you."

"I—"

He grabs my arm and spins me around, pressing my back to his chest. I'm still processing the new position when he hooks his thumb beneath the band of my jeans. It's the slightest touch, but I jump like he's zapped me with a live wire. His words growl in my ear. "That orgasm was just an appetizer, wasn't it, sweetheart? You're still feeling needy, and I have nothing but time today."

I shouldn't.

I might have learned a long time ago the necessity of separating sex from emotion, but Abel is too overwhelming already. I'm not certain I can keep my distance, avoid getting washed away through the sheer force of his presence.

I'm not sure I care. "I'm tired. It was a long night."

"You're not going to be able to sleep, not with your mind spinning out. I can help."

My chest feels like I have a gaping hole in it. I'm all too

willing to let him distract me from it, at least for a little while. I lean my head back on his shoulder and relax against him. He takes it for the invitation it is and pops the button of my jeans. The slow drag of my zipper, and then his fingers are there, dipping beneath the denim until he cups my pussy. The jeans are too tight for him to do much more than that, but it feels unforgivably possessive, as if he's claiming me.

"You didn't use protection with Eli."

I close my eyes, giving myself over to this. "I'm on birth control. We're monogamous; or at least we were before you came along."

He slips his hand almost all the way out of my jeans and then back in, this time wedging two fingers into me. I inhale sharply, barely biting back a moan. I shouldn't like how owned I feel right now. I shouldn't be fighting down the need to beg him for more. Abel holds me like this, deep and intimate, for several long moments. I can feel my heartbeat racing through my entire body, but I somehow manage to hold myself perfectly still.

He flattens his free hand to the space below my breasts, pressing me back against him more firmly. "I'd like to have you without a condom, Harlow. Have you wet and slick and pump you full of my come."

I let out a harsh laugh. "You only want that because *he* has it."

"Maybe." He nuzzles my hair off my neck and kisses me there. "But I think you want it, too. Isn't that why you're arching back against me right now? It's not because you want me. It's because you want me to erase all evidence of *him* on your skin."

He's not wrong, and I hate that he not only sees the truth

but doesn't hesitate to call me on it. "Bold of you to think that I trust you enough to go there."

"Ah, but I've never lied to you, sweetheart. And I never will, even if you hate me for it. I was tested before we came back to Sabine Valley—all of us were—and I haven't touched anyone since."

Strangely enough, I *do* believe him. I don't know if the Paine brothers plan on trying to keep any of these relationships going past the year deadline, but it makes sense that they'd prepare for the eventuality of possibly fucking their Bride more than the first night. If they're all as arrogant as Abel, they'd probably assume it's a sure thing.

"Then maybe you shouldn't trust *me*." I gasp a little as his fingers flex inside me. "Be a shame if I got knocked up and didn't know which of you was the father."

"Would it?" His voice is so dry, I can't tell what he's thinking. "I don't think so. That kid would be *mine*, regardless of whose DNA contributed to its creation. And wouldn't that be a kicker? Me and you raising his biological kid. Just another thing of his that I'll take, and gladly."

I tense. "You really hate him."

"I would think that's readily apparent." He gives my neck another light kiss. "So what will it be, Harlow? Do you want my cock or not?"

I don't understand how everything with Abel feels so inevitable, but I want what he's offering. Escape. "Yes."

"With a condom or without?"

So reckless to go without, but he's right. He has no reason to lie to me. Not about this. Not when we're stuck together for the next year. I lick my lips. "Without."

He makes a growling sound against my neck, and then he's moving, easing his hand out of my jeans and pulling my tank top over my head. My bra joins it on the floor, and then he sits on the bed and tugs my jeans down, his gaze on every inch of exposed skin. When I finally stand before him naked, he slowly peruses me as if he didn't have me pinned to a bathroom counter just this morning. He finally catches my gaze. "I want you to ride my cock, sweetheart. Use me to make yourself feel good." I open my mouth, but he catches my chin before I can speak, his eyes going hard. "I can keep fucking you from behind, but there's no pretending I'm just some asshole off the street. It's *my* cock you need right now, and you know it."

He's right. I hate that he's right.

I pull in a shuddering breath. "Stop talking and get naked.

11

ABEL

I lied to Harlow.

I told her that I'd never let something as mundane as sex cloud my vision. It's mostly the truth, but as she climbs up to straddle me, I have enough self-awareness to recognize that I want to keep her. It hasn't even been twenty-four hours, but like recognizes like. I meant what I said. This woman is a monster, just like me. Just as ruthless, just as ambitious. She'd do anything to protect the people of this faction, just like I'd do anything to keep my brothers among the living.

Imagine what we'll do together.

I skate my hands up her thighs to grip her full hips. She's soft and strong, and I have to remind myself that she's got to be the one behind the wheel for this interaction. She wraps her fist around my cock and guides me to her entrance. No fucking around. The woman might have one hell of a poker face, but it's failing her right now; her expression flickers with messy emotions as she sinks onto my cock. Pleasure and guilt and fury and determination. No matter what she claims, she still loves Eli, and what happened back in their room hurt her.

I palm her heavy breasts, enjoying the way they fill my hands. I have hours before I have to be anywhere. My brothers are all occupied with getting their Brides settled and navigating that mess. So many strong personalities under one roof will make for an interesting year.

But I don't have to worry about that right now.

My only concern is tying Harlow to me as tightly as possible, until she sees us as a team. If she's loyal to me, it will be unflinching. We'll be fucking unstoppable. I lightly pinch her nipples. "I changed my mind."

Her brows pull together in a frown. "What are you talking about?"

I'm moving her before she has a chance to tense, hauling her off my cock and rolling us so that she's beneath me. She shoves at my shoulders, but she's nowhere near strong enough to move if me if I don't want to move. I press her legs wide and settle between them. Her pussy is slick against my cock as I thrust a little, and the knowledge that she's filled up with Eli's come makes me feel a little loose around the seams. I can't decide if I want to fuck her until all evidence of him is erased, or if I want to go down on her and lick her clean.

Actually, the decision is pretty fucking easy when I put it like that.

"You're thinking too hard, Harlow." I catch her bottom lip with my teeth and bite gently. "If I want Eli in this bed with us, I'll bring his pretty ass in here and chain him to the headboard."

"There you go again, talking kinky," she whispers.

"You're mean. You liked it that he watched me make you come." I move down to drag my mouth along her neck to her shoulder. "You loved hurting him like that. Riding my mouth while he sat cuffed to a chair and totally helpless."

Her breath catches as I press her breasts together and lavish kisses across their curves to her nipples. Harlow digs her hands into my hair, not trying to guide me anywhere, just hanging on as I do what I want. She whimpers. "I'm very, very angry at him."

"Want to punish him?" I nip the underside of one breast. "Plant him face-down in your pussy while I fuck his ass. He can't run that smart mouth while his tongue is inside you."

She shivers. "There's only one tongue I want inside me right now."

"Liar." I move down her body. "But I can take a hint." It's where I was headed anyway.

I use my shoulders to spread her legs wider yet. She's pink and flushed with desire from having just been riding Eli's cock. Maybe I shouldn't like that shit so much, but I've never been one to ignore my desires. I want to taste him inside her, a mixture of their orgasms. I need it.

I don't give her a chance to brace for it. I kiss her pussy and shove my tongue inside her. Harlow's back bows, and her fingers tighten in my hair to the point of pain. "*Fuck.*"

Fuck is about right.

I'm chasing my own desire, but it doesn't matter because she's riding my face and making that sexy whimpering sound. Her legs are already shaking, but I don't care. She can come as much as she needs to until I'm finished with her.

It might take years before I'm truly sated.

I suck on her clit, rubbing my tongue against the sensitive bud as I watch her come apart. She's not one of those shy people who close their eyes and are borne along by the wave of pleasure. No, she's staring down at me as if memorizing the sight of my mouth all over her pussy. Her dark eyes are wide, and her lips are parted around each panting breath. I keep up that motion on her clit, and it's too much for her. She cries out, and only then do her eyes slide shut. Her whole body goes tense as she orgasms, her legs locking around either side of my head to keep me in place.

As if I have any plans of leaving.

I move back to slide my tongue into her pussy again, tasting her and the saltiness that is Eli. Fuck, that's hot. Hot enough that I have to fight to keep my hips still and not grind against the mattress. I don't normally have control issues, but this is hardly a normal circumstance. No, this is pure need.

She tugs on my hair hard enough that I let her guide me, crawling up her body until she claims my mouth. Harlow kisses me as if she can purge every thought with this single contact. I could tell her that shit is always there on the other side, but it doesn't matter. It's an escape, and if she gets it from me, she'll come back again and again.

She hooks her leg around my waist and shoves. I let her roll us back to our original position, her straddling me. This time, there's no conflict on her face. Just a hunger hot enough to match my own. Her lips curve as she slides onto my cock. "Abel."

Fuck, I like my name on her tongue. "Yeah?"

She leans down until our faces are kissably close, her breasts rubbing against my chest with each slow roll of her hips as she works my cock. "You want Eli." Apparently she doesn't need an answer, because she keeps riding me, keeps talking. "You just went down on me as if you could lick up every bit that he left inside me." She props her hands on either side of my neck, giving herself better leverage. "How long until *you're* fucking him?"

I grab her hips and thrust up into her. Harlow cries out and grinds down on my cock. For a moment, the only sound in the room is flesh slapping against flesh and our harsh breathing. I should keep using sex to distract her, but even if I didn't exactly promise honesty, every time I tell her the truth, I bind her to me more effectively.

I release one hip and clasp her chin. She doesn't stop moving, doesn't stop fucking me, and I like her all the more for it. Finally, I grind out, "Yeah, I'm going to fuck Eli. I said as much earlier."

Surprise flickers over her face, but it smooths out almost immediately. "Another manipulation."

"Yeah." I hiss out a breath as she plants her hands on my chest and leans back, taking me deeper yet and breaking my hold on her chin. I press my hand to her lower stomach and stroke her clit with my thumb. "I've wanted that fucker for a long time; not even hate and betrayal can take that away. I'm going to have him, and then I'm going to kick his ass to the curb at the end of this. He'll walk away knowing that I have his territory, his home, and his woman."

Harlow doesn't speak again. She simply gets down to fucking me hard enough that we're both panting and sweating, and there's no space for words. She doesn't like what I've said, but sometimes the truth is shitty. Hell, most of the time it is. She'll come to terms with it sooner or later. She's too practical, too angry, to fight against the inevitable.

And me and Harlow?

We're fucking inevitable.

She comes with a cry loud enough that everyone in this hall has to hear it. A sound that's almost a scream. I hook the back of her neck and pull her down to claim her mouth as I pound up into her, chasing my own orgasm. I clench my jaw as I come, a fierce, dark part of me elated that there's nothing between us in this moment. She's taking all of me. Everything.

She slumps to the side, and I follow her, turning onto my side. Harlow starts to sit up, but I plant my hand in the center of her chest, lightly holding her in place. "We still need to talk."

"We've done nothing but talk. I'm over it."

"Mmm." I slide my hand down her stomach and push two fingers into her.

Her eyes go wide. "What are you doing?"

"I told you I have nowhere to be for the next few hours. You didn't really think once would be enough, did you?" I fuck her slowly while I wait for an answer. She spreads her legs the tiniest bit, which is answer enough. I prop my head in my hand and twist my wrist, feeling for the spot that... Yeah, there it is.

She moans, and her eyes flutter closed. "You said you wanted to talk."

"You ready to listen?" I lightly stroke that spot, enjoying how she melts against me in response. "Or you want to come a few more times to take the edge off?"

Harlow hisses out a breath and grabs my shoulder. She doesn't try to move me; it's more like she needs something to hang on to. Her breathing picks up. "What? You can't multitask?"

That surprises a laugh out of me. Yeah, I like this woman. A lot. I watch her face as I ease her closer and closer to orgasm. "Taking this faction isn't enough."

At that, she opens her eyes. There are bright spots of pink on her cheeks. "What?"

"Come on, sweetheart. If I only wanted this faction, I wouldn't need to take the other six Brides for my brothers.

You think I chose the heirs to the Mystics and Amazons by accident?"

She blinks slowly. "You're out of your mind."

"Nah, I'm just ambitious." And I have enough rage to burn this entire city to the ground. That would only give me a momentary flare of pleasure, and it would hurt too many people whose only sin is living in the wrong place. This is better.

She lifts her hips, subtly fucking my fingers. "What's that have to do with me?"

"After you're done fucking out the worst of your rage, you're going to be my new Bride wrangler." It's a damn shame to be this close to her perfect mouth and not taste her, so I dip down and give her a thorough kiss.

She follows me as I break it, chasing down the distance between us. When she speaks, her lips move against mine. "And if I say no?"

"You're not going to say no, Harlow." I withdraw my fingers, enjoying the way she whimpers in protest, and slide between her thighs. A few minutes is a hell of a recovery time, but Harlow so sexy, it's no wonder my body's rising to the occasion. I slide into her and leverage my arm beneath her hips to guide her into an angle that will have the head of my cock rubbing against that same spot. Her harsh inhale tells me I've found it.

"Why would I say yes?" It takes her all of three seconds to have her hands on my ass, her nails digging into my skin as she lifts her hips to meet each thrust. That's my girl.

I nip her earlobe as I fuck her. As she fucks me right back.

"Because you want to be queen, Harlow. And I'm your ticket to the throne."

12

ELI

I stand in the hallway outside Harlow's room and listen
to her fuck Abel for ten minutes before it's clear that
they won't be finished anytime soon. It's just as well.
After how things fell out with us, she's not going to be ready
to see my face again today.

I'm not even pissed that she left my room and immediately jumped on Abel's cock, another indication of what
she's been trying to tell me for a very long time. She's not the
woman I thought she was. The image I built up in my head.
It's my fucking fault that she's in this mess, and she's making
the best of it. Hard to blame her for that, even if jealousy
curls through my stomach at the sound of her moans, of his
low curses.

I can't even say for certain that it's jealousy that Abel's
fucking her. It might be that she's fucking Abel. *That* is an
attraction I can't afford, but I'll use it just like I'll use any
other tool at my disposal.

Right now, Abel is distracted. I turn and head down the
hallway. My people have already been pushed out, but that
doesn't mean they're gone for good. I might have been

caught flat-footed yesterday at Lammas, but I had a contingency plan in case any of the other factions tried to stage a coup. My security people will have gathered at a secondary location to await orders.

Now I simply need to get access to a phone and call them.

I turn the corner and stop short at the sight of a blond white woman striding toward me. She's wearing tiny jean shorts, a white crop top that shows off a toned stomach, and a pair of red-tinted heart-shaped glasses that match her bright red lips. I've read that, in certain parts of the world, frogs and some insects are brightly colored to warn predators that they're poisonous. I don't know if Monroe intentionally mimics the effect, but some part of my brain shouts *danger* every time I have to deal with her.

Her lips curve when she sees me, but her green eyes behind the glasses don't warm. "Eli. Just the man I'm looking for."

I slide my hands into my pockets and give her an absent smile. It's hard to pull my chosen shield around me, much harder than normal. "Monroe."

She laughs and gives a little wiggle. Her white shirt is just thin enough that I can see the outline of her nipples through it. The wiggle just confirms that she's not wearing a bra. She takes my arm and pivots to walk next to me. "We really need to talk about our mutual Paine problem."

The hallway is empty except for us, but that doesn't mean we're not being observed. I shoot her a look. "I don't know what you're talking about."

"Sure you don't. That's not Abel Paine back there, giving it to your woman so good that she's screaming for him." When I miss my step, she snorts. "Come on, Eli. Drop the act. This goes beyond factions. We're all in the same boat."

Maybe, but that doesn't mean I can trust her. I start to untangle my arm from her grasp when footsteps signal someone approaching. A pretty, white woman with brunette hair and the kind of sweet expression that has no place here comes around the corner and stops short. She's wearing jeans and a T-shirt, and the way she looks at Monroe is exasperated. "There you are."

"Just getting a good look around and telling Eli what a pretty cage he's created for us." She pats my chest, her nails digging in through my shirt.

"Monroe, you're going to give Broderick a stroke, and it hasn't even been twenty-four hours."

"One can only hope," Monroe murmurs.

"I heard that." The woman grabs Monroe's hand, heedless of the danger she's in by keeping the Amazon heir so close, and tugs her away from me. "Come on. It's my job to keep you out of trouble."

Monroe gives me a long look over her shoulder, a clear promise that our conversation isn't over, and smiles wide. "Baby, why stay out of trouble when it's *so fun* to get into trouble?" She leans against the other woman. "I have a few ideas if you're game."

The woman is still stammering when they round the corner and disappear down the hall. I stare after them for a long moment. There is a possibility that Monroe is serious about allying together against the Paines, but I can't risk it. Not until I have no other options. The Amazons and Mystics and I might not have been in an all-out war leading into this, but that doesn't mean there's trust between the factions. Monroe might decide to take out two birds with one stone—me and the Paine brothers. If anyone can do it, she and her family can. And there are *three* of them under this roof.

I shudder. Better to get moving before someone else comes along.

The thought barely crosses my mind when a man stalks into view. He doesn't look much like Abel, aside from the similar body type of a brawler, but I instantly recognize Cohen, the third oldest brother. Their mother named them alphabetically, which amused plenty of people as she kept popping out children, but there's nothing amusing about the barely restrained violence on Cohen's face as he catches sight of me and picks up his pace. "You."

I don't take a step back, but it's a near thing. "Cohen." He's a few inches shorter than me, but he's wider through the shoulders and chest. He catches me around the throat, and I do nothing to stop it. I let him bear me back to the wall and pin me there. I merely raise my brows. "Your brother's put in a lot of work for you to kill me now."

"Don't tempt me." His voice is low and as gravelly as if he's been gargling rocks. "You deserve worse than death for what you did."

"What my father did," I gently correct.

His eyes are amber, and the color should make them warm, but they're as icy as Abel's turn every time he looks at me. "You don't get to pull that card, Eli. You were twenty-eight. Hardly a babe in arms." His fingers tighten around my throat ever so slightly.

"Not a babe in arms," I repeat. I force myself to smile as if none of this matters. "Unlike your little Bride. How old is Winry? Twenty-three? She was barely fifteen when your father was killed. Hardly a responsible party."

"She's an Amazon." Just like that, he drops his hand. "She'll pay the price, just like you will." He grabs my upper arm and yanks me away from the wall. "I don't know where my brother is, but you don't have free rein to wander the halls as you like. Get the fuck back to your room."

Frustration sinks its teeth into me, but if I dig in my heels now, it will raise all sorts of alarms. Not to mention that Cohen is just looking for an excuse to beat the shit out of me. Of all the Paine brothers, he's the most dangerous one. Abel might be the leader, but Cohen was always the knife in the dark. Their enemies never saw him coming. After eight years away from Sabine Valley, anything can be true now, but I doubt that's changed. I can't take him in a one-on-one fight. And even if I could, it serves no purpose now.

I smile, fighting down a wince when the expression pulls at my cut lip. "Sure."

He marches me down the hall. As we pass Harlow's room, another loud moan emerges. Cohen glances at the door, his expression inscrutable. I half expect him to rub my nose in the fact that Abel is fucking Harlow the same way Monroe did, but he stays silent until I motion that we've reached our destination. Only then does he release my arm.

Cohen gives me a long look. "If I had my way, Abel would have cut you down and put your head on a spike in the middle of that goddamn amphitheater."

Once upon a time, I considered this man a brother just like I considered the rest of the Paine boys brothers. Cohen and I were never close, but it doesn't change the fact that I've known him his entire life. None of that matters. It wasn't enough to alter my father's plans, and it's not enough to change what I have to do now. "That's why Abel's the one in charge." That's also why he's dangerous in a way completely different than Cohen. "You're just a dog on a leash."

Cohen starts to turn away. "I'm on *his* leash. Never forget that. The second he says the word, I'll happily rip out your throat." He glances over his shoulder at me. "Give me a reason, Eli. Just give me a fucking reason."

It's not a bluff. The Paines don't bluff. They never have.

I make myself turn away, presenting him with my back, and walk through the door. It takes everything I have to close the door softly behind me, to not engage the lock. To not show a single bit of weakness.

Fuck.

I drag my hand over my face and wince at the pain the motion causes. This isn't going to work. My people will wait to hear from me, but the sooner I get into contact with them, the better. It will prevent them from acting on their own and potentially fucking this situation up worse.

A soft sound has me spinning around. The mirror swings forward, and a familiar face comes into view. I don't exhale in relief, but it's a near thing. "You know I don't want the passageways used, Marie." Not until there's no other choice. I have no doubt Abel will find them at some point—he's too savvy not to figure out that the rooms don't quite line up where they should—but I want to keep them as a last resort until then.

Marie's expression takes on a stubborn set. "There was no other way to get access to you. We weren't sure you'd be able to get a line out." She tosses me a cell phone. "Now you can."

I catch it. It's a generic model that's no doubt pre-paid. "Thank you." I won't need to use it now. Not with her standing right in front of me. "Gather our people at the rendezvous point, and stay out of sight. Don't cause any problems. Don't engage with any of the Paines' people. Don't do *anything* until you hear from me." We'll only get one chance at this, and it has to be timed perfectly.

"Yes, sir."

"Make sure no one sees you on your way out."

Marie hesitates. "We're with you, Eli. As long as it takes, no matter what it takes."

"I know." I glance at the door. "Now go." I stride to the mirror and ease it shut. It barely makes a click, but it feels particularly loud in the silence of the room.

Well, the problem of the phone is solved. I expect Marie will be able to escape the grounds again without being caught. All my people have been trained on moving through the compound without being seen. The events from eight years ago hang heavy overhead, even after my father died. I guess part of me always knew that Abel would be returning, but even if he didn't, there was always the chance that one of the other factions would move against us.

I should have planned better.

I should have done a lot of things.

Regrets won't help me now. I can't go back into the past and change things. I can only look to the future and find a way forward.

13

I don't mean to fall asleep. I really don't. But the events of the last twenty-four hours catch up with me and suck me under. I wake in slow waves, registering the heavy arm over my stomach, the thick leg between mine, the soft rasp of breathing against my neck. Not Eli. Abel.

I open my eyes and stare at the ceiling. There's no going back now. There wasn't from the moment Eli's champion lost that last fight. There sure as hell wasn't once Eli lost *his* fight.

As much as I tell myself that I'm making the best of a bad situation, that's not all this is. I'm self-aware enough to realize that. There's something about Abel that brings out a part of me I've kept buried since I put my father in the ground. She's nothing like the woman I've become at Eli's side, the one who will smile and politick and manipulate with soft words and softer actions. No, she's dark and brutal and only too willing to cut down anyone between her and her goal.

The only difference between me now and then is that my goal has changed. It's not as simple as survival. Of course

I want to survive, but the weight of the faction hangs heavy around my neck. I can't trust either Abel or Eli to put the people first. They have too much history, too much rage between them. They'd fight each other until the entire city burned, no matter how many casualties they'd cause.

I have to ensure it doesn't come to that.

It might be possible if it were only those two I have to juggle, but Abel bit off a whole mess with the people his brothers chose for Brides. He's alienated both Amazons and Mystics. Given half a chance, they'll crush *our* faction between them for the insult he offered.

I exhale slowly. One thing at a time. First I have to get control of myself and my reactions. I can't let something as mundane as a broken heart get in the way of the greater good.

Which means I have to patch things up with Eli, at least superficially.

Fuck.

"Morning," Abel growls against my skin.

I shiver. I'm deliciously sore, and I don't know if I can go another round, but part of me wants to despite everything. "What time are we doing the parade through Old Town today?"

He props himself up on his hand and looks down at me. "Straight to business this morning, then?"

My gaze drops to his mouth before I jerk it back to his eyes. There's no reprieve there, though. I've already realized that he's just as much a master manipulator as Eli; he just goes about things with a different style. For all his talk of charging right through obstacles, Abel has a knack for finding his opponents' pressure points and using them to trigger the actions he wants. He's doing it right now.

I stretch, and Abel drags his gaze down my body as if he

can't quite help himself. *Not so unaffected, are you?* He's offered me everything I've ever wanted, but I'm not fool enough to ignore the trap it is. I push down everything, bottling it up until there's nothing for him to work with except cool confidence. "That's all this is, Abel. Business."

A muscle in his jaw twitches, but he smiles slowly. "You weren't saying that when you were coming all over my cock."

"We've already laid down parameters for that, and you know it. Sex might be enjoyable and might serve whatever petty purpose we require, but it has nothing to do with business." I sit up and start to slide out from beneath him. His arm tenses around me for the briefest moment, and I wonder if he'll let me go, but he rolls onto his back, releasing me.

I ignore the little twinge in my chest at the loss of his touch and head for the shower. I can feel his eyes on me, but he doesn't follow me into the bathroom. It's just as well. The last thing I need is to be further distracted by his body. There's too much to do today in order to minimize the damage to the faction. Abel's plan to parade through Old Town won't do a damn thing on its own. He must know that, but no doubt he's trying to tempt anyone willing to fight for Eli and remove them. It's what I would do in his situation.

It takes me about an hour to get ready. I curl my hair into gentle waves, give my eyes a subtle smoky look, and paint my lips red. I don't bother with a towel as I walk out of the bathroom. Abel lounges on my bed as if it's his, his big body taking up far too much space. He watches me the way I imagine a wolf would study a rabbit that's wandered into his den.

No matter what Abel thinks, I'm no rabbit.

I pointedly ignore him and head into the closest. After

careful consideration, I pull on a pair of dark jeans and a black top that hugs my body and does impressive things for my breasts. Boots complete the image. I'll be able to move, to fight, but I look put together. Good enough.

Abel's finally moved by the time I walk back into the bedroom. He sits at the edge of the bed, wearing jeans and nothing else. His dark eyes take me in, and he nods slowly. "That'll do."

"I know what I'm doing."

"Still can't take anything for granted." He leans forward and props his elbows on his knees then levels a severe look in my direction. "You going to knife me today, Harlow?"

"Wasn't planning on it."

He doesn't smile. "Trying to stab me in the back is going to be a fucking mistake. You're smart enough to know that, so don't let your temper get the best of you when I invariably piss you off. We both want the same thing. Remember that."

I prop my hands on my hips. "Is there a point to this fun little lecture?"

"We need to get the Brides in line. All of them. They're a pack of vipers, and they're going to be fucking things up every chance they get."

I blink. "Gee, that's so surprising. It's almost as if they were given away as prizes to their enemies and they're now handfasted to said enemies. Not to mention they're all attached to the most dangerous and powerful people in Sabine Valley. I'm *shocked* that you're expecting trouble with them."

Abel doesn't move. "You got that out of your system?"

Damn, his tone doesn't even change. Everyone's a critic. I clear my throat. "Yes, I'm finished."

"As I was saying, the Brides are going to be a problem.

They'll all be scheming and sharpening their knives and getting in the way. I need you to convince them that's not in their best interests."

I cross my arms over my chest. "Very funny."

"Who's laughing?"

Does he think I was born yesterday? I frown. "To review, you have two of the Amazon queen's daughters and her younger brother, two of the Mystic leader's children and his newest wife. Both of those numbers include the heirs. You don't need to convince them to do shit. You have the collateral in place to use them against each other. All you have to do is threaten one of their family members within your control and you have a decent chance of ensuring they're on their best behavior."

"Yes." Something like admiration warms his eyes. "But threats have a way of pissing people off. That's a last resort. I'd prefer they act like good little Brides of their own account."

It would simplify his life considerably if the Brides decided to play along. I get that. I do. But... "You're overestimating what I'm capable of. It doesn't matter that we're all Brides, which technically puts us in the same boat. They are enemy factions. They're not going to listen to me."

"You'll figure it out." He grabs his shirt off the floor and pulls it on. "We'll do Old Town at four. You have until then." Abel pushes to his feet. "You have full run of the house unless you prove you can't be trusted with it."

"Wow, what a gift."

He grabs me around the waist and hauls me against his chest. Abel tips my chin up and drops his gaze to my lips. "Keep mouthing off and I'm liable to ruin your lipstick."

Heat surges through me, but I push it down. There's a time for fucking, and there's time for business. I can't let him use his giant cock to distract me. "Don't you have some-where to be? Because apparently I do."

He chuckles, an almost rusty sound. I get the impression that Abel Paine doesn't laugh often, though this hardly qual-ifies. He gives my ass a squeeze and releases me. "The Brides will be gathered in the library."

I tense. "If they fuck up my books, I'm going to skin *you*."

"You always say the sweetest things, Harlow." He strides out of the room before I can find something to toss at his head. I find myself smiling a little and shake my head. Liking Abel was never part of the plan, but I can't deny that he's got a certain roguish charm.

I walk back into the bathroom to check my lipstick. To give myself time for the ground to steady beneath my feet again. Liking Abel can only get me mired in more trouble than I already am. There's no guarantee that he will follow through on any promises that reach past the end of the handfasting. It's just as likely that he plans to use me for the duration and then kick my ass to the curb and take all the power for himself once the faction is stabilized.

Fuck that.

I smooth back my hair and leave my room. As tempting as it is to go straight to the library, rushing in there isn't going to put me in a position of power. Instead, I detour to the kitchen.

Eli bought me a tea cart and tea set the first year we were together. It's an old-fashioned tradition, but it's always delighted me. Maybe because something about it calls to the little girl I used to be, the one who never had the opportu-nity for innocent fantasies about being a princess or having tea parties. I should have realized when Eli gave me this present that he'd never see me as an equal. He kept trying to give me back the innocence I never had the privilege of experiencing.

That ship has long since sailed. I am who I am. I just wish he'd realized that before it was too late for us.

I close my eyes, hating the burning behind my lids. I hate him and I love him and I'm simultaneously mourning the loss of our relationship and feeling trapped because there is no clean break for us.

The teakettle whistles, signaling that it's time to get back to reality. I take a slow breath and put together the cart. A careful ploy, and one that might backfire, but it's the best move.

A few minutes later, I muscle open the door to the library and push the cart through. A wave of noise stops me short. What the fuck?

I take in the scene at a glance. Aisling's daughters, Monroe and Winry, are sitting next to each other on the couch. Well, Winry's sitting. Monroe is sprawled out like a jungle cat, all long limbs and dangerously sharp claws, barely sheathed. The Mystic's youngest wife is perched on a nearby chair, her dark eyes wide in her sweet face. A muscled woman who screams bodyguard stands at her back. I vaguely remember her from last night.

None of them are the source of the yelling.

The Mystic's heir, Fallon, is a tall, lean white woman with fire-engine red hair. She looks about half a second away from ripping something apart with her bare hands. Her half-brother, Matteo, has hints of red in his thick, wavy hair, but his skin tone is several shades darker than hers. Courtesy of the Mystic's third wife's darker coloring. He's one of those guys who seems permanently stoned—from what I know about the Mystics, it's entirely possible that it's the truth—but he's got his arm around his sister's waist and is physically restraining her.

The source of their anger?

I stare at the woman standing in front of Jasper, the Amazon queen's younger brother. I *know* her. Beatrix. The Mystic's younger sister, and aunt to Fallon and Matteo. "What the fuck are you doing here?" I ask. She isn't a Bride. In fact, she's in a relationship with Jasper, who *is* a Bride.

Oh shit, this is going to be trouble.

I push the cart the rest of the way into the room and shut the door. I don't even know how she got onto the compound, but I'm nearly certain she wasn't here last night. Or at least she didn't get into the trucks with us when we were transported from the amphitheater to the warehouse. I abandon my tea and march into the mix.

I point at Fallon. "I don't care how pissed you are, starting shit right now is a mistake." Going the harsh route is a risk. The Mystic might rule with witchery and superstition and fear, but I've seen Fallon fight. She's just as deadly as Monroe. Possibly more so, because she's got one hell of a temper, and it gets the best of her often enough to make all her enemies wary.

I hold her gaze, refusing to flinch at the promised violence in her eerie gray eyes. "What do you think the Paine brothers will do if you start stabbing people? Nothing good. Dial it back."

I turn to Beatrix. She's got the same flaming red hair and pale gray eyes as her niece, though her features don't look like they were carved out of ice. Right now, she's leaning back against Jasper, and I can't tell if it's to stand between him and her niblings or because she needs his support. "What are you doing here?"

She meets my gaze. "I'm here for Jasper."

That's what I feared. Word is that she, Jasper Rhodius, and Ezekiel Paine used to be joined at the hip before the coup. An Amazon, a Mystic, and a Paine. It seemed to defy belief that their friendship would have lasted even without the Paine brothers being driven out of Sabine Valley, but she and Jasper have been together ever since. No wonder Ezekiel picked Jasper as his Bride. My chest aches for Beatrix, but her heartbreak changes nothing. The situation is what it is. We just have to make the best of it.

I shake my head slowly. "He's a Bride, Beatrix. The ceremony has happened; it's been consummated. There's no going back. If you take him, you'll never make it out of the compound, and the entire city will turn against you." Neither of their factions will be safe for them, not if he's an oathbreaker and she's the one who facilitated it.

She lifts her chin, a stubborn glint in her eyes. "I'm not taking him anywhere. I'm staying with both of them."

Well, fuck me.

I don't drag my hand over my face, but it's a near thing. This situation was already a mess, but it gets more nightmarish with each minute that passes. No matter what Abel thinks, I am only human, and he's thrown me right into this pit of vipers.

How the hell am I going to pull this off?

14

ABEL

My brothers filter into the room, one by one. Broderick and Gabriel look haggard as fuck, as if they spent the last twenty-four hours in the fight for their lives. Considering that their Brides are the heirs to the Amazons and Mystics, respectively, it's no wonder. They can handle it, but I'm reassured all the same when they meet my gaze in turn and nod before dropping onto the couch across from me.

Finnegan and Ezekiel come next. They're twins, though not identical, and the tension coming from them both is enough to change the air in the room. Ezekiel, I get—his Bride is Jasper, who was once a good friend. I know all too well how a friendship soured can turn to poison on your tongue. I think my little brother hoped that he'd come back to some sort of explanation or at least protestation of innocence. Instead, Jasper and Beatrix have moved on without him. That shit stings.

Donovan ducks into the room. He alone has a lazy kind of swagger that hasn't been affected at all by us being back in Sabine Valley. He never takes anything seriously, so why would he start now? That said...

I level a long look at him. "You let your Bride bring in a bodyguard."

He shrugs and grins. "She won't be a problem."

"You don't know that."

"In fact, I do." He sinks onto the arm of the couch next to Gabriel. "As I said last night, she's loyal to my lovely Bride, not to Ciar."

"You don't know that," I repeat. "You can't afford to take anything for granted. We're the ones who pay the price if you fuck this up."

Donovan shakes his head. "Trust me on this. The only thing she cares about is Mabel's safety. As long as I don't endanger that, she'll work with me."

Yeah, I don't trust that shit, but it's obvious that Donovan has made up his mind. With so many moving parts, I have to trust *him*, even if I don't trust the bodyguard. "Fine. But she steps out of line, you're accountable."

"Deal." He drapes his arm over Gabriel's shoulder and tugs on his hair.

Cohen is the last to arrive. He looks the way he always does—intense. We all had our ways of dealing with exile. Donovan uses jokes to deflect tension. Broderick plans things down to their finest detail in an effort to exert control in an uncontrollable world. Cohen simply cuts down both problems and threats, often literally. Giving Winry to him was a risk, but she's also the Bride least likely to inspire him to identify them as a problem needing to be *fixed*.

Once they're all seated, I begin. "We got through stage one. This is where the real work starts, because taking the faction was easy, but holding it will be significantly harder."

None of them say anything. We've gone over this plan a thousand times. I'm only repeating what we all already know. "You have to win your Brides over, at least enough to ensure good behavior. If they at least appear happy, it will make their factions hesitate to strike against us. They make good hostages, and the Bridal contract should be enough to ensure we have a year before things escalate, but we can't take anything for granted. The Amazons and Mystics broke faith before; they might do it again."

Donovan gives a slow grin. "The entire floor heard how *happy* you made your little Bride this morning. Working fast with that one."

"Harlow is an asset, and she's smart enough to realize it. We're mutually aligned for the moment." Something I hadn't planned on, but I'm sure as fuck not going to let this opportunity pass.

"And Eli?" This from Cohen. He stares at me intently. "How does he feel about how *mutually aligned* you are with his woman?"

"She's not his anymore. She's mine." There's too much bite to my words, but if there's one place I can be honest, it's with my brothers. "Eli will serve his purpose as well. I'm leaving all of you but Cohen in the compound while we do this song and dance through Old Town. Cohen, pick a team. Three people. Any more and we look like we're scared."

Cohen nods. "I'll take Maddox and Shiloh."

At that, Broderick starts to life. "Not Shiloh."

"Shiloh is one of our best, and you know it. Stop trying to shelter her."

Broderick shakes his head. "No shit she's one of the best. That's not why she can't go. Right now, she's the only thing keeping Monroe in line. I can't risk separating them for the time being."

I blink. "*Shiloh* is keeping Monroe in line."

"Yes." He looks away, his jaw clenched tight. "Monroe has taken a shine to her."

Reluctant admiration filters through me. Monroe works fast, doesn't she? It took her a single day to realize that Broderick is holding a flame for his best friend and turn it into a weapon against him. "Is this going to be a problem?"

"I have it under control."

If anyone's capable of it, it's him. He's the most even-keeled of us, the foundation that keeps us tethered when things go sideways. "Okay. Cohen, take Iris instead."

Cohen nods. "Will do."

"For the foreseeable future, patrols need to be double the size to avoid getting ambushed. Eli's people are still out there, and I have no doubt that they'll take any opportunity to attempt to stage a rescue. They'll also be undermining us at every turn." It will essentially be guerrilla warfare, but it's unavoidable. We knew the stakes when we moved forward with this plan.

Ezekiel clasps his hands loosely together between his knees. "I'll get the schedules put together. What happens if the people decide to start pushing back when it comes to supplies and resources?"

"They won't. Harlow will ensure it."

He hesitates. "You seem awfully sure of her."

"I am." If our situations were reversed, I'd be giving Ezekiel the same look he's giving me right now. Hell, I just did it to Donovan. I don't hold his doubt against him. But it changes nothing. Harlow and I are on the same page. "She's taken a look around and realized that the only people who pay the price of war—civil or otherwise—are those who can least afford it. She cares about them, so she'll do what it takes to smooth the transition. For their sake."

"Guess we'll see, won't we?" Cohen pushes to his feet. "If that's all, we got shit to do."

"Yeah, that's everything. Watch your backs."

"Always do." He moves to the door and is gone, quickly followed by the others, until only Broderick remains. He obviously has something to say, so I sit there and wait for him to work up to it.

He doesn't make me wait long. Broderick drags his hand over his close-cropped dark hair. "We might have bit off more than we can chew with this."

"Monroe is just one woman." A very dangerous, very volatile woman.

He snorts. "Yeah, no shit. But we don't just have Monroe. We have Fallon and Jasper and Matteo. Winry seems sweet as hell, but she's still an Amazon. I can't get a read on Mabel, despite the information we have on her, but the bodyguard worries me."

"Donovan says he has it under control."

"Uh-huh."

I curse. "Look, this was the only way. We've gone over this." Probably thousands of times at this point. "The Amazons and Mystics broke the peace. They gave people and resources to ensure the Paine family name disappeared off the face of the earth. If we tried to take back the faction without doing something to ensure their good behavior, they'd crush us just to get us out of the way. Having their people as Brides mean we can't move overtly against them right now, either, but we planned on that."

"I am aware of that."

I push to my feet. "We make it work, Broderick. We're committed. We have to see this through." Our very survival depends on it.

"I know. Fuck, I know." He joins me on his feet. "You should see the way she looks at Shiloh, Abel. Like a tiger who's got their eye on a nice, juicy steak."

"Shiloh can take care of herself." That's not what this is about, though. He knows that Shiloh is likely a match for Monroe—or he'd know it if his heart wasn't all tangled up over her. It's one of those unspoken things, though. He won't thank me for calling him on it, but I can't risk him being distracted when we need him most. "Just move on Shiloh like you've been wanting to do for years, and it'll be a nonissue."

His mouth goes flat. "If we're going to start handing out advice, maybe you want to talk about what the fuck you're doing with Eli? Kill him, or fuck him, but if you flaunt fucking his woman under his nose long enough, he's going to come for your throat."

I know. I plan on it. "Let me worry about Eli."

"Then let me worry about Shiloh."

He has me there. I hold up my hands. "It was just some friendly advice."

"Worry about yourself, asshole." He turns for the door. "I'll keep the compound locked down while you're out today. If Harlow can really get supplies and shit lined up, I'll need to talk to her soon to get that ironed out."

A strange possessive urge rises in me, a desire to keep Harlow away from everyone. I give myself a mental shake. It doesn't make any sense to secret her away, no matter how much I enjoy her pussy. She's an asset—a valuable one at that. Locking her away makes me no better than that fool Eli. I'm not a good man, but I'm sure as fuck smart enough to give Harlow a little lead and see what she'll do. "I'll send her your way tomorrow."

"Good."

My next stop is Eli. I wait outside his door for several long moments, steadying myself. Dealing with him means icing him out, not giving him anything to use against me. It means wrapping my rage in chains and shoving it down deep. There will be plenty of time to torment him later; right now I need him to do what I want.

I walk through the door without knocking. Eli is lying on the bed, his arms propped behind his head, staring at the ceiling. He's wearing a pair of low-slung jeans, his glasses, a pendant—and nothing else. His torso is more developed than when I saw him last, muscles clearly defined, and it's also covered in an assortment of mottled bruises. He doesn't look over as I close the door behind me. "Finished with Harlow?" There's no bitterness in his tone. He sounds perfectly detached, as if he doesn't care one way or another.

He always was a little fucking liar.

I cross my arms over my chest and lean against the door. "I'm not going to be finished with her anytime soon. You let her slip through your fingers, and she's mine now."

"Is she?" He still doesn't look at me, doesn't change his tone at all. "That might be what you believe, but I wonder if it's true."

I slap my responsive anger down. Thirty seconds, and he's already digging around under my skin. Eli's been off his stride since he lost that match yesterday, but apparently he's taken the time to find it again. Unfortunate. He's a hell of a lot less dangerous when he's reeling and all fucked in the head. I'll have to be extra careful with him going forward. "You going to play nice, or we going to have to do this the hard way again?"

He finally turns his head and looks at me. The asshole really is too pretty for his own good. Even bruised all to hell from our fight, he gives the impression of being fucking flawless. It's irritating in the extreme. He gives a slow smile that doesn't reach his eyes. "You know we both prefer the hard way. It's a wonder we never crossed that line before."

It doesn't take much to make the conversational leap with him. Even after all the time apart, I still know exactly how his mind works. "We were friends first. Friends aren't so common in this faction that I was willing to let fucking you get in the way of it." I pause. "But then, it didn't matter, did it? My father still died, choking on his own blood, and our people still burned in the house *your* people set aflame."

"I know you won't believe me, but I had nothing to do with the fire."

"True or not, you sure as fuck benefited from their deaths." I don't move from the door, concentrating on holding my tension internally. "Harlow has decided to play nice in order to protect your faction's people. Will you do the same?"

"Would it matter?" He finally sits up, his ab muscles flexing with the movement.

Fuck, I want to take a bite out of him, and I resent the hell out of my attraction. I'd never let it muddy the waters of my plan, but it's inconvenient in the extreme. "It might."

He sits cross-legged on the bed, appearing to give me his full attention. "What does playing nice look like, Abel? Standing next to you while you go through the motions of leading, despite the fact that the people don't want you here? Does it mean fucking you? Playing Bride in truth? Explain it to me."

That's about enough of that. I stalk toward him, stopping next to the bed and planting my hands on the mattress so we're eye to eye. "You'll stand next to me and offer your silent support because if your people riot, they'll be the ones to pay the price. They might outnumber *my* people, but my people have been in exile for damn near a decade. We're harder, more ruthless, willing to do absolutely anything to ensure we keep the home we've claimed. This isn't a fight you can win, and I know you're smart enough to realize that. The only thing still up in the air is whether or not you're willing to sink the entire faction in response to your bruised pride."

"You took everything from me in the course of a few hours. I hardly call that bruised pride."

I ignore that. "As for fucking... You can pretend that you're only asking out of spite, but we both know how hard your cock was when you were sucking me off. Our friendship might have burned right along with my childhood home that night, but the attraction remains. You want to do something about it?"

He inhales sharply. "Just like that?"

It will never be *just like that*, but I haven't survived this long by ignoring hard truths. There's more than a little lust for Eli simmering beneath my skin. I can hate him and want him at the same time. I'm complicated like that. "You know me, Eli. I see something I want, I take it. I want to cut you into little pieces and throw you into the river. That's not an option, so I'll settle for la petite mort."

"La petite mort." He gives a choked laugh. "*Really?* Since when did you ascribe to the French way of thinking about orgasms?"

"Since now." I drop my gaze to his mouth, letting him see a hint of the lust surging through me. "Up to you how you want to play this. I'm more than happy to hogtie you and keep you in this room for the next year. I don't *need* you for any of this shit." I lean back and make a show of looking around. "I do that, I might not have to kill you myself. You're liable to die of boredom. Your choice."

Eli looks at me for a long moment. When he smiles, alarm bells ring through my head. "With that kind of pitch, how can I resist? I'll play Bride, Abel. Shall we start by my getting on my knees and asking nicely to suck your cock?"

15

ELI

I f Abel were any other man, he'd back off and I'd win this particular exchange. But he's not any other man. We're playing a game of chicken, and we have too much history and too much stubborn pride between us to veer off into safer territory.

Too much pent-up lust. Can't forget about that.

So, instead of changing the subject or leaving the room, Abel reaches for the front of his pants, a mocking expression on his handsome face. I hate how good he looks. He's bigger than he was eight years ago, thick muscle roping his form, giving his shoulders extra breadth, his chest more definition through the thin T-shirt he has on. There are new scars, too. On his knuckles, and a faint one at his throat that his beard almost hides, as if someone tried to garrote him. Most notably is the difference in his eyes.

When we were friends before, Abel was the hot-headed one. The one who'd charge into any situation without thinking things through. He won more often than he lost, but that didn't change the fact that he let his emotions drive him more than he likely should. *I* was the one who acted as his brakes. The cooler head meant to prevail.

Obviously that's not the case anymore. He hasn't lost control once since he walked back into my life. Even the way he's been with Harlow is calculated, no matter how hot the chemistry sparks between them.

It doesn't matter. Abel might have learned how to be cold, but he's always had a fire burning deep within. Something like that doesn't just go away, not when it's such a fundamental part of the person he was for twenty-eight years. All I need to do is tap it, and he'll stop thinking so clearly. There are two ways to make that happen.

Fighting or fucking.

Fucking *and* fighting.

We have the desire for both in abundance. No matter how hard he tries to hold himself apart, eventually his walls will come down. That's when I'll strike. Until then, I might as well enjoy myself.

All in the name of my plan, of course.

I slide off the bed and sink to my knees before him. He undoes his pants in short, angry movements and pulls out his cock. I got an up close and personal experience with it the other night, but just like noticing the differences in him, this feels different. I'm not still riding a tsunami of adrenaline and fucked-up emotions the way I was after the fight on Lammas. I am myself.

Fuck, I've wanted this for so long.

I shut the thought down almost as soon as it presents itself. How I felt about Abel before the coup doesn't matter. Neither of us are the men we were. We've both changed in the near-decade apart. The attraction may remain, but that's all. There's no trust, no friendship—certainly no love. We've been boiled down to our worst parts, refined by cruelty and the need to do anything to survive.

"If you bite me, I'll knock your teeth in." He says it casually as he fists his cock, giving it a rough stroke. As if he's not so hard, I can practically see him throbbing. His dark eyes are so cold, they burn me. "Whatever plan you have going on in that twisted brain of yours, it won't work. I win, fucker. Sucking my cock doesn't change anything."

Maybe. Maybe not.

I lift my chin. "Who's to say I'm not on my knees because I want to be?" I lean forward a little. Not close enough to touch him, not yet, but closer. "You thought about it, back when we were friends."

"Back when I thought we were friends." He sounds so bitter, I can taste it on my tongue. "That's what you really mean."

No point in telling him that I considered him my best friend for all those years. It won't make a difference, and he'll just call me a liar. As I am reminded time and time again, intentions don't matter. Not only did I underestimate my father, resulting in the death of forty people, but I never went after Abel once he and his brothers were driven out of Sabine Valley. I could come up with a thousand different reasons why it was never the right time, or talk about how Abel hid the trail too well for my people to find him.

Intentions don't matter. Even attempts don't matter.

The only thing that makes a difference is the bottom line.

And the bottom line is that Abel and his brothers suffered through eight years of exile, in part, because of me. There's no coming back from that. Not even with twenty-eight years of friendship between us.

Friends and never more. We were very careful to keep it

only that. If we occasionally shared a partner in bed, it was always us sharing *them* and never each other.

An image slams into my brain hard enough to have me rocking back on my heels. Harlow between us. Riding Abel's cock. Sucking me down with that little smirk she gets when she knows she's about to make me come despite my best efforts at control.

I take one breath and then another, forcibly pushing the image away. It's not in the cards for us. It never was, even before how things played out this morning. I have to mend things with Harlow, at least enough that we're not at each other's throats, but it'd serve me right if she never let me touch her again. No, better to let that fantasy disappear with the rest of our relationship. I still don't quite understand how I've fucked things up so thoroughly with her, but the anger is too thick to think past, even now.

I look up at Abel. "You want me to suck your cock, or you want to sit here and bitch about the past?" A calculated prod.

He steps forward, backing me against the mattress. "You know, there was a time when I would have given you anything."

My throat goes dry. "There was a time when I would have done the same."

"It won't be that way again." There's no pain in his voice. He's simply stating a fact. No matter what happens in the future, we can never go back.

I could have told him the words didn't need to be said. I know better than anyone that our friendship, the partnership that was going to change the entire faction for the better, burned to ash alongside the Paine house. I lick my lips. "I can be just as much an asset as Harlow."

"You want the same deal I gave her? Partnership and

open communication? You have to earn that shit, Eli, and you haven't even started." Abel gives his cock another stroke and taps my bottom lip with the wide head. "Put your money where your mouth is. You want to play nice? Stop trying to provoke a response, and suck me off."

I drag my tongue over the head of his cock and suck him down. Down and down and down, until his width and length border on pain, until my lips meet his base. It's a fight not to gag, to muscle down my body's instinctive panic at having lost the ability to breathe through my mouth.

Abel barely gives me a chance to adjust. He brackets my head with those big hands and starts fucking my mouth. He's not holding me tightly, certainly not tightly enough that I couldn't move away if I wanted to, but there's no denying that he's the one driving the pace. Slowly and then faster, harder. I don't mean to grab his hips. I simply need to hold on to something to keep from impaling myself farther on his cock.

But then it's like my hands take on a life of their own. They delve into his jeans, pushing them down a few more inches so I can touch his skin. So I can feel the powerful flex of his muscles as he drives into my mouth.

I make the mistake of staring up at him, and the tormented look on Abel's face is so fucking sexy, I almost come in my pants.

He picks up his pace, slamming into my mouth. I'm a receptacle for his rage, and I take it willingly. It's not penance. If I have guilt about how things played out between us, it doesn't matter. My feelings never mattered when it came to what's best for this faction. Not when it came to Abel. Not even when it comes to Harlow.

He curses and shudders, orgasming into my mouth. I drink him down without a second thought, holding his gaze.

It feels so devastatingly intimate, and the sensation only gets worse as he eases out of my mouth and roughly tucks his cock back into his pants. Abel looks away. "That was serviceable."

I use my thumb to wipe the edge of my mouth. My jaw aches like a motherfucker, but I'll be damned before I show any outward indication of it. "You came pretty fast for just 'serviceable.'"

He shoots me an unreadable look. "We're going to Old Town this afternoon. If you can act right, you can come along. Prove you really want what's best for the faction like you always used to claim."

"Not wasting any time, I see." The quickest way to win over the faction is to win over the families in Old Town. They're the backbone that runs through our section of the city. I wish I could say they were loyal enough that they wouldn't take a new Paine family rule without a fight, but if I've learned anything in the last eight years, it's that this faction is filled with pragmatic people. A long as Abel doesn't do anything to fuck with their day-to-day life, they won't challenge him. Three years under my father, and then five under me, and they'll just keep going on like they were before he and his brothers showed back up again.

I don't know what about that irritates me. It's exactly what happened after *we* staged our coup. My father sat down the families of Old Town and gave them his word that they could continue to operate as before. And that was that.

Abel holds out his hand. I take it on instinct. It's not until he pulls me easily to my feet that I realize I should have slapped it away and stood on my own. Nearly a fucking decade apart and old habits still haven't completely gone away.

He raises a brow. "There's no reason to waste time. The

sooner everyone realizes we're here to stay, the sooner things get into their new normal."

I should leave it at that, but I've never been able to keep my head around Abel the same way I can around other people. "Are you planning on reversing all the things I've spent the last five years doing?" Improvements and foundational building to improve the community. To *create* a community. Most people look at this faction, see the ruler, see Old Town, and think that's an indication about how the rest of its citizens live. It's nowhere near the truth.

"Case by case basis. Some shit will stay, some will revert." He slides his hands into his pockets, expression unreadable. "No matter what else you think of me, the plans I have for this faction are the same they were when *we* talked about it." He turns away. "But then, if you trusted me enough to believe that, we would have been ruling together the last eight years instead of what happened."

That's the problem. I *don't* trust him. He's been gone too long from Sabine Valley, reminds me too much of his father now that he's back. I can't afford to believe he still wants the same things we spent countless hours talking about. "Then we want the same thing."

"Do we? I'm not so sure."

That right there is why I have to play nice. Why I suspect Harlow has decided to do the same. If she has a chance of influencing Abel's decisions, she's going to take it. A choice she shouldn't have to make, but she's been plenty clear about how little she cares about my feelings when it comes to her choices. It still makes me fucking furious, but I can put that aside for now.

Our people are the most important thing.

Playing nice means having a chance to convince Abel

that not all the changes made while the Paines were gone were bad. Hell, most of them weren't. "I'll be ready."

He doesn't move. "Don't try shit, Eli. I'd hate to have to kill you in front of Harlow. It'll upset her." He almost sounds like he means it. As if he cares one way or another about Harlow's mental health.

I want to strike at him. If not physically, than verbally. The impulse is almost overwhelming, but I manage to muscle it down. "I wouldn't do anything to upset Harlow."

"Uh-huh." Abel shakes his head. "That's one thing I don't get. You might have shoved a knife in my back, but that doesn't change that you're one of the smartest people I've ever known. The man I was friends with wouldn't let a single resource go to waste, and Harlow is one hell of a resource. Why the fuck didn't you use her?"

"She's been through enough," I grind out. "She deserves better than to be used."

He doesn't blink. "You were never such a sanctimonious prick when I knew you. You pluck her off the street, put her in your bed, and then decide you know what's best for her. Did you ever ask her?"

I'm not having this conversation, especially not with him. I drag my hand through my hair and adjust my glasses. "You don't have the high ground in this conversation. You didn't ask her what she wanted, either."

A strange little smile pulls at the edges of his lips. "Didn't I?" He heads for the door. "Be ready at four. Dress to impress." And then he's gone, closing the door softly behind him.

It's only then that I realize he never asked me a single question about my role in the coup that killed his father and burned his childhood home. A normal person would want to know why. Either Abel already thinks he knows, or he doesn't care. I don't know why that bothers me so much.

He's...different.

I never really expected him to come back here. There might be a small, insignificant part of me that wanted to see him again, but not like this. Never like this.

I should have gone after him that first night. I never should have let things stay this long unsaid between us.

I close my eyes and strive to think. No matter what kind of man Abel is now, he's still just a man. There will be a way to set things right. Even now, with rage simmering in my blood, I don't want him dead. The last few days have been infuriating, but they're two days in a lifetime. He was my friend for nearly thirty years.

Fuck, I can't afford to think like that. Abel sure as hell isn't letting some long-dead friendship color his motivations and actions. If he realizes I have a soft spot, he'll aim for it and dig his knife in deep.

No, Abel isn't the one I need to move forward.

Harlow is.

I t takes the better part of two hours to calm all the Brides down. I don't manage to convince either Beatrix or Mabel's bodyguard—Sonya is her name— to leave, but no one sheds any blood. It's not a win, but it's a solid stalemate. Breaking through to the Brides will take a lot more time and effort.

I sip my cold tea and just let myself exist for a few minutes after they all leave. Today hasn't been a win, but it hasn't quite been a loss, either.

A small creak behind me, so quiet that I wouldn't have heard it if I weren't sitting in perfect silence. The small hairs on the back of my neck rise. I'm facing the door. No one should be able to enter the library without me seeing them. And yet I am not alone.

I spin around, ready to throw my cup at the intruder's head, and barely manage to check myself when I recognize the man standing there. Eli. He's showered and changed and looks remarkably put together in a pair of slacks and a pale gray button-down. He's still got one hell of a black eye, but the swelling's gone down significantly in the last few hours. He always did heal quickly.

He's not worth ruining one of my tea cups over. Then again, he's been such an unforgivable ass, he deserves cold tea dumped over his head.

I study the wall behind him, but there's no indication of where the fuck he came from. It's not the first time he's appeared in a room when he shouldn't have been able to, but he's never answered my leading questions about how the hell he gets around. There have to be passages built into these walls, but their secret is yet another one that Eli's kept from me over the years. He won't answer now. That's for sure.

I turn back around. "Come to call me sloppy seconds again?" Damn it, I didn't mean to say that out loud. I should be focusing on minimizing the antagonism between us, but I can't quite manage it. I have too much anger pent up over too many years. I will be able to hold it together for public things—I don't have a choice—but I refuse to fold into myself to make him comfortable. Not ever again.

"No." He walks around my chair to drop into the one across from me. He moves without any stiffness at all. Either he's faking it well, or Abel didn't work him over quite as thoroughly as it appeared in the amphitheater and during the aftermath.

I sip my tea. It's unsatisfying cold, but it's better than sitting here with nothing in my hands while so much hurt spins out in the silence between us.

Finally, Eli sighs. "I fucked up."

Of all the things I expected him to say, that doesn't number among them. Still...this is *Eli*. I can't take anything at face value. I focus on holding perfectly still. "Elaborate."

"You're right. I shouldn't have challenged him to that

second fight. I put my own feelings above the good of the faction. And then I kept fucking up by increasing the animosity between the three of us instead of trying to smooth things out to ensure Abel wouldn't punish our people."

I wait, but it appears that's all. There's no reason for the disappointment that sinks its claws into me and rips its way through my heart. Did I really think that Eli would come and tell me that he loves me, he's sorry for boxing me in again and again over the last five years? Of course he has his eye on the endgame and the bottom line. That's what he *should* have done from the beginning.

This is something of an olive branch, and if I'm willing to play with Abel, then I can't turn away any resources. I stroke my thumb over the rim of my cup. "In hindsight, I'm not sure it would have made a difference. You might have handed him the faction on a silver platter, but he was already here and prepped for war. He and his brothers would have taken the compound regardless, and there would have been bloodshed. All with the same result." Abel never would have been satisfied with only me as revenge. He always meant to take the faction back. He's admitted as much.

No reason for that to sting, either. After all, I'm used to coming in a far second to the faction. One way that Abel and Eli are identical. The thought almost makes me laugh, but I swallow the sound down.

"You have so little faith in me, Harlow."

I hold his gaze. "I have exactly the right amount of faith, I think."

He doesn't quite flinch, but he makes an involuntary movement. "I suppose I deserved that."

"Yes, you did." Although I'm hardly blameless in this

situation. I stayed, after all. I could have left at any time. Instead, I let the resentment grow instead of making a clean break. I stare down into my tea. "Why are you here, Eli?"

He leans forward and clasps his hands between his knees. "I want what's best for our people."

Somehow, even when I doubted everything else, I never doubted that. Of course he does. Now that he's not reacting emotionally, he's focusing on the only thing that matters. That should make me happy. No matter what my personal feelings are, the faction matters more. I have to remember that instead of striking out at him until he reacts to *me* the way he does to Abel. I didn't even realize how much distance Eli's held me at all this time until Abel showed up and I realized how he acts when that distance isn't a factor. Oh, he might hate Abel right now, but their history is written all over them. The intimacy of being close friends for most of their lives.

No reason to feel jealous of that. I've given up any hope of my happily ever after a year ago when I realized nothing would ever change between us. All I have left is the responsibility to the people who live in this faction. That's it. "So do I."

"With that in mind, I..." He takes a slow breath. "We need to put our personal feelings aside and deal with Abel."

I stare at him a long moment. "Eli." I take a breath and cling to calm with everything I have. "Please tell me that you're not going to break your word."

"There's nothing in the agreement that guarantees his safety."

I ignore the spike of fear that sentence brings. I don't like Abel. I mean, I might kind of enjoy him, just a little, but he's not a good man. No matter what promises he's made to me, I can't trust him beyond this year. I have to remember that.

Always. "In fact, that's exactly what the Bride agreement guarantees. Peace between our people and his for the duration of the year."

"Peace doesn't mean he suffers no accidents."

For fuck's sake. Eli is just proving that he hasn't learned anything after all.

"We talked about this. Even if you managed to do something to him, he's got six brothers who will be howling for your blood and who will turn around and punish *our people* for your sins. Not to mention breaking one Bridal agreement paves the way for the other factions to do the same. They'll crush us."

"The only way I'd stage another coup is if I could take all the Paine brothers out. If I do that, the other factions will have no reason to fight us. Not when their people are returned to them."

I can't believe I'm hearing this. I carefully, oh so carefully, set my cup on the tea cart. It's either that or throw it at his head. "So what you're saying is that you haven't learned anything at all. I want no part of whatever you're planning." I lean forward and meet his gaze. "You will fail, Eli. He's too good, and his brothers and his people are too capable. And when you fail, I'll be the one who's forced to pick up the pieces and do damage control. Again."

"Damage control like fucking Abel."

I push to my feet. "I'm not having this conversation."

He drapes his arms over his chair, his expression lightly mocking. I've seen him with that look in his eyes more times than I can count, but never directed at me. He used to know better than to use his public persona on me. Even bracing for it, his words still lash me. "I thought you got over your knee-jerk reaction to run from things that scare you."

He did not just say that.

Rage sears every last bit of control I have. I plant my hands on the arms of his chair and glare. "You don't scare me, Eli. You're a fool, and I'm scared of the consequences of your actions, but I am not scared of you. If you laid one hand on me, I'd cut it off, and you know it."

Slowly, oh so slowly, he lifts his hand and presses it to my upper chest. "Prove it."

I slap his hand away, but he catches my wrist. I yank, but it's no use. Eli might be built leaner than Abel, but he's still far too strong for me. "Let go."

"No."

Playing tug-a-war on my wrist will only hurt me. So I stop trying to pull free. "You want to know why I fucked Abel? Because it was my duty."

"The first time."

"Yeah, the first time." Poison wells up in my throat, and despite my best efforts to swallow it back down again, it drips from my lips. "You want to know why I fucked him again? Because I am so angry at you, I wanted to hurt you so you'd finally *see* me. Because it didn't fucking work, and you hurt me instead. Because when he touches me, I forget everything, and that's what I need right now. There. Is that what you wanted to know? Do you feel better, Eli? Because I sure as hell don't."

He shifts his grip and strokes my wrist with his thumb. The intimate touch nearly sends me to my knees. It's something he's done more times than I can count, often when we're in a room full of people. A subtle possessive code that promises pleasure as soon as we're alone. Five years is long enough to create an entire language of small touches and significant looks, and I hate that he's using it on me right now.

"Stop," I whisper.

The mocking light drains out of his eyes, leaving a man who might be a stranger to me. He's nearly as cold as Abel is, his hazel eyes hold things I can only begin to guess at. "I've changed my mind."

There's a tight, wet feeling in my chest. I yank on my arm again. I have to get out of here, because I'll be damned before I cry in front of him. He doesn't deserve that kind of trust. Not anymore. "I don't care."

"I recognize that I fucked things up. I was doing what I thought was right at the time." He drags his thumb over my wrist again. "I understand now that that wasn't what you needed."

"Great. Congratulations. *Let go*."

He shakes his head slowly. "I love you. None of this changes that truth. And when everything is burned away and there's nothing left, we'll be the last ones standing. I promise you that."

Just like that, I stop trying to get free. "You love me? Then promise me you won't do anything reckless. Promise me that you'll be the leader you vowed to be when you took over this faction. Promise me that you won't do anything to endanger our people."

"I promise." He says it so easily, so smoothly, it can't be anything but a lie. "But you'll give me a promise in return."

I already know I won't like what he's about to say, but I can't pretend that I won't crawl through broken glass for the people in this faction. What can he ask of me compared to the depths I'm already prepared to go to? "What?"

"Promise me that you'll share my bed while you share his. We'll switch off every other night."

I blink. "*What?*"

"We're not through. I don't give a fuck if you're riding Abel's cock. That's your choice, and we both have roles to play as Brides. But you will give me a chance to heal things between us."

A sound erupts from my lips. I'm not sure if it's a laugh or a sob, but it makes us both flinch. I yank my hand back and, this time, Eli lets me go. "That's not how healing works."

He doesn't drop his gaze. "It is with us."

Is this really the worst thing he could ask of me? No, but it certainly feels like it in this moment. I trust Eli with my body, but I no longer trust him with my heart. He'll shred me every time we touch, will cut right down to my core and leave me bleeding out. I straighten slowly. "Are you sure, Eli? After all, that would put me at sloppy thirds for you."

"I'm sorry." His expression doesn't change. "I shouldn't have said that."

"No, you shouldn't have." I turn for the door, but it's like my feet have grown roots, sinking deep into the floor and holding me captive. I can't walk out of here without doing everything in my power to keep this faction safe and as stable as possible. I never anticipated that I'd be bargaining my heart in the process.

But then, what worth do my heart and body hold when weighed against so many peoples' safety?

"You want to bargain? So be it. I'll share your bed for the duration of this handfasting. Sex is off the table unless I decide otherwise, on a case by case basis. Satisfied?"

"Not yet." His lips curl into a heart-stopping smile. If only it reached his eyes. "But I will be."

17

ABEL

Old Town is almost exactly the same as it was eight years ago. It's not surprising, exactly, not when the entire point of Old Town is that is doesn't change. The shops line a street so narrow, it's been closed to vehicle traffic since before I was born. They've stretched banners from rooftop to rooftop over the street, creating a breezeway of sorts. It keeps the worst of the heat out in the summer and the rain and snow the rest of the time.

I stand at the entrance and inhale slowly. This is the second test of being back. No matter what the other factions think or what happened during Lammas, if the people here don't fall into line, our return will be short-lived.

We only have one chance.

Cohen stands at my back with Maddox and Iris flanking him. They're all dressed in black and look forbidding, though Iris is drinking in the sight of the street in a way that tells me she'll be peppering Finnegan with questions when she gets back to the compound. She's a white woman with long, dark hair that she's got pulled back from her face in a low braid. Iris isn't a Sabine Valley native; we picked her up a few years ago as we were passing through New York. Good girl. Deadly with a knife, and even more so with a shotgun. Like a fucking artist. She's got one in the scabbard strapped to her back, and despite what should be an awkward position, I've seen her draw it faster than some people can draw a handgun.

Maddox is a white guy with blond hair and the kind of good looks that would have him competing with any of the legion of blond actors Hollywood likes to employ. He's another transplant, this time from Chicago, and he and Cohen have been friends who occasionally are more for a few years now. He's only the second guy my brother has trusted enough to let into his bed on a semi-regular basis, which is saying something. He's also just as deadly as Cohen is.

Between the three of them, they are more than capable of watching our back.

Eli and Harlow flank me on either side. He's in slacks and a light-gray button-down shirt and looks like he just walked out of a board meeting. He's done something to his hair to give it a bit of a wave, and the only marring of his perfection is the bruising around his eye. Even that doesn't really detract. It simply highlights the height of his cheekbones and the curve of his lips. Eli looks like a fallen angel, and it makes me want to prod at him until the illusion of perfection shatters.

Harlow's changed into a flirty red dress that makes her tits look amazing and flares out around her thighs. She's got on black boots and a leather jacket to combat the chill in the air, and she's left her hair down. Her makeup is understated, with the exception of the bright red lips that perfectly match the dress. She catches me looking and lifts her brows, a silent challenge, but she's holding herself more tightly than the last time I saw her. Something happened today, either with the Brides or after. I'll have to get her to tell me about it once this is over.

"Behave, you two."

Harlow gives a tight nod. Eli just smiles slowly. "Of course."

He's up to something, but I knew that from the moment he said he'd play nice and then hit his knees to suck my cock. I can't afford to react, not when he's no doubt thinking three steps ahead. I have to anticipate his plans and cut them off before he can move forward with them. Either way, it won't happen this afternoon. He hasn't had enough time to plan, and no matter how fucked up his relationship is with Harlow, I don't believe he'll do something to put her in danger. He won't risk calling my bluff on it.

At least, he better fucking not.

I turn and look back down the street. This time of day, there should be a decent amount of foot traffic, but it's almost deserted. I start moving, conscious of Harlow and Eli falling into step behind me on either side. I'd feel better having Harlow between me and Eli, but that's the very reason I don't put her there. I won't do anything to let him know I register him as a larger threat than I already have.

There are a couple ways to play this, but I have to maintain a position of power. Walking door to door to talk to the owners of the shops lining Old Town isn't the way to go. Instead, I lead us down to the courtyard about halfway through the street. It used to be a four-way stop, but it's been given the same treatment as the rest of the street. There are banners filtering the light and protecting from the weather, and someone's dug up parts of the street to plant some carefully curated greenery. Tables and chairs provide outdoor seating for the scattering of restaurants in the area. There is also a trio of food trucks set up in the dead end that's been blocked off.

I sit on one of the picnic tables and prop my elbows on my knees. "Round them up. They dig in their heels, leave them be. I don't need everyone. Word will spread either way."

Cohen nods and motions to Maddox and Iris. They head back the way we came and split, ducking into three separate businesses. I keep one eye on them and the rest of my attention on the area immediately surrounding us.

Harlow props a hip on the table next to me. "You've got some balls of steel to summon them like a king. They don't like it. That's now how things work around here."

"It's how things work now. They'll learn to live with it." I speak without looking at her. "This will save wasted time on both sides."

"Not how I'd play it," Eli murmurs.

I shoot him a look. "You'd smile and come, hat in hand, door to door to tell them how grateful you are for their support and make all sorts of promises."

"That's exactly what he did." Harlow doesn't raise her voice, doesn't look at Eli. Her tone is remarkably devoid of any emotion, which tells me the source of her disquiet. As far as I know, Eli didn't leave his room from the moment Cohen marched him back in there earlier, and Harlow didn't go to him, but they must have communicated somehow.

A mystery to deal with later.

It takes Cohen and his group twenty minutes to hit every business on the street. People come out in ones and twos. I have files on all of them. The Rodriguez family who run the textile businesses. The Smiths, owners of the market and two of the restaurants, each run by one of the Smith siblings. The Phan family, clustered around their patriarch, Chinh. They handle weddings, funerals, and everything in between. All of them have been here for generations, since well before my grandfather's time.

Not everyone shows up, but I don't expect them to. These families will take the news back to the others, and Old Town will decide whether it wants to dig in its heels or roll with the new wave of things.

I wait another minute, giving them time to settle. When I speak, I very intentionally don't lift my voice, though I project it to everyone here. "You know me. You know why I'm back. I've won this faction by the laws of Lammas, and I fully intend to reclaim my rightful role. I have no interest in fucking with you. Tithes won't change. My people will ensure that everyone behaves and no one bothers you."

Chinh moves forward. He's a short Vietnamese man with a shock of white hair and a lifetime's worth of laugh lines on his face. He looks like a kindly grandpa—he used to slip peppermint candy to me and my brothers when we were kids—but underestimating him would be a mistake. He has influence with more than just his family here; he's arguably as powerful as Eli was before I took his seat.

Chinh eyes me. "Your father made promises, too. Things didn't turn out the way he said they would."

I don't bristle at his implications. I knew what I'd be pushing against when we came back. My father was a hard man, and he only got harder as time went on. I've made my peace with the fact that everyone in Sabine Valley will look at me and see the shadow of the monster he used to be. It will take time to prove them wrong, but I'm not above using their caution against them. I hold Chinh's gaze. "I am not my father."

He studies me for a long moment before he glances at Harlow and Eli at my side. "No, I suppose you aren't." He takes a whistling breath. "We'll discuss it. You'll have your answer within two days."

It's not what I want to hear, but I know better than to push my luck. Old Town doesn't bend for anyone, and they're determined to put me in my place before they roll over. Not quite a toothless threat, but I can afford to sit on my hands for two days if it smooths the way to the next step. I nod. "I look forward to hearing from you."

Chinh nods and turns. The small crowd parts around him as he walks away, his family falling in behind him. People disperse quickly after that. He's their voice, for better or worse, which means they'll be rushing to hold a meeting and discuss their options.

They don't have any, but better for them to figure that out for themselves than for me to shove the knowledge down their throat. I glance at my brother, and he nods at my silent question. Finnegan's already done his thing and we have ears in the Phan building. We'll hear every word they say and be prepared if they decide to fuck with us. Good. "That's that." I push to my feet and brush off my pants. "Let's go."

Harlow starts to life next to me. "That's it?"

"Yeah." I nudge her with my shoulder, enjoying the surprise she's not quite able to cover up. "Did you think I'd threaten and snarl and maybe beat up a few people?"

"Can you blame me?" she murmurs. "You like to threaten."

"Each situation calls for its own unique approach." I look at Eli. "Nothing to say?"

He shrugs. "You've learned how to be subtle in the last eight years. I'm still processing."

Asshole. I raise my brows. "Walk and process at the same time. We're done here."

We head back to the SUV. Cohen motions for us to stop a reasonable distance away and nods at Maddox. We all watch the blond stalk the SUV and start going over it. Eli snorts. "You think someone planted a bomb? Really?"

"It's what I'd do if I wanted to make sure someone went down and stayed down." Having Eli and Harlow with me means it's less likely to happen, but there might be people in the faction willing to sacrifice both of them to ensure a Paine doesn't sit on the throne again. Eli's father wasn't my family's only enemy; he didn't pull off that coup alone. No doubt his allies aren't happy to see us show back up again.

A few minutes later, Maddox signals the all-clear. It takes ten minutes to get back to the compound, and I don't breathe easily until the doors close behind us and I see Broderick standing at the top of the steps at the house. Another signal that everything is as it should be.

Paranoid, yes. But my paranoia has kept my brothers alive for eight long years. No reason to let our guard down now. We start to get out of the SUV, but Harlow touches my arm. "A moment?"

"Sure." I ignore the strange look on Eli's face and wait for everyone to empty out of the vehicle before I turn to her. "What do you need?"

She blinks. "Just like that?"

"I'm not saying I'm giving you anything you want, but you obviously need something because you've got shit bothering you. What is it?"

But she doesn't look reassured. If anything, she seems more confused. "How did you know something's bothering me?"

I study her face, but her surprise isn't feigned. "You're

quieter than normal, and you've been fighting not to wring your hands since you got in the car. You also won't look at Eli, which I would assume is just the new normal, but there's a tension that wasn't there earlier. So, did he figure out a way to get to you, or are you still angry about how things went last time you were alone together?"

Her mouth works, but no words come out. Fuck, he really did a number on her, didn't he? I still don't get it. Eli is too smart to fuck it up so thoroughly with a woman like this, but it seems to be exactly what he's done. I lean down until our faces are even. "Why are you so surprised that someone noticed how you were feeling, Harlow?"

"Now you're just being cruel." She looks away but only for a moment. "Everything I do, I do for my people."

"Yeah, you've said that before."

She takes a deep breath. "I'm going to be sharing Eli's bed every other night for this year. It will minimize the chance he'll try something, and it's a small sacrifice to make to see that happen."

I wait, but she just sits there, barely seeming to breathe. I could demand to know how the fuck he got to her, but it's a moot point. Eli is making his first play, and he's using the one thing Harlow can't ignore. *Guess you* can *pay attention when you want something, you fucking dick.* "No."

"Excuse me?"

"You heard me." I lean back and reach for the car door. "He wants to be in your bed, he can join us there. His choice." I climb out and turn around to look at her. Harlow's gone even paler than normal, and a little too wide around the eyes. "You got a problem with that?"

She slowly shakes her head. "What are you hoping to accomplish with this?"

"That's my business." I shut the door and head for the

stairs. Cohen and Broderick are waiting for me there. After the briefest consideration, I nod at Broderick. "Make sure Harlow gets into the house." He's too careful to push her, and I can't guarantee Cohen won't start issuing threats. He wasn't overly keen on this plan to begin with, because by nature of having a Bride, we're letting the enemy close enough to strike. A balance we have to make sure we're not on the wrong side of.

"Got it." Broderick starts down the stairs.

"Playing with fire," Cohen murmurs.

I shoot him a look. "Worry about yourself. Tell Finnegan to report anything he hears in the Old Town meeting. And then get some rest. You look like shit."

"You're one to talk." But he just heads into the house without another word. I could tell Maddox to keep an eye on him, but the other man already will. He's a fool to want more from my brother than Cohen is capable of giving, but it's their business. Not mine.

No, my business is heading up the stairs to his room. I bite down a grin and follow him up. I shouldn't enjoy going round after round with Eli so much. I can say it's all for the sake of vengeance, but there's a spark there that didn't exist when we were only friends. It's as if we've become our true selves in the intervening years; two predators sharpening their claws on each other.

I like it. Far more than I have right to. And the fool just gave me the excuse to take things to the next level.

Tonight I'll have Harlow in my bed... and I'll have Eli, too.

18

I don't make it to my door before Abel catches me. I turn without opening it. "Am I going to be locked in my room for the entire year?"

"Doesn't seem to have stopped you." He halts a little closer than he should. "How is it that you and Harlow managed to have another conversation without you leaving your room or her entering it?"

I work to keep my expression placid. "Passing notes. Perhaps a little scrying."

"Uh-huh." He leans his shoulder against the wall, the perfect study of lounging. As if he couldn't burst into motion at the slightest provocation to remove any threat he identifies. He looks me over, lingering on my hips and chest and mouth. "I've considered your request. It's denied."

Anger threatens to derail me, but I muscle it down as best I can. "Power going to your head, Abel? You can't keep her from me if she doesn't want to be kept."

"No, probably not." He doesn't move. "But the fact remains; she's not leaving my bed to go to yours."

"Are you that threatened by me?"

"Nope." A slow smile. "But I'm territorial as fuck. You want to share a bed? You can share mine. Open invitation until I decide otherwise."

I stare. Of all the things I expected him to say, that didn't number among them. "What?"

"You heard me." He pushes off the wall. "I'm feeling generous, so you can even join in if you're in the mood. Provided Harlow agrees, of course. I might be a monster, but I'm not going to pave the way for you to harm her more than you already have."

Not this again. "That's between her and me."

"Correction: that *was* between you and her. I'm here now, and I'll be doing the one thing you managed to bungle so thoroughly—taking care of her."

The chains around my anger shift, fighting to control it. They don't quite manage it. "You're such a fucking hypocrite. You come in here, take her against her will, and then act like you're...what? Boyfriend of the year? You've known her a few days, Abel. I've known her five years."

"Have you?"

That stops me short. "What are you talking about?"

"Exactly what I said. *Have* you known her? Does she know you? Because you keep that pretty little mask in place all the fucking time." He waves an idle hand at my face. "And you look at her and see a princess in need of a knight."

I clench my jaw. "If you know so much, what the hell do you see when you look at her?"

He grins, a fierce expression that's part challenge and part amusement. "I see what she is, Eli. She's not the princess." He leans forward, dark eyes intent. "She's just like us. Not the hero. Not the knight or the princess or whatever the fuck other box you can think up to shove her into. She's the fucking dragon you think to protect her against. Really, someone needs to protect you from *her*."

My mouth goes dry. He's wrong. Maybe I misjudged things with Harlow, but he's lumping her in with us. "She's not like that."

Abel shakes his head. "It's amazing that you can cling to rose-tinted glasses after everything you've done. You were never this dense before. Come to our room or don't, but she won't be sleeping in yours."

"She can tell me that herself, then. If that's really her choice."

He moves, faster than I can counter, and grabs my throat, shoving me back against the door. It's nearly an identical move to the one Cohen used in the hallway the other day, but it feels different with Abel. More sinister and somehow erotic as well. He leans down until his nose nearly touches mine. "You want to start talking about choice? What did you do to coerce her into sharing your bed again? Don't play the innocent party. I know how you think, Eli."

I swallow, the move pressing my throat harder against his palm. "Do you?"

"Yeah." He squeezes ever so slightly. Not enough to cut off my breathing, but the threat is there all the same. Desire surges through me, an unwelcome feeling that I can't stop. I can barely fight back my body's response so he doesn't realize he's affected me so strongly. "I didn't see you clearly before. I do now. I won't underestimate you again."

"Abel—"

His gaze flicks to my mouth. "Come to our bed tonight, Eli." He gives me a lazy grin. "Unless you're too scared of what might happen."

I stare. "You're honestly going to try to bait me into doing what you want?"

"Who says anything about trying?" He gives my throat one last squeeze that almost feels like a caress. Abel releases me and takes a slow step back. "You're not stuck in your room, but if you try to leave the house or do anything to endanger the future I'm building, I'll chain you to your bed and leave you there."

I don't lift my hand to my throat where I can still feel the warmth from his skin, but it's a near thing. "I'll keep that in mind."

"If you upset Harlow again, I'll beat your ass. Again." He turns and strides away, no doubt to talk to Finnegan about Old Town.

I could have told him that the surveillance is unnecessary. Old Town will cave to his new leadership. He gave them the only thing they care about—the promise to be left alone. They'll counter-offer, of course. Rolling over without a fight screams of weakness, and Chinh is too savvy not to spin this to his advantage the same way he did when my father staged his coup. I want to resent them for it, but they are who they are.

Ultimately, war is bad news for everyone. A civil war most of all. As long as Abel doesn't do anything to upset the families in power, they won't risk it.

Old Town is just one section of the faction, though. It remains to be seen if Abel will follow in his father's footsteps when it comes to his lack of care about the rest of the people who reside here. People like Harlow, who was harmed over and over again because Bauer Paine was too content in his power to bother with people he didn't see as worth his time.

My leadership has hardly been perfect, but everyone knows the consequences of stepping outside my laws, and I enforce those consequences without hesitation. No matter how much they turn my stomach.

Will Abel do the same?

Eight years ago, I'd know the answer. Half the changes I've enacted were ones Abel and I planned together. A baseline food budget for everyone. A strong presence in the streets to enforce the laws against murder and assault and abuse. Programs for the schools to help guide kids to better jobs when they finally reached adulthood.

Surely he hasn't changed so much as to take all that away? Not even to punish me.

I wish I could believe it without a shadow of doubt.

The real question is whether or not I'll sit back and allow him to fuck up what I've worked so hard to put into place. With Harlow at his side, she might shade his perspective in our favor. Or he might truly only be using her as a way to twist the knife for the next year. Impossible to say.

I step into my bedroom and stop short at the sight of a white square sitting on my nightstand. That most definitely wasn't there when I left. I glance around the room—empty —and walk to it. One single line of text.

North balcony. 2 a.m. Tomorrow night.

Damn it. Marie isn't going to listen to my order to stay away. She thinks she's helping, but this has to be played very carefully to avoid catastrophic results. There's no help for it; I have to meet her. And this time, I won't be subtle about my order for her to stay the fuck away from this house. Abel already suspects we can move without being seen. I shouldn't have tracked down Harlow in the library earlier, but the temptation was too strong to ignore. Not to mention, I doubt she'll see me without my ambushing her. I hardly had a choice.

Kind of like I hardly have a choice about picking up the gauntlet Abel has thrown. If he thinks he has the upper hand and is winning this power struggle between us, he'll relax a little. He'll have no reason to look for me tomorrow night, because he'll think that I'm retreating from the forced intimacy of sharing a bed with him and Harlow. I walk into the bathroom and methodically shred the paper into tiny squares and then dump them into the toilet and flush.

Sharing a bed with Abel and Harlow.

It's the smart move to make. No matter what they believe, sex changes things. It allows a shortcut into intimacy that is challenging to find in other ways. The problem is that intimacy can cut both ways. I don't make a habit of lying to myself, and the desire that I have for both of them, albeit in different ways, already colors my thinking. The trick is realizing and accommodating for that.

I walk back into the bedroom and sit on the bed. The question is Harlow. If she's really only looking out for our people, then she won't blink if I take out Abel and his brothers, as long as they've done something to prove they don't have the faction's best interests at heart. But if she's softened toward him; cutting him down will hurt her.

Fuck, it will hurt me. I can admit that to myself, if not aloud. It doesn't matter that we have eight years' worth of betrayal and rage and pain between us. I've never been able to cut out the part of me that sees him as a friend. The part of me that loves him. It went dormant while he was gone, but the longer we spend in each other's presence, the more prominent that feeling becomes.

It won't stop me from doing what needs to be done.

Not my pain.

Not even Harlow's.

19

HARLOW

I'm stalling, and I know it. I spend a full thirty minutes in my shower, letting the hot water numb my thoughts. The shower has always been my favorite part of my rooms, a large space with far too many showerheads and tiles ranging from copper to rose gold to a faint pink. It gives the impression of being rained on in the desert. It helps me think, or at least normally it does.

There are no revelations for me here this evening.

Once I turn off the water and get ready for bed, I'll have to make the trip down the hall to Eli's room. Something I've done more times than I can count; even after we stopped sleeping side by side, the sex was always good. The tiniest of bonds holding us together despite the ever-increasing distance between us. If I were stronger, I would have stopping sleeping with him when I realized that every time I walked back to my room afterward, the hurt inside me grew.

I thought I'd outgrown my masochistic coping mechanisms. Apparently not.

That doesn't change the fact that I'm tired. Exhausted. I just want to fall into bed and pull the covers over my head and forget for a few hours. Not fight with Abel about the fact that I've given Eli my word and, goddamn it, that means something. Not lay next to Eli for hours with five years' worth of things left unsaid between us. I don't want to do any of it.

But I'm not a coward, and I always do what I say I'll do.

I take a slow breath and make myself turn off the water. I'm not even surprised to walk out of the shower and find Abel waiting for me. I lift my chin. "I'm not going to fight with you about this."

"There's nothing to fight about. You don't want to do this, so you're not going to do it." He hands me a fluffy towel, his expression unreadable.

"I gave my word." I dry off slowly and then pad naked to the counter and grab my lotion. "It doesn't matter what I want to do, because I agreed. Eli made the mistake of trying to make me an oathbreaker. I truly hope you won't do the same."

Abel props his hip on the counter and watches me rub lotion into my skin. Heat slides through his eyes, but he makes no move to reach for me. "The terms have changed."

"That's bullshit, Abel." I finish with the lotion and turn to him. "Or is the problem that all your talk about me fucking Eli is bullshit?"

He gives me a slow smile. "Nah. Like I told Eli, I'm not jealous. I'm territorial."

"That's the same thing."

"It's really not."

My brain finally catches up with what he just said. "You talked to Eli about this."

"Come on, Harlow. You've only known me a couple days, but you're a smart girl. Tell me you're surprised."

I'm not. Abel is the kind of guy who wades into any situation and, fifteen minutes later, he's the one in charge. Part of it is sheer strength, part of it ruthlessness, and the rest is a strange sort of charm that isn't quite charisma but draws people all the same. The way he handled Old Town was brilliant. No posturing. No threats. Just a calm and clear declaration of intent. I could barely take my gaze off him, and the rest of Old Town obviously felt the same.

That doesn't mean he gets to bulldoze me now.

I drag a brush through my hair, wincing when I yank too hard. Abel tilts his head to the side. "That won't do." He catches my wrist and takes the brush from my hand. I watch, my throat tight, as he comes to stand behind me and carefully begins brushing my hair.

"What are you doing?" I whisper.

He's got a look of concentration on his face that I've seen before, both in the fights during Lammas and when we fuck. The brush is a gentle tug on my hair, a soft touch at the hands of a man capable of so much violence. It makes me shiver. Abel's eyes flick up and meet mine in the mirror. "It strikes me that you've never been taken care of, Harlow. It's a damn shame."

It takes me two tries to speak. "I can take care of myself."

"No doubt." He finishes one section, drapes it over my shoulder, and moves to the next. "But just because you can doesn't mean you should have to." Still holding my gaze, he leans down and presses a kiss to my shoulder. "You'll share a bed with Eli. You'll keep your word. You'll just do it in a way that will minimize harm."

I feel like I'm standing in the middle of a pyre and he just tossed a match at my feet. Every time I think I have a read on Abel, he does something like this and sends me spinning out into confusion. "Why are you doing this?"

"I take care of what's mine. You're my Bride."

"So is Eli."

His eyes flash, and he goes back to combing my hair. "Eli requires a different approach."

Every instinct demands I put as much distance between us as possible. I already know that Abel won't tolerate me doing it physically—not right now—so I do the only thing I can think of. I change the subject. "It's very important to me that the programs Eli and I have created over the last five years aren't eliminated."

Abel doesn't look up. "Tell me about the programs."

I try to focus. This is what I want, after all. The entire reason why I've submitted to Abel. *Maybe not the entire reason.* I ignore that last bit. "Only a part of the tithes go to the compound, only enough to keep it running. The rest go to ensuring no one goes hungry in the faction. We have grocery drops twice a week in several set locations." He still seems more focused on my hair than on what I'm saying, but I don't miss the way his expression tightens.

I take a breath and keep going. "We've also had more regular patrols, mostly to have a visible presence, but also so that our people are available for any reports that need to be handled."

"Reports."

It's not a question, but I answer all the same. "Domestic violence has gone down more than seventy percent since Eli took over. Other crimes like assault and murder have also decreased substantially. He spent a year making examples, and it's worked." No matter what else I feel about Eli, I cannot fault him for what he's done to improve this faction. If someone like him had been in charge when I was a child, I wouldn't have endured years of living under my father's roof, subject to his mercurial moods and abuse.

"I see." Abel idly drags his fingers through my hair. "Your

programs are safe, Harlow. I promise."

I want to press him, to demand more, but Abel's already said that he'll never lie to me. Why would he lie about this? I take a slow breath and let it go. "In that case, we need to talk about the Brides. They're going to be a problem. Or at least some of them are. Beatrix of the Mystics is here. Jasper didn't seem particularly happy about it, but the one you really have to watch is Fallon. She's a powder keg about to explode. Monroe is, too, but in a different way." Of the two, I'd be hard-pressed to decide which is the most dangerous.

He pauses briefly and then keeps brushing my hair. "Ezekiel will handle things with Jasper and Beatrix. It's messy, but likely for the best that he has both of them here."

Because, once upon a time, they used to be friends. Everyone knows the story, though it reads more like a fairy tale than reality. A Paine, an Amazon, and a Mystic—the best of friends. For most of their teen years and into their twenties, they were nearly inseparable despite their respective parents' best efforts. Until the coup against the Paines. And then Jasper and Beatrix's friendship turned to something more in the years since. It has to sting for Ezekiel to come back to that. "What will he do?"

"That's his business." Abel sets my brush down and runs his fingers through my damp hair. "Aside from the heirs, what was your impression?"

"Matteo is classic Mystic. Sort of checked out and chill. It could be an act, but if it is, he's never once slipped in the time we've been watching the Mystic faction." He's several spots down the line for the throne, so I honestly think he's just a strange anomaly in the ruling family. The rest of them are feral. "Mabel, the Mystic's youngest wife, is a mouse. She didn't say much and basically hid in the shadow of her bodyguard."

Abel makes a face. "The bodyguard is a complication."

"You should have known she would be. The Mystic leader inherited her with the marriage." I have to fight not to lean back into his touch as his hands land on my shoulders, thumbs digging into the tight knots there. I hiss out a breath and have to close my eyes. "Winry is exactly what she seems to be. She's the favorite daughter, the sheltered one—as much as an Amazon can be sheltered. She's a good kid, and she's scared out of her mind and trying not to show it." I force my eyes open to find him watching me with a strange expression on his face. "What?"

"Nothing." Abel slowly releases me, pausing when I weave on my feet a little, and steps back. "Winry will be fine. She's made of stronger stuff than everyone expects."

Maybe so, but... I turn to face him. "Why did you give her to Cohen? Of all your brothers, he's the..." I hesitate. "Coldest." More like terrifying and icy and deadly. Abel is deadly, too, but he's got a fire inside him that makes him feel a thousand times more human than his younger brother.

"I have my reasons."

"Maybe one day you'll explain them to me."

He steps closer. "Do you really want to know?"

I open my mouth but reconsider before I can speak. Abel's already too close. Asking this question, allowing him to invite me into his confidence, might be the smart play to make, but I'm suddenly afraid that I won't be able to keep it separate. That I won't be able to identify it as a *play* and not as a developing relationship. It's the first step down the treacherous slope to falling for him, and I'm farther along that path than is comfortable.

Instead, I make myself turn from him and walk to the robe hanging from a hook by the door. "Another time."

"Sure," he says quietly. "Another time." I must imagine

the disappointment coloring his tone. I must. If it's there, it's a lie.

I might have come to the conclusion that I can trust Abel with my body the same way I can trust Eli with it, but my heart is no safer within his grasp. Even if he's right there with me, tipping toward the point of no return, he won't let that change any of his actions. If it ever becomes necessary, he'll throw me under the bus without hesitation, soft feelings or no. Abel's worked too hard to accomplish this coup to let a little thing like soft feelings derail him.

My robe feels like a completely inadequate shield. I reach the door and push through, only to stop short at the sight that greets me.

Eli.

On my bed.

He sees me and raises his eyebrows, the very picture of a lounging king. "I've decided to play by Abel's rules. I'm sure you have no objection."

Oh, I have *every* objection. Bad enough to share the bed with one of them, to alternate between the two shades of uncomfortableness, to deal with it as best I can. To share a bed with both?

The thought leaves me weaving on my feet. I'm strong. I've had to be to get to where I am, to survive what lies in my past. Faced with this, it all means nothing. I might be strong, but I'm nowhere near strong enough. Any hope I had of surviving this year with my heart intact is disappearing before my very eyes.

I turn around to find Abel filling the door behind me. "I am not a bone to fight over."

"You're the one who put yourself in that position." He shrugs, as if this is a minor inconvenience. "We'll make it work."

That is not an answer, but I suppose I didn't ask a question. I spin back around to find Eli sitting up. He's wearing what he usually starts the nights in—lounge pants and nothing else. The bruises on his face and chest have already started to fade, the swelling completely gone. And, damn it, he looks good. It's not fair that he looks so good when he's regularly shattering my heart into a thousand pieces. He catches my gaze. "I'll play nice. Tonight."

"That's not exactly the reassurance you seem to think it is." Play nice. What does that even mean? There was a time when we played nice, but the last few days have broken what little foundation we shared. I don't know what he is to me anymore, but *nice* does not apply. Neither does *safe*.

"I'll keep him in line." Abel's voice is closer, and I barely jump when his hands land on my hips, and he pulls me back against his chest.

Eli's smile goes sharp. "That won't be necessary."

Oh gods, what is happening? I try to breathe past the strange panic fluttering in my chest. "Since when are you two in agreement on anything? This is a terrible idea. Everything about this is a terrible idea."

Eli's gaze flicks to Abel and then back to me. "We're in alignment for the night. Don't think too hard about it."

As if it were really that easy. I wave my hands at the bed. "Even without the threat of violence or the other very obvious pitfalls of this plan, the bed isn't big enough for three people." When I set up this room, I picked out a queen-sized bed because I had no intention of sharing it. It's barely big enough for me and Abel, and I'm one hundred percent sure that his feet hang over the end when he stretches out.

"Then we'll go to the other room. Grab the shit you

need." Abel gives my hips a squeeze and nudges me forward.

The shit I need?

How about a flamethrower and a suit of armor?

Strangely enough, the hysterical thought calms me. Wasn't I just thinking that I'm physically safe with them? They won't do anything I don't want them to. That might not help my emotional state, but it still gives me something to focus on. "I—"

Abel squeezes my hips again. "We're not going to do anything you don't want, sweetheart. You say stop, it stops."

It's on the tip of my tongue to say stop now, but I swallow the word down. I don't know what strange alliance is going on between the men in this moment, but I already decided I'd do anything for this faction.

Except...

I can't pretend that I'm saying yes solely because the faction. No matter how much this scares me, I want it. I won't lie to myself and say I don't. "Okay," I whisper.

"Let's go."

I take a deep breath and then another. It's not enough to slow the racing of my heart, but it's enough to help me think. I duck back into the bathroom to grab my toothbrush, and then there's nothing else to do but walk in a strange little group to Eli's room.

The door barely closes behind us when Abel pulls his shirt over his head and drops it on the floor. I don't miss the way Eli's gaze catches on his chest and lingers, but I can hardly blame him when I'm doing the same thing. The man is built like a fucking tank and having all that power focused on sex is a heady thing.

He jerks his chin at us. "Get in bed."

Holy shit, is this really happening.

20

Harlow is skittish as fuck, but she drops the robe and walks to the bed, her chin raised as if about to step in front a firing squad. I check out her round ass and thick thighs, enjoying the little jiggle with each step. She's built like the mythical Amazons the faction in Sabine Valley get their name from, but my girl likes to eat. I love that shit.

I lift my gaze to find Eli watching her, too. For just a moment, before he locks himself down, he has the expression of a man standing in a desert who's just laid eyes on an oasis. No matter how ugly things have gotten between them, he obviously still loves her. The thought sends an unwelcome pang through me. Love or no, he fucked up his chance. She's mine now.

They both are.

Like I told him earlier, I don't give a fuck what the status quo was when it was just the two of them. I'm here now. Harlow can think what she wants. Eli can keep hatching plans in that impressive brain of his. It doesn't matter. I'm not going anywhere.

Harlow skirts the edge of the mattress closest to Eli and climbs on the other side. She scoots to the top of the bed and leans against the headboard. She catches me watching her and raises an eyebrow. "Big talk, but you're just standing there."

There you are.

I give her a slow smile, enjoying the way I can see her catch her breath even from across the room. I stalk forward and grip the back of Eli's neck when I come even with him. He tenses like he's going to throw me off, but I don't miss the way goose bumps rise over his exposed skin. Eli likes being handled roughly, and fuck if that knowledge doesn't tie me in knots.

"The same thing I said in her room goes for you, too." I say it quietly. "At any point, if you want this to stop, say so and it stops." No matter how much I want to punish him, to fight him until we're at a standstill, I'm not interested in forcing anyone into my bed who doesn't want to be there.

He leans back against my grip, just a little. "Even after all this time, you know me better than that, Abel."

"Do I?" The question feels ripped from my chest. I thought I knew him, once upon a time. I thought I knew a lot of things.

Eli twists a little. Not trying to break my hold on him; just moving enough that he can meet my gaze. "People don't really change. You're the one who told me that."

I remember that night. How could I forget? It's the night everything changed. My father had just pulled some fucked up shit with Cohen, and I'd had to step in. It'd fucked me up. I knew my father was a monster, but having that violence turned on *us* had rocked my world view in a way I wasn't prepared for. I was twenty-seven at the time.

That was the night that I realized working at the ground

level to change things in the faction would never do a damn thing as long as Bauer Paine ruled.

Eli's the one who found me on the roof, sitting there in silence in the freezing night, unable to release the storm of emotions inside me. He'd offered me what comfort I'd allow, sitting close with his shoulder a reassuring steadiness against mine, and asked me what I wanted to do. I'd told him that people didn't change and my father is a threat.

Threats needed to be eliminated.

I still don't really understand how the fuck we ended up here. If people don't really change, then how could the man who was always the steady presence at my side suddenly shove a blade in my back?

I search his face, but there are no answers there. Eli always did have a damn good poker face, but tonight isn't about digging into the useless *whys* of the past.

It's about Harlow.

I'm not quite sure how we landed in this strange place of agreement, but as I lean in, he relaxes into my touch. I study the look in his hazel eyes. Fierceness and determination and no small amount of lust. It'll do. I give his neck a squeeze. "You've been fucking up."

"So you keep telling me."

I use my hold on him to turn his face to Harlow. "Seems to me you have some groveling to do."

She shakes her head. "Not interested."

"Not with his words, sweetheart. With his mouth." I guide him forward until our knees hit the mattress. "What do you say, Eli? Gods know you'll fuck this up if you talk, so just nod if you want Harlow's pussy all over your face."

He shoots me a hard look. "Watch yourself, Abel."

Fuck, but I like it that his charming facade has cracked. I can't help but poke at him further. "Nah, I'm good." I give him a little push, urging him onto the mattress. "Unless you just want to sleep. Seems like a waste with all this potential in bed."

He snorts. "You mean with *you* in bed."

"I said what I said." I focus on Harlow. "What do you say, sweetheart? You willing to let him do a bit of oral groveling?"

She's a bit too wide around the eyes, looking as spooked as she did earlier. It's like now that the worst of her rage has drained away, she's easily bruised. At least easily bruised by Eli. All I have to do is kindle that angry flame. I give her an arrogant grin. "Though if you're not in the mood to play, you can just scoot on over, and we'll have some fun without you."

"Fun," Eli grinds out.

"Sure. Fun. What else would you call me fucking your ass?"

He startles and gives me a long look. "Well, when you put it like that, how am I supposed to argue?"

"Easy answer: you're not." I wave at his hips. "Lose the pants, Eli." While he does that, I round the bed to Harlow. She's blinking up at me as if she's never seen me before. Earlier, in the bathroom, the gentleness felt right. It won't work for this situation. I put one knee on the mattress and lean down to wrap my fist around her long hair, tugging her head back and baring her neck. "I meant what I said before. You change your mind, you let us know."

Her breathing picks up, and she licks her lips. "This isn't going to change anything."

"No shit." I lean down and drag my mouth over the long line of her throat. "But it'll let loose a little steam. Tomorrow we can go back to being at one another's throats. What do you say?" I can't pretend that I'm entirely selfless when it comes to this. Shit with Eli is complicated in the extreme, and I'm not sure what the hell will happen if it's just the two of us fucking. Blow jobs are one thing. I can maintain some control there. But taking his ass? Having so much of me pressed against so much of him? Even as jaded as I am, I can't deny that it might shift things. We have too much messy history.

With Harlow in the mix, it gives us both something to focus on that isn't each other.

Her eyes narrow, some of the shocked look bleeding out of them. She reaches up almost tentatively and presses her hand to the center of my chest. "Do you want me to do this?"

Half a dozen replies spring to mind, every one of them designed to increase the distance between us. I don't know how she got so close to me, but even if I mean to keep her, vulnerability isn't on the agenda. I've learned what happens when you trust people, and evidence of that is kneeling on the other side of the bed, watching us with a frown on his handsome face. Eli's betrayal carved my heart out because I cared about him. Because I trusted him. If I give Harlow the same opportunity, will she slice out what's left?

I'll never find out.

Still, when I finally answer her, it's the truth that emerges. "Yes."

She searches my face and finally nods. "Okay."

It strikes me that Harlow trusts me to see us through. That thought might stagger me if I think about it too closely, so I shove it aside. I snap my fingers at Eli. "You know what to do."

"You snap your fingers like that again, and I'm going to break them."

I grin. "You're welcome to try." This is normal. Or, rather, the new normal. Sharp edges and sharper words.

Instead of answering, he crawls across the bed to Harlow. Without a word, Eli hooks her thighs and drags her down the mattress, settling between her thighs with an ease that speaks of familiarity. He doesn't say anything to her, doesn't hesitate, just wedges his hands beneath her ass and lowers his mouth to her pussy. She gasps a little and starts to reach for his head before she seems to catch herself. She fists the sheets on either side of her body as he works her with his tongue, a pretty pink stealing over her skin.

They look good together. Really fucking good. He's all long, lean strength, and she's soft skin and parted lips and a mass of light red hair.

They look like *mine*.

I pull off my pants and drop them onto the floor. There are a thousand ways to play this, but I let instinct guide me. Eli would call that being impulsive, but my impulsiveness has landed both him and Harlow in my bed, so it's not like that's a deterrent. I crawl onto the mattress and, after considering my options, I kneel at Harlow's side and palm her generous breasts together. Her pretty pink nipples look neglected, so I lean down and taste first one and then the other, alternating with licks and sucks and little nips. She moans, and then her fingers are in my hair, holding me to her as Eli eats her pussy.

She's all flushed skin and harsh breathing, but he's just playing around right now, teasing her. He's not actively trying to make her come. I shift down so that I can skate my hand up the lean line of Eli's spine. He tenses beneath my touch, but the moment I wrap my hand around the back of his neck, he gives a growl that has me going painfully hard. Fuck, he's sexy, even if he drives me up a wall when our cocks aren't involved.

I keep hold of his neck as I move to stretch out on top of

him. We're nearly the same height, which puts his pert little ass right against my cock while still giving me access to his neck and Harlow's thighs. I give her a light nip, and she jumps. There's almost too much sensation, almost too much pleasure, and we've barely gotten started.

She presses herself up onto her elbows and looks down her body at us. I'd pay good money to see it from her perspective, because her eyes go wide, and she bites her bottom lip. It takes her two tries to speak. "Are you going to fuck his ass, Abel?"

Beneath me, Eli goes perfectly still. I plant my fists on either side of his ribs and leverage up a little, pressing my cock more firmly against his ass. "Do you want me to?" The question is for both of them.

Harlow nods so fast, her hair flies around her head. "Yes."

I give another slow thrust against Eli's ass. "And you?"

He lifts his head just enough to turn his face in my direction. "Yes." A ground-out word, permission to do something I've wanted for far longer than I care to admit. This feels different than him sucking my cock. This whole night feels different than anything I've done with either of them to date.

This could change everything.

I want to take his ass, want it so bad, my hands are shaking, but I'm also not ready for this to end too soon. I bite the sensitive spot where his neck meets his shoulder. "Then earn it."

He curses, and then his mouth is back at Harlow's pussy. There's no finesse this time. He's going after her like salvation is on the other side of her orgasm. I snake one hand around and down his stomach to wrap around his cock. He jolts, and then his hips are moving, fucking my hand and grinding back against my cock as he eats Harlow out.

Fuck, it feels good. Having his whole body available to me. Building each of our pleasure in steady, rolling waves. All of it.

We don't need much in the way of words when there's sex involved. And without words, we have nothing to fight over. The past doesn't matter. The future is nonexistent. There is only the three of us in this bed. Time stands still until we decide otherwise.

"On your back." I barely sound like myself, but that's okay.

I slide off Eli, and he wastes no time obeying, rolling onto his back and taking Harlow with him. She lets out a cute little squeal, and then she's straddling his face. Her surprise flips right back to pleasure as Eli sucks on her clit.

Playing this slow is the right way to go. Teasing Eli until he's fucking panting for me, until he can't think past his need for my cock.

I can't do it.

Every encounter I've had with him in the days since Lammas have been tense and filled with things unsaid, things undone. None of that matters right now, not with lust so thick in the air that I can taste it on my tongue.

It's not the only thing I want to taste on my tongue.

Before I can think too hard about it, I lean down and take Eli's cock into my mouth. He's not as girthy as I am, but he's longer and has a wicked curve. I press my hand to his stomach as I suck him down, enjoying the way his muscles flex beneath my palm as he fights not to arch up into my mouth.

I explore him with my tongue slowly, forcing myself to go easy instead of sucking him off until he loses control and comes. I want that, want it more than I can say, but I can't shake the feeling that the moment he does, he'll find a way to end this.

I can't remember the last time I felt anything resembling peace, the last time I set down the burdens that weigh so heavily on my shoulders. Even when I'm in bed with Harlow, focused entirely on her, part of me has always been wondering what bullshit Eli is getting up to.

They're both with me tonight. I don't have to wonder. I don't have to watch for a knife in the back, not until the sun rises and this strange peace dissipates like the morning dew. Tonight, there's nothing on the agenda but pleasure and I didn't expect the sheer relief that knowledge brings.

I'm not ready for this moment to end.

With that in mind, I drag myself off his cock. "Get over here, Harlow."

She whimpers a little, but I'm not in the mood to argue. I hook her around the waist and lift her off Eli's face and down to perch astride his hips. "Take his cock."

"Abel—"

I catch her chin in a light grip and drag my thumb over her bottom lip. "Take his cock, and take mine, too."

Her breath catches. "I thought you were going to fuck his ass."

"I am. I will. But he hasn't earned it yet." I hold her gaze and give her a slow smile. "Before I fuck him, we're going to fuck you. Over and over again until you can't take any more. Right, Eli?"

"Right."

I skate my hands up her thighs to her hips and look over her shoulder at Eli. "You have lube stashed in here somewhere?"

His grin is slow and arrogant. "Yes..."

"She's going to need it."

Harlow's jaw drops, but she recovers quickly, her expression settling into the familiar challenge that I enjoy so much. She looks at him and then at me. "You think you can outlast me?"

"Sweetheart, I *know* we can. Now, where's the lube?"

21

ELI

Trust Abel to turn this into a competition, to somehow know it's exactly what the three of us need keep things from spiraling out of control. At least in theory. I feel completely untethered as he wraps a fist around my cock and guides me to Harlow's entrance. She sinks down slowly. This is nothing like the last time we had sex, with ugliness bubbling up between us and spilling from our tongues.

Here, there is only pleasure.

She looks down at me, her hair a tangled mess around her head, her skin flushed from pleasure, her lips parted around each ragged exhale, and it's almost like all the bad shit doesn't exist anymore. There's just us and our love, and things make sense again.

And then she leans over and takes Abel's cock into her mouth.

I wait for the anger I felt last time I watched them together, for the pain and jealousy and rage. There's a faint pang in my chest, but it's different. Diffused. Maybe because this feels different. This isn't us or them. It's the three of us meeting on a somewhat even playing field. No one's trying to prove a point, at least not one beyond the fact that we could be good together.

Can't afford to think like that.

Except it's nearly impossible to resist the siren call of what could be as Harlow starts rocking on my cock, slowly fucking me even as Abel thrusts into her mouth. It's seamless, and it feels like we've been here before, like this isn't new but merely a continuation of what was.

Dangerous thoughts. Ideas I should tuck away and forget as quickly as possible. Any future with either of these people is an ask I'm sure as fuck not entitled to.

But then, I've always been a selfish bastard when it comes to what I want. I don't want to let Harlow go. And, even knowing it's impossible, part of me still craves a future similar to what Abel and I once dreamed of. Not the same one, not when we've both changed so much, but a future where we stand side by side.

Impossible.

And yet...

I arch up and capture one of Harlow's nipples. I use one hand on her back to hold her to me and slide the other up Abel's inner thigh to cup his balls. He curses and then gives a rough laugh. "So, it's like that."

I lift my head enough to glance at him. There's something in Abel's dark eyes that I can't define, but it looks a whole lot like possession. There was a time when he looked at everyone he cared about that way, with an emotion that went beyond love. I never thought to have it aimed my way again, and even as my mind tries to reason its way through it, part of me can't help responding. "It'd be a shame if you came before Harlow did."

He gives a rough laugh. "Uh-huh. Since you're not

getting the job done..." Abel moves down to straddle my thighs. I realize what he's doing a second before he lifts Harlow off my cock and impales her on his.

She cries out and falls forward, bearing us both back to the mattress. It's the most natural thing in the world to kiss her; it's something I've done a thousand times in the past without thought, but it feels different now. Of course it does. We have so many things that were left unresolved between us for far too long. They might be out in the air now, but I'm fucking terrified that it's too little, too late. I know better than most that sex isn't enough to bind Harlow to me, but I'll be damned if I don't at least try.

As Abel fucks Harlow in short, brutal thrusts, I slide my hand between us and stroke her clit. She starts to retreat, but I'm having none of it. This closeness might never happen again, and I'll be damned before I miss a moment of it. I hook her neck and tow her back to my mouth, kissing her even as she moans and whimpers against my tongue. She clutches at my shoulders, her whole body going tense. I know her signs as well as I know my own, and I keep up that steady, light touch against her clit as Abel pounds into her. Her thighs tighten on either side of my hips, and then Harlow is moaning her way through an orgasm.

Abel barely lets her finish before he's moving us again, a conductor of our bodies and pleasure. He ends up leaning against the headboard with her between his legs and leaning against his chest.

I kneel between her thighs and spread lube over my cock. She just came hard enough that I can see evidence of it all over her thighs, but I meant what I agreed to; we're going to fuck her over and over again until she can't take any more.

And then Abel's going to fuck my ass.

I have to pause, to let the thought wash over me and away, or I run the risk of blowing my load the second I penetrate her. It's been a long time since I had anal. Harlow and I have engaged in some pegging, but it's more an extra little spice than a regular occurrence. And her dildo is *not* Abel.

Fuck, I have to get control of myself.

Abel's watching me closely as he palms Harlow's breasts. He's playing with her, keeping her riding that edge, touching her body with a familiarity that I crave and resent at the same time. "Problem?"

"No problem." I drag my cock through her pussy folds, watching her part around me. The sight does nothing to drive back my desire. Gods, I'm already in trouble, and we've barely gotten started. I clench my jaw and press into her.

Abel takes the opportunity to hook his hands around her thighs and pull them up and out until her feet touch down on either side of his knees. The position allows me to sink even deeper into her, and she whimpers in a way that tells me I'm rubbing against her G-spot with every stroke.

He presses three fingers to her pussy above where I enter her. Not stroking her clit so much as providing the tiniest bit of friction as I fuck her. The tips of his fingers brush my cock with every stroke, the light touch nearly sending me out of my mind with need.

How many years did I fantasize about Abel's hands on my body? How many partners did I have while we were still friends? People who were great but simply not him?

Harlow is the first person I was with who didn't come with that baggage. I was never thinking about him when I was with her, because she's overwhelming in a completely different way.

It's as if eight years of missing him, decades of wanting

him, all of that time spent not having him, roll into this moment.

Even as I try to hold back, it feels like the most natural thing in the world to press my body to Harlow's, to lift my chin until my mouth is even with Abel's. We share a breath, a harsh exhale as I drive into her, and then his mouth is on mine.

Abel kisses me like he owns me. Like he has just as much pent-up, thwarted desire as I do. He keeps strumming Harlow's clit, and I keep fucking her, but he laces his free hand through my hair, keeping my mouth to his.

Her cries escalate, reaching a pinnacle well before I'm ready to break the kiss. Harlow digs her nails into my ass as she comes around my cock. I try to hold out, to resist the feeling of her pussy clamping around me, but it's too good. I curse against Abel's tongue, and then I'm following her over the edge, pumping into her and filling her with my come.

Finally, a small eternity later, Abel leverages my face away from his. He's grinning in the low light. "That's a good start."

Harlow curses, but I don't have to look at her to hear the smile in her voice. That strange feeling in my chest gets stronger as I ease out of her, and Abel makes an impatient motion for the bottle of lube I dropped near his feet. I raise my brows but retrieve it. A few seconds later, he's lowering Harlow onto his cock.

She makes a keening noise. "Not even a little break?"

"You can take it. Can't you, sweetheart?"

She whimpers but finally nods. "Yeah. I can take it."

I kneel between their spread thighs and watch Abel fuck her. Or, rather, watch him use a grip on her thighs to lift and lower her on his length. The sight of his thick cock spreading her pussy has *my* cock giving an answering twitch. It'll take me longer than this to recover, but hell if my body isn't doing its damnedest to make a liar out of me.

He's so much bigger than she is. And the look of intense concentration on his face as he shifts his angle to hit a spot that makes her whimper is just as sexy as everything else happening. Her breasts shake with each heaving breath, and a light sheen of sweat dusts her skin.

I start to lean forward, but Abel gives a sharp shake of his head. "Not her mouth, Eli."

He doesn't need to elaborate. Not when we're moving like two parts of a whole. Or, rather, *three* parts of a whole.

I slide down to settle between their thighs. Harlow makes a whimpering noise I've never heard before, and it feeds my fucking soul as much as this connection with Abel is right now. I drag my tongue over her clit, and she jolts so hard, Abel has to grab her hips and pin her down on his cock. So I do it again. And again.

Fuck, I lose myself in this moment, in the taste of her and him and me, all mixed together. And I'm a glutton for desire, because I dip down and give the base of Abel's cock the same thorough treatment.

He reaches past her hip to dig his fingers into my hair and yank me back up to her clit. "You can suck my cock later, Eli. She needs another."

Harlow gives a thready laugh. "I can't come again."

"You're not done yet, sweetheart."

I obey the unspoken command in his tone and flutter my tongue against her clit in the motion she loves above all others. She moans, but Abel holds her steady. In fact, he's the one that starts to move, thrusting up into her in slow strokes that, combined with my mouth, have her panting and speaking in words that are barely comprehensible. Her hand joins his in my hair, and I look up her body to find her reaching back behind her head with the other to hang on to his neck.

She's shaking, but she's not there yet. Harlow writhes as much as she's able. "Oh gods, that feels so fucking good."

"You can take more, can't you?"

"Yes," she sobs. "I can take more."

Abel gradually picks up his pace, while I keep mine the same. She needs the steady touch to bring this home. From the way she's whimpering, it's going to be one hell of an orgasm. She always gets loud with the big ones.

"More, Eli. Suck my clit. Please."

I obey, watching her closely. My cock is already hard again, and it's everything I can do not to fuck against the mattress like a wild thing. The need to bury myself in her, in him, is nearly overwhelming.

Not yet.

My tongue is getting tired, but I don't give a fuck. I could do this for hours. I *have* done it for hours. I let my tongue and lips do what I haven't been able to with words.

Apologize.

Start the first steps to try to make things right between us.

Fucking is only the gateway, the path to soften Harlow enough that she'll actually listen to me instead of shutting me out. Even with that, we're still a long way off.

With that in mind… I slow down.

I can't think. Can't move. Can't do more than take the pleasure that Abel and Eli deal to me in wave after wave. My toes feel like they're permanently curled. My body is shaking, both from exertion and from the orgasm hanging just out of reach. I just need a little more. Just a little more, and I *know* it'll blow the top of my head off.

But Eli is slowing down.

I yank on his hair, but he's too strong to be moved until he's ready to. My breath sobs out. "Eli, please. Stop teasing me."

"Not yet," he murmurs against my pussy.

Beneath me, Abel stills. "So it's like that?"

"Yeah, it's like that."

Abel gives a rough chuckle. "In that case, time to move things along." He lifts me and eases me off his cock, and I can't help an involuntary sound of protest. Without his cock inside me, I feel so fucking empty, I can't stand it.

I curse them both. "I'm *so close.*"

Abel kisses my temple. "Eli's still apologizing, sweetheart. Let him do the work." He eases out from beneath me and carefully sets me on the bed.

Eli barely pauses in eating me out, following me down and pushing my legs wider yet. He can get focused when we're fucking, but this feels like another level entirely. Surely it's all for show. No matter what Abel's projecting about Eli using his mouth to apologize without words, I *know* Eli. There's no way he thinks he's wrong when it comes to how things played out. He barely looks in the past for faults, not when he's always been so focused on the future. Plotting and planning.

That's what this is. That's what it has to be.

Eli nips my thigh hard enough to make me flinch. His hazel eyes seem darker than normal, and I'm not entirely sure I can blame the shadows in the room for it. He holds my gaze as he licks the aching spot, soothing it with his tongue. "Stay with me, Harlow."

Layers upon layers beneath those words. Or maybe I'm just a fool for this man and hearing what I desperately want to hear. They say insanity is doing the same thing over and over again and expecting a different outcome, but I can't help the hope that blossoms in my chest. "I'm here," I whisper.

Abel half drags me farther up the bed until I'm nearly pressed against the headboard. Eli, of course, follows me without hesitation. He shoves his tongue into my pussy as Abel moves down the bed, stroking a hand along the center of Eli's back until he gets to his hips. A little urging, and Eli shifts up onto his knees, putting his ass in the air.

Abel squeezes Eli's ass. "Ready?"

Eli barely lifts his head enough to say, "Yeah."

Abel hesitates, his gaze on the back of Eli's head between my thighs, but he finally smacks Eli's ass. "Get your tongue out of her pussy long enough to answer a few questions."

Eli chuckles against me, making me moan. He drags his mouth across my thigh. "What questions?"

If he could see the way Abel looks at him, I don't know if he'd be laughing, even a little. Abel looks at Eli like he wants to tattoo his name on Eli's very soul. It's similar to how Abel looks at me when we're fucking but even more intense. He squeezes Eli's ass again, parting his cheeks. "You've done this recently?"

Eli finally pauses and lifts his head. "It's not like you to be coy, Abel. If you want to ask if you can pound my ass, then fucking ask."

Abel clenches his jaw, but it's not in anger. It's in barely restrained need. Fuck, he's thought about this a lot, hasn't he? I don't have the breath to ask, and even if I did, I wouldn't. This moment feels like we're poised on the brink of something. One wrong word, one hasty action, and we'll tumble down the wrong side and ruin everything.

"I'm going to fuck your ass, and I'm going to do it rough. Can you handle it?"

Eli's breath shudders against my thigh. "Yes."

I half expect Abel to question him, but he takes Eli at his word. "Harlow's pussy is looking needy. Get to work."

Eli doesn't need to be told twice. He loops his arms under my legs and presses his hands to my lower stomach, holding me in place as he ravishes me with his mouth. It's intense, but so is the way Abel watches us for a moment, a possessive little smile pulling at the edges of his lips. As if we're his in truth and he's pleased with how Eli's working me.

He squirts lube onto his palm and coats his cock in lazy strokes, his gaze still on Eli eating me out. More lube on Eli's ass, and Abel's hand dips down. From the sound Eli makes, Abel just pushed a finger or two into his ass. I can't see properly from my position.

And then Abel moves, fisting his cock and working into Eli's ass in slow little thrusts. He's watching so closely, I can't shake the impression that he's waiting for Eli to be proven a liar. For him to flinch or make a pained sound. I could have told him it wouldn't happen, but Eli's reaction speaks for itself.

He moans against my pussy and arches back, the curve of his spine achingly beautiful. It looks like he's offering his ass up to Abel, which is exactly what he's doing. It's so sexy, I can barely stand it, and just like that, I'm hovering on the edge of orgasm again. "Eli," I gasp.

"Not yet." He gentles his kisses, avoiding my clit as Abel works his cock farther into Eli's ass.

It doesn't take long before he's seated to the hilt. Abel's broad chest moves with every ragged breath, and sweat beads against his skin. I can see him shaking from restraint, or maybe I'm the one shaking because I need to come. I need it now, and Eli is playing with me. Each exhale sobs from my lips, but he doesn't seem to give a shit. I hate edging, and I love it, and I both want him to never stop and need him to end it now.

Abel gives a few slow pumps and then reaches around Eli's hip. From the way Eli jerks, Abel just wrapped his fist around his cock. My suspicion is confirmed by the fierce grin on Abel's face. "Seems like your mouth isn't doing the job, friend."

Eli presses his forehead to my stomach. He's breathing just as hard as we are. "Can't promise I won't come the second I get inside Harlow. Your cock feels good, Abel. Too fucking good."

"Mmm." Abel's muscles tense in another slow thrust. "Hold out until she comes."

I shove my sweaty hair off my forehead with a shaking hand. "Do I get a say in this?"

"Do you want Eli's cock, sweetheart?" Abel's big hands grip Eli's hips. "Do you want him to fill you up while I fuck his ass?"

Desire nearly shoves me over the edge all on its own. I have to take two ragged breaths before I can form an answer. "Yes."

"Thought so." He keeps up that slow thrusting. "You feel too good to stop fucking, Eli. Figure it out."

I barely have a chance to register the words when Eli rears up and grabs my hips. He drags me down the mattress, wedging one arm beneath the small of my back and lifting me up in a practiced move that has his cock pressing against my entrance. He shoves into me, drawing a little shriek from my lips. "Oh fuck, that feels good."

And then Abel plants his fists on either side of our hips, sinking deeper into Eli, which causes Eli to sink deeper into me, and it feels even better. Eli curses against my throat. "If you don't stop—"

"Not until she comes," Abel repeats.

He was just playing around before, testing Eli's ability to take him entirely. He's not playing around now. His face takes on an expression of utter concentration, and then he starts fucking Eli in earnest. Long, rough strokes that have Eli's whole body rocking against mine. It creates a grinding kind of fuck that has me biting back a moan. Their combined weight keeps my hips pinned to the mattress, and not being able to do more than take it makes the whole thing hotter.

We don't speak. There's no need for words. The only

sounds in the room are our harshly commingled breathing and the wet, slick sounds of the best kind of sex.

My orgasm catches me by surprise. One moment I'm kissing Eli's shoulder, his neck, his jaw, and the next, my entire body clenches and pleasure nearly makes me black out. I think I scream, the sound muffled against Eli's skin.

He curses, and then his hands are on my ass, moving us as much as he's able to in our current position. With a muffled grunt, he follows me over the edge, and I swear I can feel him fill me up with his come.

Abel simply keeps fucking him. Each rough stroke has us shifting against each other and draws out the pleasure until it's nearly unbearable. My muscles are liquid. It's all I can do to cling to Eli through it. And then Abel's fingers lace through mine on both of Eli's shoulders, and his thrusts lose their rhythm. He extracts one hand in time to pull out and come across Eli's back, and then he slumps down next to us, his fingers still tangled with mine.

I whimper as Eli eases out of me a few moments later. I'm going to be sore tomorrow, but I can't bring myself to regret it. This was too perfect. I can't let myself hope it means something, but there's a strange feeling coursing through me, as if my body is too large for my skin.

This is what it could be like. If we worked together instead of fought each other every step of the way. This seamless give and take between the three of us, nearly perfectly balanced in a way that isn't quite accomplished with only two.

I'm afraid to hope that it means anything at all.

But... I suddenly want it to.

I don't quite have sensation back in my legs when Abel hauls both of us into the shower. We clean off quickly, but there's no salvaging the sheets. It feels like far too much effort to change them, but Eli and Abel don't seem to need my help. They strip the bed and change the sheets quickly.

No one's speaking, as if we're determined to preserve the peace as long as possible. They haul me into bed between them, but I don't miss the way, their hands linger against each other's on my skin. Then Eli shuts off the light.

I expect to lie awake. I'm not used to sleeping next to someone anymore, and having *both* of them in bed with me...

I don't know what I think about that. I fall asleep before I can come to any conclusions.

23

I wake up plastered to Abel's chest with Eli's weight at my back. Late morning light presses against the sheer curtains covering the windows. The temptation to close my eyes and simply go back to sleep is almost too much to ignore. I have no business feeling safe sandwiched between these two, but I can't shake the certainty that, no matter what else is true, they would both put themselves between me and danger without hesitation. Not to mention, for a few hours, I saw how things could have been between Abel and Eli. An unbeatable team, their strengths perfectly complementing each other.

I never questioned Eli's father's coup. No matter what I think of Abel, I know what the faction was like under his father's rule. So many suffered because he didn't give a fuck about anyone who couldn't further his own interests. Which compromised most of us.

But now, I have to wonder... What would have happened if Abel had been allowed to take over, if Eli and he were allowed to mature into a team that would tackle any challenge that came at them?

The thought makes me sad, and I'm not quite sure why. I try not to worry about what could have been. My life is what it is, and that's what I have to work with. Worrying about some fantasy version of it and the choices I would make there is a recipe for even more unhappiness. Asking these men to do the same is something I won't do.

But it still makes my chest ache.

I start to slide out from between them. Abel rolls easily onto his back, his face relaxed in what appears to be sleep. I don't trust that for a second. He's the type to burst into wakefulness at the slightest sound, and he sure as hell doesn't trust us enough to allow this kind of deep sleep. Which means he's intentionally giving me space.

I don't understand this man. I don't get how he can hold such violence and such thoughtfulness within him at the same time. I certainly can't figure out how he's come to mean so much to me in such a short time. I want to blame the sex, and it's certainly playing a part, but it's more than that. He gives me space to expand. He trusts me to take care of things for our faction. He insists on seeing parts of me that no one else bothers to.

It's terrifying. I both love it and hate it.

Padding to the bathroom feels a little like running away. It's nowhere near far enough to clear my head, but closing the door between me and the men allows me to take my first full breath since we all climbed into that bed together.

Feeling strangely numb, I turn on the shower and wait as steam slowly fills the room. I'm not even surprised when the door open behinds me, but when I turn to look, it's not who I expect.

Eli shuts the door behind him and leans against it. He looks tired and deliciously rumpled, and I can't help but think of how many mornings we started like this. We let each other so close, but somehow we never covered that last little distance, the important part that would cement us together forever. I've never felt the loss as keenly as I do now. Gods, we fucked this up so thoroughly. I can't pretend it's all his fault, though. It took two of us to get to this place.

I can't quite dredge up a smile. "Is the truce over so soon?"

He doesn't move. "I never wanted to hurt you. Trust that if you trust nothing else."

The messed up part? I do. I might have doubted so much, but I don't doubt Eli's love for me. Or at least the love he used to feel. No doubt it's ground to dust now, no matter what he claims. "I never meant to hurt you, either. Not really. Intentions are nice, but they don't really change actions and words."

"I know." He sighs and leans his head back against the door. He's got whisker burn on his neck, and there's a trail of little bruises up his inner thighs from my and Abel's mouth. He looks like some kind of golden god who's tumbled down to earth for a little pleasure. If only our lives were that simple.

I wait, but he doesn't say anything else. No reason to feel disappointment. Last night might have felt earth-shattering for me, but it doesn't mean it changed anything. I can't afford to stumble, no matter how the ground moves beneath my feet.

To distract myself from the way everything suddenly hurts, I turn and walk into the shower. I'm not even surprised when he follows me in. Of course he does. Eli closes the distance between us, backing me against the cool tile, but he doesn't touch me. "You're only half right, though. Words don't mean anything. Only actions do."

I lift my chin. "Thank you for the reminder. I definitely

wouldn't have thought of that on my own." I hate that I can't help holding all the words he's said in the last twenty-four hours up against this truth. *I love you. I won't let you go. I'm sorry.* They might cut me to the quick, but they're barely worth the air he uses to expend them.

"Harlow—"

But I'm done. We can talk ourselves in circles until the end of time, but I can't afford to be distracted from the thing that truly matters. The people of Raider faction. "If you really care about this faction, you should try to actually work with Abel."

Instantly, his expression closes down. "We're not talking about Abel."

"We can't talk about us without him. Not anymore. I would think last night made that startlingly clear." Slowly, hesitatingly, I press my hands to his wet chest. It doesn't matter how much we hurt each other; I still want Eli. I can't seem to stop wanting Eli. My life would be so much simpler if I were able to walk away from this man. "You need to talk to him, Eli. Really talk to him. He might never forgive you for everything that happened that night, but the least you could do is explain your side of things."

He stares at the spot where I touch him. "It doesn't matter what my side of things are, and you know it. Weren't you just telling me that intentions don't mean a single damn thing? Forty innocent people died, Harlow. That's unforgivable."

I don't disagree, but he's not the one who made that call. "You didn't even know about the house fire, not until after the fact. If you just—"

He kisses me before I can continue. A soft press of his lips against mine, barely long enough to register. Eli lifts his head. "Some things can't be fixed. We can only go forward."

Something akin to fear blossoms in my chest. The way he says that... I can't shake the feeling that he's not talking about the coup eight years ago. He's talking about something much closer to home. I reach up and dig my hands into his hair, tugging until he lowers his head and meets my eyes. "What have you done?"

"Nothing." I can't exhale in relief, because he follows it up with, "Yet." Eli's speaking so low, it's almost lost in the sound of the water hitting the tile. "I've already sold my soul for this faction, Harlow. I can't let all those sacrifices be for nothing."

Gods, he makes me want cry. To scream. To shake him until he gets the concept of a compromise. "Do I need to explain the sunk cost fallacy to you? The past doesn't have to define you."

"I wish it were that easy." He kisses me again before I can keep arguing.

I should shove him back, should drag him out of the bathroom to talk to Abel, should do a lot of things. Instead, I let him kiss me with everything he has. I open for him, providing the escape he's silently asking me for. He shifts forward, pressing me hard against the tile, and the contrasting sensation between his warm body and the coldness at my back has me moaning.

Eli steps back just enough to spin me around, and then he's bracketing my throat with one hand and sliding the other between my thighs to cup my pussy. His low voice in my ear hardly sounds like the man I've shared the last five years with. "Do you really think it's that easy, Harlow? We have a conversation and all the sins of the past are forgiven?" He bites my shoulder hard enough to make me jump and then shoves two fingers into me.

It feels like he's possessing me, like he's owning me. I

don't know if I hate it or crave more. I can't think past the feel of him, the pleasure of him slowly fucking me with his fingers, dragging the heel of his palm over my clit in the same rhythm. Fuck, that feels good. My eyes threaten to flutter closed, but I can't lose the thread of this conversation. "Why not? The only rules are the ones we make."

His chuckle almost sounds like a curse. "And what happens then? Do we live in a happy little throuple until we're old and gray? Since when do you chase fantasies like that?"

I don't. I never have. I never will. But it still hurts for him to demolish the possibility of that future before I even allowed myself to contemplate it. I press my palms to the tile, arching back against him. His cock is a hard length at my ass, and the feeling has me moaning nearly as much as his hand playing with my pussy. I try to focus, to gasp out the words that need to be said. "Better to strive for that than to become your father—old and angry and alone until the day he died."

Eli freezes, and for one delirious moment, I'm sure I've gone too far.

But then he drags me to the bench and sits down on it, pulling me astride him. "You're so fucking mean now, Harlow." His hazel eyes have a light in them I've never seen before. He looks downright feral. "Why do I like that so much?"

I wrap my fist around his cock and position him at my entrance. I'm so wet, I slide down his length with barely a hitch. The full sensation steals my breath, but we're finally sharing a degree of honesty, and I'm not about to stop now. "Because we're not lying to each other anymore." I start riding him. The tile bites my knees, but I don't give a fuck.

I'm too intent on my pleasure. "Because, after five years, you're finally *seeing* me."

He might be right. It might be too little, too late. I don't know. I don't know anything anymore. We're well off the map and in uncharted territory. *Here be monsters* and all that. I don't know what the future holds for us.

Perversely, that knowledge slows me down, until I'm barely moving on his cock. He's got his hands on my hips, but he doesn't seem interested in rushing this, either. Eli leans back against the wall, and though his gaze skates over my body, it's my face he lingers on. As if trying to memorize this moment, this vulnerability between us. This *truth*.

Pleasure builds in slow waves, cresting higher and higher despite our pace. I start to close my eyes, but Eli moves one hand to cup my face and shakes his head. "No. Stay with me, Harlow."

The one command I'm not sure I can fulfill. Not when we have so much stacked against us. "I'll try," I whisper. In this moment, I'm not sure if I'm lying or simply wishing on a future that will never come. It doesn't matter.

I try to hold out, to slow down further, but we've gone too far. My body goes tight and hot, and then I'm grinding down on his cock, chasing an orgasm that has white spots dancing across my vision. It's so good, it hurts. Or maybe I'm just always hurting with Eli.

He pounds up into me, chasing his own pleasure. When he comes, he says my name almost like a curse. I start to climb off him, but he wraps his arms around me, loosely holding me in place. "Just give me a minute."

I should probably fight this; the feeling of being held by Eli is almost too sweet to bear. The feeling of time slipping through my fingers, faster and faster, shoving us toward some inevitable end... It keeps me in place. I don't want this to end. It doesn't seem to matter that we already *have* ended. I wrap my arms around his neck and hold him as our breathing slowly evens out. An act somehow just as intimate as sex; maybe more so.

My ability to keep a healthy distance falters with every moment that passes. The wall I've painstakingly built around my heart crumbles a little more after each interaction with these men. If I were smart, I'd say to hell with keeping my word and run. Just flee into the unknown and take my chances in another city with another set of people. Anything but kneeling at their feet, bowing my head, and hoping neither Eli nor Abel swings the sword that will end me. Not physically, never that, but a sword cuts through a heart as easily as a neck.

I'm suddenly sure that mine won't survive the year.

For eight long years, my plan has been simple. Survive. Return to take my rightful place as faction leader. Make Eli pay for all the pain and suffering he's caused me and mine. There is absolutely no reason that last night should have changed anything. Sex is sex is sex. Yeah, we put aside our fucked up past to take care of Harlow, but that's the only reason we were on the same page, and even then it didn't last past the moment we all felt into an exhausted pile and slipped into sleep.

The first thing Harlow did upon waking was flee.

The first thing Eli did was chase her.

Both expected things, as long as I don't fall into the trap of assuming that all the orgasms and pleasure meant something. It obviously didn't to them. It shouldn't have to me, either.

But then, my rules have always been frustratingly flexible when it comes to Eli. Why should heartbreak, betrayal, and eight years of grief change that? It pisses me off so much, I can barely breathe past the rage. Last night is a glimpse of what we could have been. A future that he set on fire right along with my childhood home.

The bathroom door opens, and Harlow strides out, stopping short when she sees me awake. She looks frazzled. She hasn't taken the time to dry her hair, and she's got that too-wide look around her eyes that says she and Eli had another altercation.

I sit up. "Hey."

She glances back at the bathroom and lowers her voice. "I'm going to change and then go check on a few things. I..." Harlow takes a deep breath and marches to the bed. She hesitates and then reaches out and takes my hand. "Abel, could you talk to him? Actually talk, not just posture and threaten and end up with his mouth around your cock again?"

I have to fight for an arrogant grin. "Why bother, when I love him sucking me off so much?" Despite my best efforts, the words fall flat.

"Abel..." She gives me a small smile, though her eyes are sad. "If you two ever managed to work together, you'd be unstoppable." She frames my face with her hands, leans down, and presses a light kiss to my lips. The casual intimacy shocks me as much as her words.

I capture her wrists in a loose grip, holding her touch to me. "You're asking for the moon, sweetheart. No matter if it would be a good thing or not."

Another of those achingly sweet kisses. "If anyone can get me the moon, it's you. At least think about it. Please?"

It's not as if part of me has already been considering future possibilities. Not forgiveness. I don't know if it's in me to forgive Eli, and he obviously doesn't crave that from me. But I haven't been able to get what Harlow said yesterday out of my head. The policies Eli's put in place, the very same fucking ones that we planned together all those years ago.

I want to know why, if his goals were always the same as mine, he did what he did. I want fucking answers. I don't know what I'll do with them, having spent eight years telling myself that they don't matter because I'm going to set the scales right. But I want them all the same.

Am I actually considering this?

I finally release Harlow. "I'll think about it."

"Thank you." She turns away and walks to the closet, disappearing inside. A few short minutes later, she returns. She's wearing jeans and a tank top and has pulled her hair back into a ponytail. It strikes me that she still has clothes in this room even if she's moved most of her stuff down the hall. She gives me a faint smile. "Is there anything specific you need from me today?"

No, but I don't like the thought of not seeing her until tonight. "Check in on Fallon and Monroe."

"That's where I'm headed now." She makes a face. "How are you going to play things in the long run with them? They both have jobs and responsibilities in their respective factions."

A reality I was hoping to put off for a bit longer. "After you talk to them, we'll figure it out. Feel free to negotiate on my behalf."

Surprise flares in her eyes, quickly followed by a warmth that I crave the same way I crave dawn's light after a particularly brutal night. "You trust me enough to give me that power?"

"I trust that you and I are in line with wanting the best for the faction." Which isn't quite the same thing as trusting her entirely. But it's still a huge admission. "Do what you need to do."

Harlow opens her mouth, seems to consider what she's about to say, and finally nods. "Thank you." She reaches for the door. "See you tonight?"

"Yeah, sweetheart. I'll see you tonight." I don't imagine the pleased look on her face as she leaves the room.

I don't get a chance to enjoy the knowledge that I pulled Harlow out of her head, because Eli chooses that moment to pad naked into the room. His skin is still damp from the shower, and he's slicked his hair back from his face. Without the pretty-boy blond waves, his features are almost too perfect. He looks like a sculptor crafted the high arch of his cheekbones, the strong line of his jaw, the sensual curve of his lips. It pisses me the fuck off.

He sees me and stops. "Last night changes nothing."

"Agreed." But I can't get Harlow's request out of my head. I can't imagine a future where I trust Eli at my back the way I once did, but there are questions still churning in my gut that only he has the answers to. I almost snort. Turns out Harlow is right, after all. We do need to talk.

I shove the sheet off and climb to my feet. "Let's find some coffee. It's about time we had a conversation."

Eli disappears into the closet and returns a few minutes later with jeans and a white T-shirt. The simplicity of the clothes does nothing to detract from his attractiveness. Or maybe I'm just getting sidelined because now I know how he tastes. A distraction I can't afford, but a necessary one. The only real way to neutralize Eli would be to kill him, and I'm not ready to take that step.

THE LONGER WE SPEND TOGETHER, the clearer it becomes that I'll never be ready to take that step.

We stop in Harlow's room so I can change clothes and

then head down to the kitchen. I checked it out the first day here, and I'm reluctantly impressed all over again by how well outfitted it is. It's commercial grade and commercial size. There was a chef and with two assistants on staff to take care of all the meals for everyone in the house—and another team that handled only the barracks—but we haven't replaced them yet. Poison would be a great way to remove the threat we represent, and my people are the only ones I trust.

We haven't had the luxury of keeping a chef on staff, not when we've been more or less on the move since we left Sabine Valley. We'd settle for a few months, or even a year, but something always happened, and we always had to move again. Even if we'd landed in one place, it wouldn't be home the way Sabine Valley is.

There's coffee made, but from the thickness of the liquid, either it's been there overnight or that someone let Donovan brew it. I shake my head and dump it down the sink, pause to wash the pot, and then start the process for a new round of coffee.

Once it begins dripping, I turn to face Eli. He's got his carefully neutral expression in place, and he leans against the counter across from me. "I see Harlow got to you."

I shrug. "She's tired of being the bone between us. Or the bridge. No matter which way you spin it, it's not fair to her."

"Agreed."

I wait, but he doesn't seem inclined to continue. Fine. The agreement, the fact that he's here—it will have to be enough. I take a moment to look around the kitchen. All the stainless steel surfaces shine, the tile below our feet barely scuffed by so much foot traffic. It's like the rest of the house. High-end and yet comfortable and practical. "You know, when we were younger, we talked a lot about how we'd fortify a place."

Eli's expression goes perfectly blank. "Did we?"

"Did you think I'd forget?" Honestly, I had. Our plans for the faction always took the forefront in my mind. We went over them time and time again, finessing them to the smallest detail, considering different paths to get to the same result.

Talking about the home we'd someday build for our people was more of a footnote. One I forgot until yesterday, when the mystery of how Eli managed to upset Harlow had the memory flickering in the back of my mind.

I walk from one end of the kitchen to the other, measuring it with my steps. "Especially when so many of these rooms don't line up the way they should." He's not reacting, but that's as much as an admission when it comes to Eli. "It's not mapped out the way we planned, but the basic details are the same."

"There isn't a question in there."

"No, there isn't." I already know he won't show me any of the entrances to the passageways, but that's fine. I'll figure them out on my own. It's more the fact they exist at all that fucks with my head. "Harlow lined out the things she won't compromise on yesterday." He doesn't respond, but I don't need him to, not when I'm watching him so closely. "A food program so no one goes hungry. A concentrated effort to shut down violent crime against people who can't defend themselves. Imagine my surprise at how familiar that shit sounded."

Still his expression doesn't change. "You have a point."

"Yeah, I have a fucking point." The sudden desire to cut through all the bullshit and find out the truth nearly over-whelms me. I cross my arms over my chest and stare. "I doubted the intel I had on you. It doesn't make any fucking sense. We had plans together for this faction, for how to change things. When you betrayed me, I figured it was all bullshit, that you just wanted the power for yourself. But then I find out that you went ahead and implemented most of them. Why the fuck would you do that? Why would you do any of it?"

Eli sighs and looks away. "They were good plans."

"Yeah, they were." It feels like there's a knife in my heart, the blade scraping against muscle and rib bones with every word. "Did you really think I had to be dead to make them happen?"

"I..." He scrubs a hand over his face. "The past is the past. We both have plenty of sins to lay at our feet. What the hell does rehashing this accomplish?"

I don't know, but the fact he's dodging this question means I need to hear the answer. "Indulge me."

"Nothing I can say will make a difference, Abel. Not a single damn thing. If I tell you that I had no idea my father was going to set fire to the house, you won't believe me. If I tell you that I lost no sleep over *your* father's death but that I'm still haunted by those forty people, you'll call me a liar."

My chest feels too tight. For the first time since I walked back into his life, the polished edge of his voice is gone and there's only raw pain there. The side of Eli that only I ever saw, the ragged edges and harsh truth. I don't know if I can trust it, but fuck, I want to. "Is it the truth?"

"Would you believe it if I said it was?"

I don't know. I've spent eight years being driven by Eli's betrayal. His old man didn't surprise me; Deacon Walsh always was a mean son of a bitch, and he and my father never saw eye to eye on anything for all that Deacon was his second-in-command. That betrayal stung, but nowhere near as much as Eli's. It's not like we were kids. He was twenty-fucking-eight when this shit went down.

I didn't expect to miss him so much. I sure as fuck didn't expect for that feeling to get stronger now that he's back in my life. We're different people than we were eight years ago, but somehow we still fit. It doesn't make any damn sense to me. I should want to string him up and leave him for dead for what he did, but I can't help wondering if Harlow is right.

If there's some way to salvage this.

Love or hate, trust or not, I've never been able to claw out the part of me that cares far too much for Eli Walsh.

To buy myself time, I grab two mugs and pour us each one before I pass his over. I burn my tongue on the hot coffee, but the sting settles me a little. "Tell me what happened, and I'll decide what to believe from there."

25

No matter what Abel says, he's too stuck in his beliefs to let something as complicated as the truth derail him. When I stood in the ashes of his home, I knew that there was no going back. It doesn't matter how large or small a role I played; I was partly responsible for that massacre. I don't deserve forgiveness, but I had to move forward in order to ensure that sacrifice wasn't for nothing.

If he'd asked me this yesterday, I would have told him to fuck off or said something designed to provoke him. But now?

Last night shouldn't have changed things. Sex *never* changes things, not in any permanent way. Even knowing that, I can't deny that I'm conflicted for the first time since I dedicated myself to the path that ended with me leading this faction.

And then there's Harlow.

I can still taste her on my lips, feel the slide of her skin against mine, see the sadness in her eyes as she mourns the future we could have had. I don't know if she's right. Abel's been gone a long time, and he reminds me of his father more than ever now. Or he did when he first appeared. Now I'm not so sure. There are cracks, and through those cracks I can see the shadow of the man he used to be. The one that I once dreamed of partnering with to bring this faction into a new future.

I take a tiny drink of my coffee and set it aside. "Your father was a monster. Under his rule, the people of this faction were suffering, were dying, because he was too busying chasing his fights and his glorious victories."

"You don't have to tell me what my father was like. I know as well as anyone. We talked about it after he hit Cohen, after I stepped in. You knew what I planned on doing." There's no heat in his tone, but he watches me carefully. "Your father planned the coup before I had a chance to."

"Yes." It's tempting to pick up the coffee mug, to keep something in my hands, but I've trained myself too well to fidget. "I knew he was going after your father and I didn't tell you." This part's harder. Harder to say, harder still to believe. "I thought if we could get Bauer out of the way, we could undermine my father as well. He wasn't as bad as Bauer, but he wasn't a saint, either."

"Why not come to me with that plan? You know how I felt about my father. You knew there was only one endgame for me, and it resulted in my father six feet under."

Yeah, I knew that. It's why I did what I did. I take a slow breath, shoving down the past. "That's exactly why I didn't tell you. He was your father, Abel. No matter how fucked your relationship, how much you hated him at the end, I couldn't let you bear the burden of his death."

His face goes slack with shock for half a second before he recovers. "You're shitting me. Are you seriously trying to tell me that you did this so I wouldn't have to kill Bauer myself?"

I've gone this far. I might as well finish it. I never considered myself naïve, but it's impossible to paint me as anything else for believing things would work out that night. That it would end in anything other than disaster. "You're able to push through a whole hell of a lot when you're furious, but cold-blooded murder? That was a stretch, let alone planning patricide."

"I don't blink at murder any longer," he says softly.

Maybe not, but if there's one thing I don't regret, it's that he wasn't the one who ended his father's life. I spared him that much, at least. It doesn't make up for the rest, but it's a small consolation. "I didn't realize my father had brought in the Mystics and the Amazons. Not until I smelled the smoke."

I'd been down the street, on my way to tell Abel that he was finally free of his father. I still remember the way my stomach dropped out at the sight of the flames against the night sky. I'd stood there for hours as firefighters showed up to ensure the flames didn't jump to nearby buildings, as the neighborhood came outside to bear silent witness, as the flames finally burned away to nothing, leaving only ash and death in their wake.

My stomach churns at the memory. I'd thought Abel was in that fire. That, in implementing the action that would set us free, I'd inadvertently caused the death of my best friend. Of the man I loved. Realizing that he survived, that he got all his brothers out... It only made that feeling worse.

Because I knew what he'd believe. That I was behind all

of it. That I'd committed a betrayal there was no coming back from.

That *everyone* would believe it.

I clear my throat. "By the time they realized you and your brothers weren't among the bodies in the house, you were gone. I knew looking for you was an invitation for them to finish what they started, so I disrupted the hunts as best I could." It wasn't enough. Not even close. Every time one of the people my father sent returned a failure, I breathed a sigh of relief.

Until I was able to kill my father and end the hunts once and for all.

Unlike Abel, I have no problem making the cold, unforgivable decision when it means the greater good.

Abel studies me over the rim of his coffee cup. "If that's the truth, why didn't you come after me? The transfer of power wouldn't have been easy, even if Old Town got behind him. The two of us could have done what we'd planned."

I swallow hard. "What would you have done if I'd shown up in the first year? In the second? Third?"

"Put a bullet between your eyes." He says it without blinking.

"That's why I didn't. There's a chance that if I found you, my father would finish what he started. But more than that, I couldn't do it to the faction." I laugh bitterly. "Forty innocent people died, Abel. I couldn't let it be for nothing. I couldn't let him rule for years and do even more damage to the people in Raider faction."

He's still watching me with that unreadable expression on his face. "You let your father live for three years past that night."

I grimace. "He was a canny old bastard and paranoid as

hell. I had to let things stabilize, but more than that, I had to wait for him to let down his guard. He died in his sleep." With a pillow shoved over his face, and my weight holding it in place. The death wasn't anything closed to the misery he deserved, but if there's a hell, he's suffering plenty in it right now.

Eventually I'll join him, as payment for my sins.

"He died in his sleep." Abel snorts. "I'll just bet he did."

"I'll do anything for the good of this faction. Anything."

Abel stares for a long moment and then shakes his head. "You and Harlow are quite the pair, aren't you? Both such noble martyrs. It'd be sickening if it weren't so goddamn cute."

He drinks his coffee, still watching me. "Let's say I'm in the believing sort of mood. You've done this much for the faction. Can't imagine you like the idea of handing over all that power just because I'm back."

I don't, but it's more than that. I can't let the faction go back to where it was before we killed Abel's father. Too many people suffered during those days, and I'll commit further unforgivable acts to ensure they don't suffer again. My father? Abel's father? They saw the throne as power that was their due. Neither of them felt the weight of ruling, the sheer responsibility for every life within the faction.

Not like I do.

"That depends on what your plans are."

His smile is knife-sharp. "Yeah, that's not an answer. You planning on pulling a repeat of eight years ago, Eli?"

It's the only way to ensure the faction's safety. No matter what cracks Abel has shown me, the truth is that he's a stranger to me now. I can't guarantee that he's not an even worse version of his father. Waiting to see is just paving the way for him to hurt those who can least afford the harm. It won't be me or Harlow or even Old Town that bears the brunt of his ruthlessness. It will be kids like Harlow was all those years ago. I couldn't save her then. I can save those nameless kids now, though.

I lift my mug and let the warmth of the coffee seep into my hands. "It would be the smart play to make. You're an unknown quantity."

"Oh, I think you *know* me pretty well by now."

That surprises a chuckle out of me. "Fucking is different, and you know it."

"Yeah, I guess I do." He drains the rest of his mug and sets it on the counter. What little joking there was in his expression bleeds away. "I'll think about what you said, Eli. I've had eight years thinking you betrayed me, and I think you'll understand that I'm not all that willing to pull a one-eighty just because you say so."

I expected nothing else. Honestly, I didn't expect a single thing. I wouldn't have broached this conversation if he didn't push it, if *Harlow* didn't push it. I'm not sure what she's trying to accomplish, but it aches to talk about this shit. That night is a wound that never quite healed right, and I suspect it's the same for Abel. We've had too long to move through the world with those wounds; they've shaped us into the men we are now.

We were friends all those years ago. We might have been more if either of us ever made a move. None of that matters now. The only thing that does is what we do next.

My coffee tastes bitter on my tongue. "Believe what you want, Abel. I know I don't deserve forgiveness for what I've done, but I'll do worse to keep the people of Raider faction safe."

He stalks to me, crowding me back against the counter

with his bigger body. His proximity goes through me like a bolt of pure lust, and it's everything I can do not to respond physically. I hold perfectly still. Fuck, I even hold my breath.

He reaches out and loosely brackets my throat with his calloused hand, his expression contemplative. "Come to bed with us again tonight."

I swallow hard. I want to say yes more than I've wanted anything in a very long time. "Doesn't seem wise to go without sleep for too many nights in a row."

Abel gives me a slow smile that has my cock twitching despite my best efforts. "No one's getting sleep tonight, and I think you know it." He squeezes lightly then steps back. "Your choice."

I watch him walk away, my chest too tight. Yeah, I want to climb back into bed with him and Harlow—the sooner, the better—but there's no avoiding the meeting with Marie tonight. She's already pushing against my orders; I can't afford for her to act on her own because I'm otherwise occupied. She's never had a problem following orders before, but we're in uncharted territory in a number ways at the moment.

It's not until I'm walking the halls, heading for my room, when I realize that Abel didn't react at all like I expected him to. No instant denial. No telling me that it didn't fucking matter. Just a mild comment that he'd think about my version of events. I don't know what I'm supposed to do with that.

I open my door and step into my room. What if—I can barely let myself contemplate it, but—What if Abel believes me? What if he simply lets go of the version of that night he's believed for so long? What if the future we always dreamed of isn't actually ash?

I can't afford to hope, can't let that desire cloud my decisions and my vision. But I'm only human, and I've spent so long mourning the loss of him that the fact that he's here, that he's still himself—at least in part—is fucking with me.

For the first time in a very long time, I don't know what the right path forward is.

Being in a room with Monroe and Fallon is a little bit like being trapped in a cage with a tiger and a feral wolf. They smile and trade barbs and sharpen their claws. The impossible feat is to get them to stop snarling long enough to agree to something, but it's been thirty minutes, and now I'm just waiting them out.

Monroe examines her nails. She's found time to paint them a bloody red since I saw her in the library yesterday. She's wearing a sleek, short black dress and her blond hair is an artful tumble around her face. As always, her lipstick is bright red.

Ironically, Fallon and she are a matching pair. Fallon's wearing a black tank top, black pants, and black heels. The dark color makes her skin look ethereally pale and her hair sinfully bright. She's lounging in a chair with her ankle on one knee, and the way her hand keeps drifting to that ankle makes me think she has a knife stashed there.

Just what I need. Fallon and Monroe getting into a knife fight in the library.

Monroe grins suddenly. "So, Fallon, how is that baby

Paine in bed? He seems awfully *eager*." She leans forward, all happy smiles and sharp eyes. "Did he come in his pants when he saw you naked the first time?"

I have to fight not to roll my eyes. Gabriel Paine might be the youngest of the Paine brothers, but he's twenty-eight. Hardly a baby by any definition of the word.

Fallon lifts an imperial brow. "You Amazons are always so vulgar."

"We prefer the term *earthy*." Monroe leans forward in her chair. "But it's sweet of you to throw stones from that pretty glass house of yours. Vulgar, Fallon? Really? I know what kind of kinky rituals the Mystics get up to when they think no one is looking. Someone's started believing their own hype."

"Shut your filthy mouth, Amazon."

Monroe inches forward. "Make me, Mystic."

In another second, they're going to be fighting and this will have been an even larger waste of time. I sip my tea and sigh dramatically. "That's enough, children. If I wanted you to brawl, I'd put you out in the yard and at least give the people some entertainment."

Just like that, I have two pairs of eyes cutting in my direction, one green, one eerie gray. Monroe tilts her head slowly to the side. "I knew you were a lap dog, Harlow, but you're really taking the cake with this. Is Abel's cock that good? Or were you always an opportunistic bitch?"

I let the insults roll off me. She's said worse in the past. We're enemies, after all. Enemies, and yet in a very similar situation. "Lap dog or no, I'm still free to move around as I see fit while you're confined to your rooms. I didn't anticipate you'd be one for captivity."

Her lips curl into a sneer before she catches herself. "I'm biding my time."

I glance at Fallon. She hasn't moved since I spoke, hasn't seemed to breathe. The expression on her face makes me think that she's visualizing her knife going into my throat repeatedly right now. I keep my tone mild. "And you, Fallon? Are you biding your time as well?"

She finally moves, shifting farther back into her seat. "I take it you have a reason for calling us here. I'm listening."

Monroe snorts. "Just like that?"

"Unlike you, I'm able to think with my brain and not just my pussy." She flicks her fingers at me, a clear command to continue.

I have to pause to keep from snarling. It doesn't matter what these women think of me. It only matters that the faction benefits from this situation that Abel's created. He's guaranteed peace in Sabine Valley for the next year, but that doesn't mean shit for those in power. Underhanded plays and shady deals will be the name of the game for the next twelve months. In order to cut off avenues for a good portion of that, I need these two women on my side. "You have two choices. You can keep fighting and pushing buttons and bickering and stay in this house for the next year. Or you can work with the Paines."

"Pass," Monroe says.

I ignore her. "I'm sure you have responsibilities and other things requiring your attention in your respective factions. Obviously you can't go home, but we're willing to loosen the leash a bit. There's no reason for your companies and factions to suffer simply because you're Brides." The jab isn't my most subtle, but I'm irritated and trying hard not to let it get control.

Monroe goes still. She might play like she's a loose cannon, but it's a ploy just like Eli's easy charm is a ploy.

People see the pretty face and the irreverent attitude and, despite her being the Amazon heir, they underestimate her.

"Are we expected to run things remotely from Paine territory?" Fallon's fingers drift to her ankle again. "That's a potential security breach that won't be ignored by our people. You might as well keep us under lock and key and be done with it."

This, I expected. I wrap my hands around my cup of tea. Like last time, neither of them took me up on my offer to share. "I'm merely opening up negotiations. I'm sure there's a compromise that can get the job done."

"I doubt it."

I give Fallon a long look. "It's your choice, but with you and Matteo gone, do you really think Juniper won't take advantage of this opening?" Fallon's sister was third in line for the Mystic throne, and she is actually a loose cannon if ever there was one. Cruel and petty and with no impulse control to speak of, if she took over, both the Mystic faction and Sabine Valley as a whole will suffer. Even Matteo with his dreamy demeanor would be a better option.

Then again, positioning Juniper to take the throne would be a brilliant way to undermine the Mystics and set them up for a hostile takeover from one of the other two factions. It's ruthless in the extreme and required playing the long game, but I wouldn't put anything past Abel at this point.

Fallon clenches her jaw, and her eyes flare. "She wouldn't dare."

"She would, and you know it. She's probably already started." I turn to Monroe. "Your mother followed in the Amazon tradition of teaching her oldest two daughters to rule so that if anything happened to you, Thea will be able to step in and your people will be fine."

Monroe loses her smile. "I'm not dead; she's the spare for a reason."

"You might as well be dead, Monroe. If you stay here for the next year without reasserting your position, you might not have a position to come back to." I sit back. "Look, call me a lap dog if you want, but the truth is that I want what's best for my faction. That means that I will do whatever it takes to smooth the way as long as the Paines don't fuck with our bottom line. That also means that I have no interest in war. Both of your factions are too strong to take on without bleeding Sabine Valley dry—at the moment." I pause meaningfully. "In a year? That might be a different story."

"Bitch," Monroe snarls.

"If you want to insult me, you're going to have to try harder."

Monroe shakes her head slowly. "Okay, fine, you have us over a barrel. What do you want?"

"Speak for yourself." Fallon's tone could freeze the entire room several times over. "But I will listen to your proposal."

This is going better than expected. I can only open the door. It's going to be up to the Paines to enforce it. "We can negotiate you returning to your factions on a limited basis to maintain your power and continue whatever projects you have going right now—with some conditions." I tick them off on my fingers. "You will not transport anything to or from this faction. Your family members who are Brides will remain behind to ensure good behavior. And you will give your word that you will uphold the Bridal agreement, which means doing nothing to harm, directly or indirectly, the Paine brothers or the Raider faction."

"You ask too much."

Monroe laughs. "Get that stick out of your ass, Fallon."

She pushes to her feet and smooths her hands down her body. "I agree, on one condition."

"I'm listening."

Her grin is razor sharp. "We limit the definition of harm as physical and financial when it comes to Broderick Paine. I won't bloody him, but I'm going to spend the next year tormenting the fuck out of him."

I open my mouth to say no but change my mind halfway through. She's going to do it anyway. If I give her this concession, then there's a decent chance Monroe will keep her word, and it will negate the risk of larger consequences. I've only seen Broderick in passing, but if he's even halfway as capable as Abel, he can handle whatever Monroe throws at him. If he's not? Well, that's a him problem, not a faction problem. "Deal."

"Perfect." She flips her hair off her shoulder. "Are we done here?"

"That was about it."

"Good." She turns and walks out of the room, her hips swaying dangerously. No doubt off to start her torment. Or, more likely, continue it.

I focus on Fallon. "And your answer?"

Her face is completely locked down. "You really only care about this faction, don't you?"

"Yes." The word feels like a lie on my tongue, but I ignore the sensation. The faction is my end all, be all. Whatever confusing feelings I'm housing for Abel and Eli have nothing to do with that.

She nods slowly. "I'll take this devil's bargain as well." She rises to her feet, a human-shaped pillar of ice. "Just know that if this is some ploy to get the Mystics' secrets, it will be for nothing."

That remains to be seen. But I'm reasonably sure that

neither Monroe nor Fallon will do anything to endanger their family within this house. I nod, holding her gaze. "I'll take that into consideration." I rise as well. "It will take some time to get the details finalized, but we should be able to put this into motion next week."

"Good."

I wait for her to leave before I sink back onto the chair and exhale slowly. That went better than expected. It's still going to be a complicated situation to maneuver through, but as long as we can keep both Fallon and Monroe on leashes, I suspect the rest of the Brides will follow suit.

I pour myself another cup of tea. Despite my best efforts, my mind goes back to Abel and Eli. I don't know if either of them will listen to me long enough to sit down and have a conversation with each other. It's impossible to say if that will help or hurt things, but the stark truth is that we can't go on like this. If we're too busy tearing into each other, we're not going to be able to face any threat that arises.

No matter what Eli thinks of the Paines being back, even he has to admit that they're likely preferable to us losing the faction altogether. At least as Abel's Brides we have a chance to influence the situation.

Not to mention... Abel isn't what I expected at all. He's brutal and harsh, but there are threads of kindness and caring that appear at the most unexpected times. He might seem very similar to his father on the surface, but the core is different.

That makes what happened the night of the coup all that much more tragic, but Eli did what he had to. I believe that even if I stopped believing in us.

Except...

Have I stopped believing in us? I don't know. Things were complicated before Lammas, and the last few days haven't uncomplicated them. I thought my love for Eli had turned to hate, but last night...

I shake my head and lift my tea cup to take a sip. After all this time and all my certainty, it seems foolish in the extreme to let an outstanding night of sex change how I feel. But did it really change things? Or did it bring what was already there to light?

I don't have answers. All I have are more questions.

"Do you believe him?"

I stare at the beer bottle dangling from my fingers. I don't drink much these days, not when any blurring of the senses can be the difference between survival and death, but today just flat-out called for a beer. "I don't know."

I've spent hours going through the compound with Broderick to oversee the changes and ensure all the security features are up and running. Tomorrow we'll officially get our answer from Old Town, but from Finnegan's spy tech, we already know what they'll say.

They won't fight us.

That public support will go a long way to smoothing the transition of power, and having Eli and Harlow publicly at my side will go even farther. I should be feeling victorious right now, should already be considering what changes I want to implement.

Instead, all I can think about is the past.

Broderick's the only one of my brothers I can talk to about this. He's the most level-headed of us, the one who likes to weigh all the facts before making a decision, the steady one that keeps all seven of us grounded. It's why I gave Monroe to him; if anyone can handle her dangerous recklessness, it's him. I have no right to be leaning on him now, but fuck if I can get my thoughts in order.

He pops the cap off his beer bottle and sinks onto the chair next to the desk. We've co-opted Eli's study for our own, but really it's Broderick's now. I've never been comfortable being idle for long, and being locked in a room with a shit ton of paperwork is my idea of hell. Another way that we're fundamentally different.

Finally, he says, "That's one thing about that night that never sat well with me. Or at least our version of events. No matter what else Eli is, he was your friend."

"You know as well as I do that friendship doesn't mean shit when it comes to power."

Broderick sighs. "Yeah, I know. I just think that it's entirely possible that he's telling the truth. It seems like some roundabout shit that Eli would do."

That's the crux of it. Killing my father so I wouldn't have to is exactly something the Eli I knew would have done. Some high-handed bullshit designed to save me from unnecessary pain. "It doesn't change the end results."

"No. It doesn't." Broderick leans forward and looks at me. Where some of our brothers take after our mother's red hair and freckles, Broderick and I are purely our father's sons. Sometimes I wonder if looking at me bothers him the same way sometimes I see the ghost of our father's face in one of his expressions. He frowns. "What are you going to do?"

"I don't know." It seems to be the answer of the day. No matter how confidently I projected to Eli, the truth is that this isn't playing out at all like I expected. I didn't anticipate

Harlow, and I sure as fuck didn't anticipate feeling anything but loathing for Eli. "If I were smart, I'd kill him now." The words ring hollow.

"You can't. Maybe you could have before you made him a Bride, but if any harm comes to any of the Brides, we'll have the entire city howling for our blood."

I give a mirthless smile. "They're already howling for our blood."

"Harming one of the Brides will give them the ammunition to strike without worrying about the consequences."

"I know." I drag my hand over my face. The truth is that I don't want Eli dead. I did when I came back to Sabine Valley, but that desire died within the first twenty-four hours. No matter how angry, how hurt, how betrayed I felt, the truth is that this man was my best friend for more than two-thirds of my life. My father might have been cold enough to strike him down without hesitation, but apparently I retain enough of my soul that it's an impossible ask.

Maybe that makes me weak. I don't know anymore.

Eli isn't the only one I have to worry about, though. "Harlow wants us to figure it out."

"Harlow, huh?" Broderick shakes his head. "She could be playing you."

"She could be," I agree. "But I don't think so. She's not great at lying, and her priorities are the Raider faction above all others. She's an asset, and she could be one hell of a leader if she had a long enough leash."

"You've let her negotiate with the Brides on your behalf." His tone is careful, but he can't hide the tension there. Not from me.

I look at him. "Yeah. You got a problem with that?"

"Only that Monroe came back to the rooms happy as a pig in shit earlier today, and that can only mean she's about to unleash some chaos to make my life harder." He takes a pull from his beer. "She's still spending a lot of time with Shiloh."

Ah. That's one complication I should have seen coming. I knew Broderick held a flame for Shiloh, even if he never made a move to morph their friendship into something else. Giving him a Bride was destined to fuck with that, but I didn't expect Monroe to pick up on that unrequited situation so quickly—or to use it as a pressure point against Broderick. "Like I said the other day, there's an easy enough fix for that."

"No, there isn't. Shiloh is my friend, and even if I wanted to do something about it, I have a Bride now."

"A Bride who's an enemy. All that you had to do was consummate the handfasting Lammas night. You never have to touch Monroe again."

"I won't." There's something there, something haunted in those two words.

What the fuck happened between him and Monroe on Lammas night?

I can't ask. He won't thank me for prying, and if it's not something fixable, it will just rip open a barely closed wound. Still... "You have shit handled?"

"Yeah." Broderick gives a steady smile that doesn't fool me for second. "Don't have a choice, do I?"

"It's only a year."

"Only a year," he repeats. He takes another pull from the bottle, a longer one. "So the only question is what you're going to do about Eli. Rekindle the friendship, or spend the next year tormenting the fuck out of him?"

When he puts it like that, it turns out I've already made my choice. I don't know if I can trust Eli again, but sometime in the last few days, I've lost my desire to see his head on a platter. "I'll figure it out. The one person who most deserves to suffer is Deacon Walsh, and that fucker is already dead."

"Not only him." Broderick's blue eyes are stark. "Both Aisling and Ciar have blood on their hands because of that fire. Maybe Eli knew about it, maybe he didn't, but we *know* those two did. The drugs that put everyone to sleep came from the Mystics, and the Amazons set the fire. We know that as truth."

"I know." I drain my bottle and set it on the desk with a clink. "First we get this faction in order. Then we start looking to their borders. We have the year to prepare, to put our plans in motion. No matter how things fall out with Eli, we won't be turned from this. I promise."

"Good." He pushes to his feet and sets his bottle next to mine. "Honestly, if you can bring Eli around to our side, it would simplify matters. The less time it takes to bring our faction to order, the faster we can move on to the next part of the plan." Broderick turns and walks out of the office without looking back.

He's been the steady one for eight long years, so I don't know why it surprises me so much to see the hairline fractures in his control. I'll have to keep an eye on him. The pressure he's under is already astronomical—and that's without Monroe adding gasoline to the situation and gleefully lighting a match.

A knock sounds before I can leave the room. I grab the bottles and toss them into the trash under the desk. "Come in."

Harlow slips through the door. She gives a little smile when she sees me, and fuck if that doesn't brighten up my whole day. I hold out a hand. "Come here."

She walks into my arms without hesitation and, yeah, I like this a whole hell of a lot, too. I kiss her, and she goes soft against me for a long moment before she steps back. "I know this might be hard to believe, but I didn't come here for a quickie on your desk."

"Sweetheart, you wound me. There would be nothing quick about it."

She shakes her head, that little smile still pulling at the edges of her lips. "Did you talk to Eli?"

"First I want to hear about how things went with Fallon and Monroe."

She gives me a long look. "I didn't peg you for a man who avoids hard topics."

"Play your cards right and you can just flat-out peg me."

She blinks. "You have yourself a deal."

I motion for her to sit. "Tell me how the meeting went."

"Fine." Harlow takes the seat Broderick had earlier and gives me a quick rundown. It's about what I expected. Having multiple members of the family is the only way that will ensure anything resembling good behavior. The Amazons and Mystics might have little in the way of honor when it comes to dealing with us, but they won't fuck over their own. I eye Harlow once she finishes. "You threw Broderick under the bus."

"Correction: I assumed Broderick was more than capable of dealing with anything Monroe brings to the plate and negotiated accordingly."

She has me there. Before my conversation with my brother, I wouldn't have doubted that, but there's a lot about this situation that I didn't anticipate. "We'll figure it out as we go."

Harlow studies me for a moment. "I'm assuming that the required escort will be planting more of those fancy listening devices like the ones you used with Old Town."

I allow myself a satisfied grin. "That would be telling."

"They're paranoid enough to sweep the place after your group leaves every day."

I shrug. "At first. But human nature is always to do as little as possible, and familiarity breeds even more laziness. After a few weeks, they won't be as diligent. Our people will just be another normal occurrence in the other territories." I should leave it there, but Harlow's operated in good faith to this point. "And where do you think Fallon and Monroe are going to get the clothes they wear to all those meetings?"

Surprise and appreciation flare in her dark eyes. "You're going to bug their clothes."

"Yes." Not a foolproof plan on its own, but cast the net wide enough and we'll pull something useful. We have a year to play this game, and once our faction is stabilized, we can afford to use up every bit of that time.

"Clever." She sits back and crosses one long leg over the other. "Now, about that conversation..."

I bite back a sigh. I could kiss her and let sex distract us, but Harlow's too stubborn to let this go, and we'll just be having an identical conversation when we finally surface from the orgasms. "Eli and I talked."

She's back to watching my expression closely. "He never would have hurt you or your brothers."

"No, he just facilitated my father getting his throat slit."

She raises her eyebrows. "Do you know what it was like living in the faction under your father? I'm not talking Old Town or those in his immediate circle. I'm talking about the rest of us."

Guilt bites at me, but I shove it down. "Yeah, I know. I would have moved on him within the year. I was just getting things into place." And, if Eli is to be believed, he moved first so I wouldn't have to.

The fucked up thing is that I *do* believe him.

I just don't know if it changes anything.

"Eli's father was just as much a monster as yours," she says quietly. "Things didn't get better right away, but once he died and Eli took over... He's done a lot to help the people who most need it. Not just funneling resources their way and enforcing the laws. He's set up programs and funding and all sorts of things."

The programs she mentioned this morning. The same ones that Eli and I spoke about all those years ago. Eli fulfilled the promises we made in a way I wasn't able to once my brothers and I were driven out of Sabine Valley. It's a strange sort of relief to realize that the people have benefited even if I wasn't here to see it. The only ones who bore scars from that coup are me and my brothers. And, I'm now beginning to understand, Eli.

Some would say it's a small price to pay, that the benefit of the faction outweighs any pain we experienced.

I can't quite argue that they're wrong.

"Harlow," I finally say. "If I told you to simply forgive Eli for all the shit he's pulled in the last five years, for all the times he's pushed you back to safety instead of letting you stand on your own, you'd shove those words right back down my throat."

She opens her mouth, seems to reconsider, and finally sighs. "Probably. I still care about him, but that doesn't change the fact things are complicated."

"Things are complicated with me and Eli, too. I talked to him. I'll think about it. That's all I've got right now."

She looks like she wants to keep arguing but finally nods. "I guess that's fair."

"So kind of you to realize it." I take her hand and pull her to her feet. "Let's go find something to eat and go to bed."

"Abel, it's like six."

"Yeah, I know." I tug her against me and slide my free hand down her spine to cup her ass. "I haven't had you naked in twelve hours. I'm going through withdrawals."

"You poor thing." She slides her hand up my chest and loops her arms around my neck. Harlow goes up onto her toes and presses her body against mine. "If you're that deprived, I suppose we could have a little appetizer before dinner."

"How thoughtful of you."

"Mm-hmm." She brushes her lips against mine, and then she's sliding down my body until she perches on her knees. I hold still as she undoes my jeans and pushes them down enough to free my cock. She gives me a slow smile, and then she's sucking my cock down, my length disappearing between her red lips as the wet warmth of her mouth encloses me.

In this moment, I can admit what I really want. Harlow as a full partner. Eli as a full partner. The three of us together in a carefully balanced trio that is all the stronger for the fact that it's not particularly traditional. From a purely analytical point of view, our strengths balance one another's perfectly. My brutality to Eli's twisty brain to Harlow's moral center. We could bring this faction to new heights.

We *will* do it.

Together.

28

ELI

It's been so long since I felt guilty that I barely recognize the sinking sensation in my chest as I move soundlessly through the passageways to the meeting place. All I can think about is Harlow's plea for me to work with Abel instead of against him, of how fucking much of a relief it was to finally air the truth between us.

Abel might be different than the man I grew up with, but I was wrong before—he's not his father. He hasn't lost his soul. If there's even a sliver of the man I used to know, we might have a chance to build the future we always dreamed.

But if I'm wrong, the people of this faction will pay the price.

I press my ear to the door, listening closely. It's late enough that most people aren't wandering the halls, and even if they are, they have no reason to be in the north wing. It was previously used by staff that we kept here, but it's been empty since the Paines took over. Still, it pays to be cautious.

Silence greets me.

I wait another thirty seconds, but when I hear nothing

concerning, I flip the latch that sends the door swinging soundlessly open. I step into the dark room and ease the door shut behind me. Nothing moves except me, which is how it should be, but I can't shake the feeling of being watched as I pad across the room and slip out the door and onto the balcony.

We're close to the wall here. Too far to jump, but I can still look down over the wall and to the street below. All is silent and still, but the feeling of being watched only intensifies.

If Abel found me here, it would shatter what little trust we've managed to build up between us.

Fuck, what am I doing?

Harlow is right. If I'm really intent on putting the faction first, then that means working with what we have instead of trying to wrest control away. I won't be able to take the faction back without killing Abel and all six of his brothers, and that's too steep a price, no matter how ruthless I've been in the past.

I turn for the door, but a shadow breaks away from the corner of the balcony, morphing into the familiar features of Marie. Even in the relative darkness, I can see the circles beneath her eyes. I glance at the door and shift closer, speaking barely above a whisper. "Disband the people. Call the whole thing off."

She jerks as if I've struck her. "You can't be serious."

"I am."

Marie leans forward. "I don't care what he's threatened you with; we'll see it through. You just have to hold out a little longer."

Something like true fear coats my tongue. I move before I can think twice about it, shoving her against the wall. I lean down until our faces are even. "Listen closely, Marie, because I will not repeat myself. If you move against Abel without my permission, I will cut down you and every single person you bring with you. I will not spare you, and I will not show mercy."

"You really are serious," she breathes.

"Deadly so."

"But..."

I step back and drop my arm. "I did not ask for or need your input. The safety of the faction is what matters, and this is the best way to ensure it. You will do nothing to endanger that."

For a moment, I think she'll argue with me, but she finally nods and drops her gaze. "Yes, sir."

"It's over, Marie. It's time for you to move on now. Let your people know." A bitter pill to swallow, but even if this works out with Abel, he won't trust any of my people at his back. Nor should he. All it takes is one misguided person to think that shooting him will be enough to put things back to how they were before. It's too big a risk to let them close.

Disbanding them means failing them in a way, but Harlow is right—the stability of the faction as a whole is greater than any one person or small group. All of my people are capable. They'll land on their feet.

They'll just do it without me as their leader.

"Yes, sir," she repeats. Her tone is off, no doubt because she's fucking furious with me, but she'll get over it eventually. Or she won't. Either way, I have bigger things to focus on now.

"Don't come back to the compound." I turn and walk through the doors and off the balcony.

I stop short, peering into the darkness. The feeling of being watched is so intense, I spend a good five minutes staring at the shadows and waiting for someone to reveal themself. But there's no one there. The room is empty, and I'm being paranoid. I shake my head and move to the door in the wall.

Fewer than ten minutes later, I'm back in my room.

I take a quick shower, but it does nothing to settle me. Ever since Harlow basically moved out, this room has felt like it's missing something vital. Some*one* vital. After last night, that sensation has only grown. I can barely look at the bed without remembering everything we did there. The sex, yes, but also the heady comfort of sleeping with Harlow and Abel. Something outside of the realm of possibility until last night.

I want it again.

I don't want to wait.

Despite the late hour, I pull on a pair of lounge pants and head down the hallway to Harlow's room. After the briefest debate with myself, I open the door without knocking. The room is dark, but she left the curtains open, allowing moonlight to spill into the space. It highlights Abel's large form at her back, his arm carelessly wrapped around her, holding her to his chest. The sheet is tangled around their hips, leaving both their torsos bare.

Longing nearly takes me to my knees.

I'd hoped they'd be awake, but I can hardly crawl into bed with them while they're both asleep. And the idea of waking them feels like shattering a perfectly rendered piece of art. No matter how bitter the idea of returning to my bed alone is, it's still the right choice.

I've been selfish enough for several lifetimes when it comes to these two. The least I can do is leave them in peace for tonight. I turn for the door.

"Eli." Harlow's soft voice stops me short.

I should leave. I've already done what I told myself I wouldn't; there's no reason to make it worse.

But I can't make myself walk away from Harlow. Or Abel, for that matter.

I turn and pad to the bed. She lifts a hand, and I let her take mine and tug me down to the mattress. It really isn't big enough for three people, but Abel's pressed against the wall, and there's a little space for me to stretch out next to Harlow.

There was a time early in our relationship when we were still so giddy and drunk on love that we would stay up most nights and lie just like this, sharing secrets in the intimacy of the dark. It's how she told me about her father and what she'd done to be free of him. It's where I confessed the truth of the night of the coup. Big secrets and smaller ones, too. Like how I'd always wanted a sibling but had seen the Paine brothers as stand-ins for those roles. How she loved kids but wasn't sure she wanted them for herself.

She runs her fingers over my knuckles. "Hey."

"Hey." This moment feels as fragile as a soap bubble. One wrong move will send us hurtling back to the space we were in during Lammas and immediately after. Hurt so intense, it feels like hate. Poisoned words and bitter actions.

I glance over her shoulder at Abel, but he's still relaxed in sleep. I don't believe it for a second, but I also appreciate him giving us the illusion of privacy. I lift our intertwined hands and kiss her wrist "I have something to say, if you'll hear it."

"Asking my permission now?"

I barely fight down a grimace. "Occasionally, I'm a slow learner." I hesitate, but she finally nods in the shadows. An indication to continue. "I'm starting to realize how thoroughly I've fucked up when it comes to you."

"Yes." The word is so soft, it's barely an exhale. "But I think we can agree it's a mutual fuckup."

She's giving me an out, but I want this verbalized between us. Five years of doing what I thought was right and ignoring all signs to the contrary. "I don't know when I stopped listening to you. You've just gone through so much, survived so much, that I wanted to provide you with a safe haven." She tenses, but I keep going. "But that was *my* goal, not yours. I realize that now. You never wanted safety."

"There is no safety in this world, Eli." She squeezes my hand. "Not really."

"Yeah, I get that now." I close my eyes for a moment. "I know apologizing isn't enough, but I'm sorry, Harlow. I could see how bad things were getting, but I thought if I just held you closer, if I just did all the old things that used to work, it would all figure itself out. I didn't realize I was suffocating you."

She exhales, long and slow. "I should have tried harder to talk to you."

"I don't know if it would have made a difference. I had a narrative in my head." It's humbling as fuck to realize how intensely I messed things up between us. A truth that it had taken Abel less than an hour to divine. "I meant what I said yesterday. I still love you. I'm not ready to let this go."

She's so still, I'm not sure she's breathing. "You told Abel the truth."

I glance over her shoulder, but he hasn't moved. Yeah, there's no way he's sleeping right now. I give a wry smile. "Yeah, though I don't know what difference it makes."

"It makes a difference." She reaches out a tentative hand and feathers her fingers over my jaw. "This is going to be messy, Eli. No matter what else is true, that is."

"Seems to me that the payoff is worth the mess." Guilt

feels like an almost physical thing in my chest and throat. "It took him an hour to realize what I'd spent five years intentionally not seeing. Even now, part of me wants to protect you. I *know* you're capable, Harlow. I've always known that. But my instinct is always going to be to step between you and harm."

She gives a sad little laugh. "I'm starting to realize that's a quirk of yours that doesn't only apply to me."

No, it doesn't. There's a reason I let so few people close to me. "That doesn't make it right."

"No, it doesn't." She strokes her hand down my neck and presses it against my chest over my heart. "Maybe we were always missing something, Eli. Maybe we were always missing *him*."

"I have no right to expect his forgiveness. Or yours."

"Maybe not." I can hear the smile in her voice even if I can't see her face clearly. "But the decision to forgive isn't about whether or not you deserve it or expect it. Either way, it takes time. We... Eli, we *have* time. We have an entire year to figure out if we can make it work." She presses her hand more firmly against my chest. "Will you promise to try?"

As if there's any question of it. "Yes."

"So will I." Harlow lifts her voice. "And you, Abel? I know you're awake."

He gives a dry chuckle. "I was giving you privacy for your chat."

"Well, you're involved in this, too." She keeps her hand on my chest and shifts over a little until she's on her back. Abel moves to accommodate her and props his head on his hand. Harlow reaches up with her free hand and presses it to his chest, too. "Will you try?"

"You already know what I'm offering."

She tenses. "I'm not talking about you and me, and you know it. Will you try with Eli?"

I find myself holding my breath. With everything between us, I have no right to expect this. Fuck, as recently as this morning, I was planning to do whatever it took to take Abel down. Just because I've decided to cling to hope doesn't mean he feels the same.

I can't blame him if he doesn't feel the same.

"Yes." The simple word lands like a bomb in this bed. "I'll give him the same deal I gave you, Harlow. Full partnership, open discussion over any changes I have planned for the faction. And at the end of the year, if you want to stay, Eli..."

I barely register that he's saying when he reaches over Harlow and hooks the back of my neck, jerking me to him so he can claim my mouth. "If you tell me want to stay, you better be damn sure that's what you want, because I'm playing for keeps."

Holy fuck, this is happening.

It's really happening.

It's not in my nature to trust. If something seems too good to be true, it undoubtedly is. The three of us in a real relationship... That feels the very essence of fantasy. We're too messy, too fractured as individuals. One of us will fuck it up.

But not tonight.

And maybe not tomorrow.

Maybe we'll have just enough time to sink into the possibility of us before it's ripped away.

As I lay between Abel and Eli, their breathing low and even in the darkness, I don't know how to battle the thought of what the future brings. I want this. I want this so bad, I have to fight not cling to these men until they have bruises of my fingerprints in their skin. At the same time, I know that giving myself over to this is simply a faster route to heartbreak.

We will fuck it up. How can we not when we're all still so new to the idea of happiness?

My breathing is coming too fast, too harsh. I think I might be panicking. The hysterical thought rolls through my head that I won't have to wait for my heart to break because I'm having a heart attack right now. Surely that's what's causing this horrible pain in my chest, the tightness that I can't inhale around. It's the only thing that makes sense.

I start to sit up, the need to move overpowering thought and reason, but both men tighten their arms around me. Abel shifts closer and props his chin on the top of my head, a strange sort of anchor, while Eli moves until his face is pressed to my neck, his breath a warm and steady exhale against my skin.

They anchor me, but it's not enough.

Here, in the dark, it's horrifyingly easy to spill my fears onto them. "We'll fuck this up."

"We'll stumble." I feel Abel's words against my back as much as I hear them.

I can't twist to look at him, not with them effectively pinning me between them, but it wouldn't matter anyway. I can't see him. "That's what I said."

"Stumbling is not failing."

Eli presses a kiss to my throat. "We won't fail, Harlow. Not now that we've decided on this path."

If I could draw a full breath, I might scream at them for being so calm, so collected right now. "One day ago, you were ready to literally kill each other. That kind of hate doesn't just go away."

"Neither does the friendship we had for twenty-eight years." Eli shifts down and presses another kiss to my upper chest. "Like Abel said, there will be stumbles. We're human, and we're bound to fuck up. The stumbles matter less than how we deal with them."

Abel strokes his hand down my side to squeeze my hip. "Don't shoot us in the knee before we're even out of the gate, sweetheart. Give us a chance to prove that this is possible."

Their calm, the weight of them against me, the feel of their skin sliding against mine... It starts to slow the frantically spinning thoughts in my head. The tightness in my chest doesn't entirely abate, but the urge to scream fades a little. "I'm afraid."

Afraid that I already care too much. It doesn't matter if this falls apart in a week, a month, a year. Or if it falls apart in ten minutes. I've loved Eli for years, and there's no denying that I've gone and fallen for Abel. There is no way I leave this situation intact.

Strangely enough, the realization settles me the rest of the way. The worst has already happened. I'm emotionally compromised. There's no reason to fear it happening because it already *has* happened. Now all that's left is to ride this roller coaster to the finish and hope it doesn't hurtle me off a cliff.

I take a slow breath. "Okay." Another breath, slower yet. "Okay," I repeat.

It's only then I understand what's happened. I frown into the darkness. "Neither of you were asleep."

"Hard to sleep when you're tense as a brick between us," Abel rumbles.

"I know you, Harlow." Eli shifts closer yet, sliding his leg between mine. It's not exactly sexual, but I'd have to be dead not to react to him touching me. Especially with Abel still tracing idle patterns on my hip and outer thigh. Eli presses another light kiss to my throat. "You don't trust it when things take a turn for the good."

I swallow hard. "Can you blame me? My track record proves that it's better to expect the other shoe to drop than to believe the situation is as it first appears."

"No, I don't blame you." His breath ghosts against the skin damp from his kiss, raising goose bumps over my skin and causing me to shiver. Eli's thigh slides higher to press against my pussy. "How can I when I'm part of the history you hold up to come to this conclusion?"

I open my mouth to deny it, but I can't lie to him. Easier to say nothing at all, but that's the coward's way out. "It took the two of us to get here."

"And it will take the three of us to get out again." His hand slides past me, and I don't have to see to know he's drifting his fingers over Abel's arm. "We should sleep."

"In a little while." Abel moves, wedging his free arm under me so he can reach around and cup one of my breasts.

I give a little breathy laugh. "You can't solve everything with sex."

"This isn't about solving things." He plucks my nipple, and I instinctively arch back against him. He grabs my hip and pulls me back even farther, until his cock is pressed against my ass. "This is about bolstering the foundations. Sex is the one time none of us are fucking this up. We'd be fools to ignore that asset."

Eli's rough laugh hardly sounds like him. "Sounds to me like you just want to get your dick wet again."

"With the two of you in my bed, can you blame me?"

"No." Eli slides down my body. Abel brings his other hand up so he's cupping both my breasts, pressing them together in a way that feels like he's offering them to Eli, who lavishes my breasts with kisses until I'm writhing and reaching for him.

Abel releases my breasts from one hand and snakes it between my thighs to stroke my pussy. I jolt, and then Eli's hand is there, too. They take turns toying with me, squeezing my thighs, dragging their fingers through my folds, spearing me with one finger and then two, and then both of them fuck me at once. It's overwhelming in the best way possible. Abel begins circling my clit while Eli wedges three fingers into me and, after a little adjustment, flicks his fingertips against my G-spot.

I'm trapped between their larger bodies, trapped with their hands on my pussy, trapped by pleasure. And just when I think it can't get any hotter, Abel's voice rumbles in my ear. "You're ours, sweetheart. No matter how bumpy the road gets, that's the fucking truth. And tonight, we're going to prove it to you."

Eli nips the underside of my breast. "Ours," he agrees. He keeps up that agonizingly good stroking against my G-spot. Abel shifts his touch, lightly rubbing back and forth over my clit with the length of his blunt fingers.

I open my mouth to say... I don't even know what. Instead a moan erupts from my lips, and then I'm coming, clamping down around Eli's fingers.

The bastards don't stop.

The orgasm swells to new heights, my body locking muscle by muscle and turning my lungs to lead. I make a gasping sound that might be a curse, and then it sucks me under entirely.

Eli and Abel do one of those silent communication things again. I don't know how they manage it when we're all barely more than shadow, but they turn me in their arms so that Eli is at my back, and Abel pulls my leg up around his hip.

Eli drags his hand up the back of my thigh to the small of my back. Such a small touch, but so fucking tender that I can barely stand it. Just another indication of how well we're balanced when we get out of each other's way. Soft and hard and intense and sweet. We can have all of it. Eli kisses my neck and presses a fingertip to my ass. "Let us claim you, Harlow."

It takes my pleasure-drugged brain several moments to understand his meaning. "Both of you?"

"Yeah."

I'm already nodding before I can think better of it. "Yes."

Eli rolls away for brief moment, and then he's back, pushing a lubed finger into my ass. "Let us do all the work."

I make a sound that might be a laugh. "That's probably for the best. I can't feel my legs."

Abel cups my chin and lifts my face to his. "Better get used to that, sweetheart." He kisses me as Eli pushes his cock into my ass.

We've done anal enough times that I know the drill. I shiver and relax into the penetration. He goes slow, working into me in short strokes that take him a little deeper each time, until he's finally sheathed to the hilt. He releases a shaky exhale. "You good?"

I shift back against him, rocking a little, and grin when he curses in response. "Yeah, I'm good." Better than good. Now that the aftermath of my orgasm is easing, my desire ramps up again. I stroke my hand down Eli's arm. "This isn't going to be the best position for this."

"I know." He gives a rough chuckle. "Hang on." He bands an arm across my hip and rolls onto his back, taking me with him.

Abel follows us, ending up kneeling between our spread thighs. I can't see his face clearly, but the way he drags his hand down the center of my body feels possessive in the extreme. He pauses to cup my pussy, idly pushing two fingers into me, and then his hand is gone, and Eli jerks under me. No doubt Abel is playing with his balls.

Eli curses. "If you keep doing that, I'm going to come before we even get going."

"Have to work on that restraint." But Abel says it almost kindly, almost like a promise.

He wraps his fist around his cock and presses it to my entrance. The slightest movement forward and he's pushing inside me. Both he and Eli are large enough on their own, but with both of them inside me...

It's almost too much.

I can't catch my breath. "Fuck, fuck, fuck."

Abel hesitates, his cock half buried inside me. "Sweetheart, talk to me."

"You're too big."

He goes still for one eternal moment and then laughs. It's a deep, happy sound, and I've never heard him make it before. He leans down and catches my mouth in a rough kiss. "You know how to turn a man's head."

"I'm serious."

"I know." He hesitates. "Do you want to stop?"

"Fuck no."

"Thought so." He gives another low laugh. "Eli."

Apparently no further words are needed because Eli starts kissing my neck, zeroing in on the spot that makes me go melty, and reaches between me and Abel to lightly circle my clit. I'm still so sensitive that I can't take much more pressure than he's giving me, but after a tense moment, I give myself over to it. To all of it.

Still, Abel doesn't move for several long seconds. "Ready for more?"

Eli sets his teeth against my neck. "You can take it, can't you, Harlow? Just let him sink in a little more. All this cock, just for you."

"I can take it." The words burst out, an instinctive

response. I don't want this to stop. I don't ever want this to stop.

"Good girl." Then Abel is slowly sliding the rest of the way into me. I fight to relax, to simply let him do the work, but a steady pressure begins to build to the beat of my racing heart. They hold perfectly still, caging me between their bigger bodies and, gods, it's almost too much.

Almost, but not quite.

Slowly, oh so slowly, I catch my breath. "I've got it."

Abel begins to move, fucking me in slow strokes. From the way Eli's hands tighten on my hips, he can feel every inch, too. Abel gives me a wicked grin. "Next time we do this, we're both going to fuck you, sweetheart."

"You're both fucking me right now."

"No, we're not." He executes another slow thrust, filling me again. Over and over again. It's too much, far too much, and then suddenly it's not enough. I start moving to meet his thrusts, which has me sliding on Eli's cock in my ass and, *holy shit*, that feels good. But it's still not enough.

"Please." I sob out the word.

Abel moves first, guiding us onto our sides and shoving one of my legs up and wide. He holds me easily and glances over my shoulder at Eli. They begin to move as one, easing out of me, leaving me horrendously empty, and then filling me up with both of them. I'm helpless to do anything but take it, and I'm barely able to do even that.

Between one stroke and the next, I come. I orgasm so hard, my toes curl and my foot cramps. Eli's seated in my ass, and he curses, barely pulling out of me before his come lashes my back. Abel isn't far behind, pounding into me and then orgasming with a curse. He kisses me and then leans over me to kiss Eli. "Shower, and then let's switch the sheets."

"We're going to have to buy more sheets if we keep doing this," I mutter.

"Worth it." Eli stretches in one long move, and then he's tugging me up and to the bathroom. Abel follows us into the shower a few minutes later, and when we return to the bed, it's to find he's already replaced the sheets.

This time, when we all lie down together, I'm too exhausted and content to do anything but sleep.

Happiness is a strange sort of thing. I'm normally inclined to align with Harlow's mistrust of it, but I can't help thinking that with the three of us finally on the same page, there's few forces in this world strong enough to tear us apart.

In theory.

The truth is, as always, significantly more complicated.

"Abel."

I open my eyes to find Eli on his side, his head propped on his hand. He's watching me with a strange look on his face. "You're heading out soon."

"Yeah." As tempting as it is to spend the day in bed, I need to trek out to Old Town to get their official answer today. My father would have demanded they deliver the answer to the compound, but they're going to agree to my rule; there's no reason to ruffle feathers with an unnecessary power play. I doubt I'll take either Harlow or Eli for this one, though. The first impression was the big thing that mattered. Now it's just tying up some loose ends.

"I..." He hesitates and huffs out a breath. "There's one

last thing that needs to be said."

"Eli—"

"I'm sorry I didn't come after you. I'm sorry I let eight fucking years go by without finding you... That I would have let more years pass." For once, he's not even attempting to bullshit. That raw tone is back in his voice, though I don't need to hear it to know this is the truth.

I reach out and lightly clasp his throat. "It wouldn't have mattered. We intentionally made ourselves hard to find, and even if you were successful, I might have killed you."

"I might have deserved it."

I shake my head slowly. I believed that when I first came back to Sabine Valley. I don't believe it any longer. "No. If I'd been thinking clearly back then, I would have realized that you'd try to handle shit so I wouldn't have to." I stroke the line of his throat with my thumb. "Love makes fools of us all, doesn't it?"

"That's what they say." His voice is so hoarse, it's barely above a whisper. "I want to make things right."

"We will. Harrow's right, though. It's going to be a long road." I slowly retract my hand. "When I get back from Old Town, I'd like to sit down and go over some plans with you and Harrow. I want more details on the stuff you've already implemented, a look at the finances, and to put together some ideas for the next few months."

His slow smile has my goddamn heart skipping a beat. Eli grabs my hand and presses a kiss to my palm. "I'd like that. I...I never dared dream that you'd end up back here, that we'd actually put into action everything we talked about when we were younger. It makes me happy."

Is that what this feeling is in my chest? Happiness? It's like sunshine in the middle of the night. "You might not stay happy once we start negotiating."

"Maybe. But I've missed our negotiations, Abel. I've missed a whole hell of a lot when it comes to you." He releases me. "You should go. Being late to meeting up with Old Town is a bad idea."

"Yeah." But I don't immediately get out of bed. "I'm glad you found her, Eli. I'm glad we both did."

We look down at Harlow, sleeping between us. The balance we never realized we needed, might have never looked for if shit didn't get so fucked up eight years ago. I'm not one to say that everything happens for a reason, because I don't believe that there's some higher power out there who's invested in humanity's suffering. But even I can't deny the gift Harlow is.

I carefully slip out of bed. Harlow was right last night. Her bed isn't anywhere near big enough for all three of us. We'll have to officially move into the other room tonight. Eli and Harlow might have some shit to say about that, some desire to create a little bit of distance now that we've blasted through so many walls.

Fuck that.

I have them. I'm keeping them. I'm tired of dicking around while I wait for them to come to terms with it. I brush my hand over Harlow's head and then Eli's and pull on my clothes. I feel his gaze on me before I make it to the door. Sure enough, when I turn around, Eli is watching me. "Take care of each other while I'm gone."

"You won't be gone that long. Be careful out there." He yawns. Without his glasses and with his hair a mess, it's like seeing him without his armor. It's just another reminder of how well I know this man, regardless of what pitfalls this life has thrown at us. When push comes to shove, there's one truth I can't escape.

I love him.

I doubt I ever stopped, even if rage made that love feel a whole lot like hate for a number of years. I open my mouth to tell him but change my mind at the last moment. Now isn't the time. He's even more skittish than Harlow is, but at least we have enough history that he might not call me a liar to my face if I told him the truth. Harlow, though? It will take time and patience before she accepts the thing I've recognized since that morning when she fucked me to purge away the memory of Eli. I don't know if it's love, but I've fallen hard for her. Eventually, it *will* be love, as long as we don't get in each other's way.

Eli closes his eyes and rolls over to throw an arm over Harlow's waist. Maybe I should feel threatened by how quickly they seem to have patched things up, but it's just one more barrier demolished between me and the ultimate end goal I've decided on.

The three of us. Together in every way that matters.

I force myself to turn away from them and slip out the door. I take fifteen minutes to shower and change, and then I go down to the kitchen for coffee. It's early, but Broderick is an early bird, and I want to sit down with him and start going over how to vet the people we need to hire to staff this place. We're getting by on our own right now, but eventually we'll have to start entertaining and the like, and we can't pull off that shit on our own. I'm sure Aisling and Ciar wouldn't be surprised if we served them grilled cheese— we're Raiders, after all—but to play the game properly, we need the proper weapons.

That means a chef. It also means either bringing a tailor in to work on retainer or losing our shirt in bargaining with Old Town. I'm not quite ready to take that step, and no doubt Broderick has ideas.

Eli will have some ideas as well. I'm still getting used to

the idea I can trust him. I don't *really* think this is all a ploy to get close enough to strike, not when he could have sunk a knife between my ribs or shot me dozens of times in the last few days. Plus, doing something underhanded like recommending a chef who intends to poison me and my brothers puts both Harlow and the rest of the Brides at risk. He might succeed in killing us, but the other two factions of Sabine Valley would come for his blood, so victory would be short-lived.

No, I believe him when he says he wants to try. I don't think that's simply the past talking, but I'm being cautious all the same. I want him, I love him, but I'm gambling with more than my life and safety. I have my six brothers, their six Brides, apparently now a bodyguard and Beatrix of the Mystics. Not to mention the people who have chosen to follow me over the years, currently housed in the barracks. They're all trusting me to guide us through.

I can't make decisions with my heart.

Fuck, I didn't think I even had a heart anymore.

I have the coffee going when I sense someone behind me. I don't hear him, but then I never hear Cohen when he walks. When we were kids, Donovan and Ezekiel once ambushed him and tied a bell around both his wrists so we'd have some kind of warning when he moved around. He didn't find it as funny as the rest of us, but then Cohen's never had much of a sense of humor. Being exiled from Sabine Valley killed what little softness he had. Or maybe that was losing Samson at the same time. Impossible to say.

One look at his face, and I know I'm not going to enjoy this conversation. "What happened?"

He glances at the coffee. "Enough in there for two?"

"There's a whole pot," I say mildly. Normally, that would be enough for several people, but Cohen doesn't sleep much, and his coffee intake reflects that. I grab two mugs and pour us each one. I pass his over. "It's not like you to stall."

"Not stalling. I'm fucking exhausted." He takes a long drink of coffee, apparently oblivious to the fact it should be burning the fuck out of his mouth. "I was doing rounds last night."

Another quirk of Cohen's, and one that's saved us more times than I care to admit. Ever since the fire, he can't rest until he patrols the entire premises of wherever we're staying. I lean against the counter. It's not like him to pussyfoot around. "What did you see that you think is going to piss me off?"

He lowers his brows. "Your boy was having a late night meeting on one of the balconies on the north side of the building. I just happened to see him, but if I'd been even a few minutes off either way, I would have missed the meeting entirely. It was that woman, the one heading up security when we got here. Marie."

Something cold sinks its roots into my chest, but I ignore it. Either I trust Eli, or I don't. "Did you hear what was said?"

"No. I was too far away. Light's not great there, either, which is probably why they chose that place to meet." He hesitates. "The conversation looked tense."

"I see." Hard to say one way or another what that means, but no matter how fucked up my trust is right now, I trust my instincts. Eli wasn't lying last night when he asked Harlow's forgiveness, and he wasn't lying this morning when we talked about the future. I don't know what the hell was going on last night on that balcony, but I refuse to believe he betrayed us and then crawled into bed with us. There's no fucking way.

"I followed her."

Of course he did. I bite down a sigh. "I don't suppose you took backup."

"I can handle myself." He doesn't have the grace to look apologetic for the fact he endangered his life. Again. "Besides, she didn't see me. Some fucking security person she is; she didn't even circle around before she went back to her little hidey-hole."

I make a winding motion with my hand. "And the rest."

His amber eyes go hard. "They're all there, Abel. At least a dozen people and a cache of enough weapons to level a small town. He's got them set up to take this faction back."

No.

I take a drink of my scalding coffee to avoid voicing the instinctive denial. No matter how much my brothers trust me, they know I have something of a soft spot for Eli. They'll focus on that instead of on my instincts saying this isn't what it looks like. "I'll take care of it."

Cohen gives me a long look. "You sure? You don't exactly see clearly when Eli's involved in a situation."

That's exactly why I can't claim this is all one big misunderstanding without evidence. I *know* Eli didn't betray us. I just do. But that doesn't mean the woman and her people aren't dangerous. Will Eli be willing to turn them over to prove his loyalty? *That*, I don't know. Still, I can't fix any of this shit right now, and I need Cohen to stop looking at me like he's about to crack my head open and check to see if I have any brains left. "I have it under control."

"The more you say it, the less I believe you." Cohen shakes his head. "I know you won't put off the meet with Old Town, but you *will* let me handle security. It'll be subtle, but now isn't the time to be reckless."

"No."

"Abel."

I shake my head. "No, for two reasons. I won't go into Old Town with excess security today for the same reason I wouldn't two days ago. It reeks of weakness and insecurity, and they'll see it as a sign that I'm afraid of them and react accordingly." I pause meaningfully. "And we flat-out don't have enough people to both defend the compound and put together that kind of security. I'm not going to leave this place and all of you defenseless."

He curses. "Fine, but you'll take me and the same two as last time."

"Agreed, as long as you understand you can't shoot first and ask questions later. Not in Old Town. We can't strike first, even if you see Eli's people."

He glares but finally nods. "If you get shot, don't come crying to me."

"Wouldn't dream of it." With that out of the way, I can't help needling him a little. "How are things going with your Bride?"

"It's best we stay the fuck away from each other."

Surprise stops me short. Cohen isn't exactly the most expressive of my brothers, but he sounds almost concerned. "What happened?"

"Nothing." He gives a long sigh. "Nothing important. She's just...soft. I know I'm a monster, but she really makes me feel like one." Something must show on my face, because he holds up a single hand. "She's not doing anything. We've just spent our lives around a certain sort, and I don't understand how a fucking Amazon princess is so goddamned soft and sweet. It's a head trip. Better for both of us that I stay away and Maddox handles things."

I consider whether I want to wade into the meaning behind *that* statement, and ultimately decide it's not my fucking business. "Let me know if there's anything I can do."

"Sure, I'll start now. Don't get fucking killed because you're thinking with your cock. I get it with *her*, because Harlow's priorities are obviously in order. But we have a whole lot of history with Eli, and the good doesn't outweigh the bad. You'd know that if you weren't all fucked in the head whenever it comes to him."

"He didn't know about the fire."

Cohen snorts. "You say that like it matters. His father and his people did it. If he didn't know, that just means he's incompetent. It doesn't absolve blame."

This is the other component of choosing to keep Eli— my brothers. Some of them will be more open to the idea than others, and that's a whole different battlefield to step onto.

It won't be necessary if Eli's betrayed me. Again.

No, damn it, *no*. He hasn't. I honestly believe that.

I still want to stalk upstairs, drag him out of bed, and shake him until he gives me some answers.

I take another long drink of coffee. I have to keep my head in the game. Right now, the priority is getting Old Town's official response and checking off that box. Once they've publicly declared their support, I can deal with Eli and his people. If he doesn't give them up...

I don't know what I'll do. Maybe offer them exile, but I won't be able to trust that the fuckers leave without some kind of proof. Exile didn't keep me and my brothers out of Sabine Valley indefinitely, after all.

A problem to deal with this afternoon.

Add it to the fucking list.

I try to go back to sleep, but the conversation with Marie still bothers me. It should be as simple as I gave her an order and she'll follow it, but I also gave her several orders since Lammas that she ignored. For her to stay out of the compound. For her to wait for my next move. She ignored all of them. I stew on that for far too long, running possibilities and not liking what I come up with. Ninety percent of the outcomes end with Marie striking on her own without my input.

I open my eyes and sit up. Harlow makes sleepy sound of protest next to me, but then she opens her eyes. There is no easing into wakefulness with her. She's asleep one moment and fully coherent the next.

She frowns up at me. "What's wrong?"

"I may have fucked up." It pains me to admit it, but it's glaringly clear that this isn't the first time. "Again."

Harlow sits up. "What's wrong?" she repeats. "What did you do?"

My instinct is to stay silent and take care of it myself, but I've tried doing it that way, and I almost lost Harlow as a result. Still, it takes more effort than it should for me to form the proper words. "Marie was in the compound last night."

"*What?*"

I hate the look on her face, the suspicion. "She left a note in my room, and so I had to meet her. I wasn't plotting."

Harlow stares at me a long moment. "Did you tell her and the others to stand by?"

Guilt flares, hot and poisonous. "Yes, on the first day. Last night I told her it was over. That I'm not going to fight Abel, and neither are they."

"Eli." Harlow drags her hand over her face. "What the hell were you thinking? No, don't answer that. I know what you were thinking." She flings the covers off us and climbs out of bed. "You have to tell Abel."

"He'll think I'm plotting against him."

"You *were* plotting against him." She turns around, glorious and fierce and naked in the late morning light. "Do you love me? Do you love him?"

I open my mouth to form the safe answer, but we've gone much too far for safe. Trying to withhold anything will result in losing the possibility of the future I've barely dared imagine. I'll lose Harrow for real. I'll lose Abel before I've truly come to terms with having him back in my life. I take a slow breath that does nothing to steady me. "Yes. Yes, to both."

"You have to tell him." She looks at the clock next to the bed and curses. "He'll be going into Old Town soon. How likely is it that Marie will decide today's the day to strike?"

I think back over our conversation and grimace. "Likely enough. She'll know that Old Town is delivering their official answer today. There's no telling when Abel will next be out of the compound, and she's not the most patient sort.

She has the time and place and opportunity. It might be months before another chance presents itself."

Harlow's face goes even paler. "You have to tell him, and you have to tell him now. We can fight about the fact you met her last night and didn't say a single damn thing to us later. If Abel dies, we won't be able to fight about anything at all."

If Abel dies.

If Abel dies.

Funny how the idea shocks me to my very core. Funny since a few days ago, I wanted him dead for what he'd taken from me, for what I assumed he'd done to Harlow. Or not so funny at all, because the thought of the world without Abel in it leaves me dizzy with fear. "He can't die."

"He's human. He's just as vulnerable to death as the rest of us." She says it so calmly. "There's also a chance they'll use the opportunity to strike the compound instead. I have to find Broderick and tell him."

"Yes." Of course she'd see the possible moves just as easily as I do. Harlow's always been more capable than I've allowed her to be. We stare at each other for a moment more and then simultaneously burst into action.

Harlow runs into the closet while I pull on the clothes I was wearing last night. By the time I yank my shoes on, she emerges wearing jeans and a T-shirt. "Find Abel. Tell him the truth."

"I will." Even if it breaks the fragile trust that's bloomed between us. I can live with that as long as *he* lives. With each minute that passes, I become surer that this is when Marie will direct her team to strike. Old Town might have agreed to Abel's terms, but they won't move to defend him if he's attacked on their street. Hell, they wouldn't move to defend *me* even after five years of ruling this faction because Old Town doesn't give a fuck about anything but Old Town.

Harlow and I part ways at the door. She heads toward the hall where Broderick and some of the other Brides are staying, and I rush to the stairs and down to the main floor. The house isn't exactly quiet, but I can't shake the feeling that I'm going to be too late.

That I'm already too late.

I catch sight of a familiar figure near the front door. I haven't seen him since Lammas, but I'd recognize Gabriel Paine anywhere. He used to follow me and Abel around when he was just a little kid. Fuck, we used to essentially babysit him. I shove the thought away. "Gabriel."

He tenses, and his expression is unreadable as he turns to face me. "Eli."

"Where's your brother?"

"You're supposed to be in your room."

Obviously Abel hasn't updated the rest of the household on our new status, not that I blame him, but it's slowing me down right now, and I don't have time for this shit. I don't hesitate, stalking to Gabriel and grabbing him by his collar. "Listen to me, you little shit. Abel is in danger, and I need to get to him right now. Where the fuck is he?"

Gabriel sinks a punch into my stomach. Even bracing for it, it knocks the breath out of me. He breaks my hold on his shirt and steps back. "If you ever touch me again without my permission, I'll fucking kill you."

I nod and draw in a rough breath. "Where is your brother?"

"Old Town. He left fifteen minutes ago."

Gabriel definitely pulled his punch, but my stomach still feels like it's lodged in my chest. "Harlow has all the info. She's looking for Broderick."

"Then she has it covered." Gabriel turns to the door. "Let's go."

Alarm flares. "You're not coming with me." I used to change this kid's diapers. It doesn't matter if he's twenty-eight now. When he was five, he couldn't say his Ls well and called me Ee-eye. If I take him and he gets killed, I'll never be able to live with myself.

"You seem to think you have any say in the matter." Gabriel pulls a phone out of his pocket and types out a quick message. "If you pull some shit, my brothers will know."

Which means he just texted them all. Good. I eye his phone. "Any chance of getting Abel on the phone?"

"No. He doesn't check it when he's doing business. And Cohen's shit at texting, so he just ignores the group chat." Gabriel shakes his head. "Let's go."

Arguing will just waste further time. Maybe it's paranoia that has the voice in the back of my head screaming that every second counts, but I'm not willing to ignore it. "Okay."

We grab a truck from the parking lot of the compound, and Gabriel climbs behind the wheel. "If you're trying—"

"Stop threatening me, and hurry the fuck up. My former head of security has at least twelve people organizing an assault on your brother. How many people did he take with him?" I don't believe in the gods, but I find myself praying as Gabriel takes the turn out of the compound on two wheels. Surely Abel was as smart and paranoid in this as he's been about everything else up to this point.

"He took Cohen, Iris, and Maddox."

I wait, but the list stops there. "Last time, he had people on the street."

"Last time was different." Gabriel tightens his grip on the wheel. He favors their father's coloring the same way Abel does—dark hair, dark eyes—though his build is leaner. "It's just them this time."

"Fuck." I brace my arm against the doorframe as we take another corner. We're at the east entrance to Old Town, but Gabriel doesn't stop there. He rounds the block and takes the street that runs parallel. I recognize where we're headed a few moments before Gabriel slams to a stop near the dead end in the center of Old Town that houses the food trucks.

This is where Abel will meet with Chinh and the others.

It's also where I would set up the ambush if I were Marie.

The years peel away, and I'm twenty-eight, sprinting through the streets with Bauer's blood on my hands, seeing the haze of fire against the night sky and knowing that I'm already too late. I didn't reach the house in time that night.

I have to reach Abel in time today.

I barely wait for the truck to stop before I throw open the door and jump out. Gabriel is right on my heels. I have the thought that he's making sure I don't escape or some shit, but it doesn't matter as long as he stays close. It's not until I'm squeezing through the gap between one of the food trucks and the wall that I realize a gun would be really useful right now. I have no weapon, nothing but my body and my words.

It will have to be enough.

But as I hear voices raised in anger and fear, I already know it won't be. Too late. Too late. I am always *too fucking late*.

Gabriel and I burst out from behind the food trucks and into chaos. A shot sounds somewhere close, and the midday crowd of Old Town scatters. Some people duck into businesses. Some hunch over against the walls as if that will do a damn thing to protect them from a shooter.

We sprint for the knot of people in the middle of the tables. I catch sight of Chinh being bodily carried away by two of his grandsons, and then I see Abel, Cohen, and the others.

Time seems to slow down between one step and the next. I register things in flashes. Abel's clenched jaw. The woman standing in front of him, her dark hair shining in the sunlight. The gun in her hand. So unassuming, almost boring, and yet representing the end of my and Harlow's chance at happiness.

A mere ten feet separate them.

Marie will go for a body shot. She's got a sadistic streak, and she'll want to slow down Cohen and the others. Either to pick them off or to get away.

She's going to *shoot Abel*.

I pour on the speed. I hear Gabriel curse behind me as he gets knocked off-course by a pair of men running in the opposite direction, and it's just as well. This will all be over shortly.

Fuck, I should have apologized to Harlow earlier. I should have tracked Abel down and told him the truth the second I realized he didn't die in that fire, instead of letting the years spin out between us. I should have done a lot of things.

Five feet between us now.

Abel catches sight of me, and the look on his face is horrible. I expect resignation or anger, but he looks fucking terrified. Not for himself. Of course the bastard is never worried about himself. His mouth moves and I might not be able to hear the words through the rushing in my ears, but I can read his lips well enough.

Eli, stop!

No. Fuck that. *Fuck that.*

I mourned this man during the long hours it took to put out that fire the night of the coup. And then I spent eight eternally long years mourning him a second time. I can't survive a third. I refuse to.

I wish we had more time.

I wish the three of us had all the time in the world.

It's okay. Harlow and Abel will take care of each other. They'll be okay. Better than okay. The knowledge gives me one last burst of speed.

Marie's hand moves on the gun, her finger tightening on the trigger.

I throw myself forward with everything I have, covering the distance between Abel and me in one giant leap. I hit him in the chest as something hot and painful blossoms in my back.

A woman is screaming. Someone fires a gun, and the screaming stops.

None of it matters because Abel's got his arms around me, and he's lost that terrified look. No, now he's fucking furious, and it's the most beautiful thing I've ever seen.

He lowers me to the ground, which is a good thing because my legs don't seem to be holding me all that well. "What the fuck is wrong with you?"

It takes me two tries to speak. "She was going to shoot you."

"And now she shot *you*." His face spasms as if he's holding back too many emotions. "I'm laying you down. Do *not* pass out. Do you hear me, Eli? If you fucking die on me, I will march down to the doors of hell and fight the devil himself to get you back." He eases me to the ground on my stomach.

This is nice. The world spins a little less now that I have

my cheek against the concrete. I laugh a little, but it hurts, so I stop. "Harlow would kill us both."

"Yeah, she would. So don't die and get us in trouble."

I open my mouth to tell him that I won't, but darkness takes me before the words can leave my lips.

They say you never know what you've got until it's gone. I kneel in a pool of Eli's blood and feel him slump into unconsciousness. Two things become terrifyingly clear in that moment.

The fool really does love me, or he wouldn't have jumped in front of a bullet with my name on it.

If I don't do something, and fast, he will die.

The world around me snaps back into motion. I register my youngest brother, Gabriel, and relief almost makes me weak. If he's here, we have a chance. I yank my shirt off and shove it against the bleeding wound in Eli's back. The woman who shot him lies in the street a few feet away, her eyes gazing sightlessly at the sky. Cohen doesn't miss.

I put pressure on Eli's wound and look at Cohen. "Find the rest of them and kill them. Gabriel will handle this, and I'll watch his back. Hurry, before they scatter."

For once, he doesn't argue with me. He simply motions at Iris and Maddox, and they take off, following the trio of men who appeared with the woman. They won't be the only ones, not if Cohen's estimates are correct, but we'll flush out the rest later.

Gabriel reaches us and drops to his knees. He peels the bloody shirt away from Eli's back and then presses it into place and gives me a long look. "What do you want to happen?"

My brothers are loyal to the bitter end. This would be a clean way to get rid of Eli. No one can say that we were behind this, not when his own people shot him in front of witnesses. The thought of him dying leaves me so fucking cold, I have to focus hard on not shaking. "Save him, Gabriel."

He nods slowly. "I'll try, but you're asking the impossible. The bullet is lodged inside him. I don't think it hit an artery based on the fact he's still alive, but that just means it will take him a few minutes longer to bleed to death. If we try to put him in a truck and drive him back to the compound, you might do more damage." He pauses.

"Tell me the rest." My voice hardly sounds like me. It's almost as if the words come through a long tunnel that's closing in around us.

"I'm not a surgeon, Abel. I can do simple bullet wounds, but I'm liable to do more damage than the bullet did if I start digging around in him." Another pause. "I'm sorry."

Gabriel, because he's Gabriel, even sounds it.

"I can help."

I look to find a petite Vietnamese woman standing before us, two of Chinh's sons at her back. It takes my brain several long seconds to kick into gear and identify her. Cam, the only daughter of Chinh's only daughter, Tien. Cam doesn't work for the family business, so my information on her is less complete than on the others in the family. She's a... "Surgeon."

"Yes." She nods, all business. "I can try to save this man." She gives me a hard look. "In exchange, you'll owe my grandfather a boon."

I almost laugh. Of course Chinh would have me bargaining while the man I love is dying beside me. I clear my throat, trying to think, but it's no use. All I can focus on is the stickiness of the street beneath my knees and Eli's increasingly faint breathing. There's no time for bargaining. Chinh could ask for the sun, and I'd do my damnedest to find a fucking rocket ship and go lasso the fiery bastard. "Done."

She looks over her shoulder at her uncles. "The stretcher."

Things happen quickly after that. They produce a stretcher from somewhere and load Eli onto it as carefully as if he were made of spun glass. Cam directs them to take him to the main building where the Phan family resides and then turns to me. "You'll wait here."

"The hell I will."

"You'll wait here," she repeats slowly, as if I didn't hear her the first time. "I will need to focus if he has a chance of surviving, and you pacing and glowering will distract me. Sit with your brother, and wait." Apparently she doesn't need a response because she disappears after her uncles.

Gabriel hauls me to my feet and guides me to a nearby bench seat. He pulls out his phone and frowns at it. "Broderick has the whole compound locked down. There was a small team that tried to climb the wall, but Ezekiel and Donovan took care of them." He grimaces. "Cohen hasn't checked in, but it's only been a few minutes."

"He'll be fine." I still sound too distant, too empty. If Eli dies... Fuck. Thinking about it hurts. I should have made the time to talk to him again this morning after I found out about that late-night meeting. If we'd talked, it would have given him a chance to come clean, all three of us the opportunity to make a plan that doesn't involve Eli bleeding to death on the street like a fucking dog.

If he dies, Harlow and I lose everything.

Harlow.

I give myself a shake. "Have Broderick send Harlow here with Finnegan or one of the others. It doesn't matter who, but don't let her come alone."

Gabriel's thumbs hover over the phone screen. "You sure that's a good idea?"

I'm not sure of anything anymore. For the first time in so long, I'm not thinking shit through. I'm scared out of my mind, and I just want Harlow here so we can wait to hear about Eli together. "Do it."

"Okay."

We settle down to wait. Ten minutes later, Cohen, Maddox, and Iris appear. Maddox is cradling his arm, and Iris has a spattering of blood across her face, but they look otherwise unharmed. Cohen drops onto the bench next to me. "It's taken care of."

I nod at Maddox. "You okay?"

"Just a scratch."

Knowing Maddox, that could mean anything from a literal scratch to a stab wound needing stitches. I motion at Gabriel. "Take care of it."

Maddox rolls his eyes, but after Gabriel disappears behind the food trucks and reappears with a first aid kit, he allows my brother to patch him up. It's not nearly enough of a distraction, but his snarling and Cohen telling him to shut the fuck up and let Gabriel take care of it fill the pocket of silence that's formed around our little group.

People have come out of the buildings, but most of them

wisely decide they had somewhere else to be, and the street is nearly deserted. It's just as well. I'm not eager for a witness to this shit.

I stare at the body of the woman who shot Eli. Who would have shot me. Marie, his former head of security. She's just a fucking human on the small side with a normal face; she hardly looks like the type of person who can burn my entire world down with one bullet.

I jerk my chin at Cohen. "Get her out of here."

He nods and hauls the body over his shoulder, disappearing down the street in the direction of where we parked. Iris shadows him, her shotgun held easily in her hands. She'll watch his back.

That's when Harlow shows up.

I've never seen a more welcome sight in my entire fucking life. I swear to the gods, the clouds part and a sunbeam shines right on her light red hair as she rounds the corner, moving at a fast enough clip that Finnegan is obviously struggling to keep up despite having a good six inches on her.

She sees me and changes course, picking up her pace until she's running. I meet her at the perimeter of the tables and pull her into my arms. "I'm so fucking sorry."

"Where is he?" She clings to me, but she's looking over my shoulder. I can tell the exact moment she recognizes the stain on the concrete because she goes tense. "Is he alive?"

"He's in surgery. Chinh's granddaughter is handling it."

Harlow leans back to look up at me. "He didn't betray you. I know it might look like that with the ambush, but I swear he didn't."

"I know." It's the truth. Eli wouldn't be Eli without some underhanded bullshit going on. Loving him means accepting that about him. "That fucking fool jumped in front of a bullet for me."

Her hands tighten on my shirt. For one moment, I think she might pass out, but Harlow's made of stronger stuff than that. Hell, I think she's made of stronger stuff than either Eli or I am, too. She takes a slow breath. "Let's get in there, then."

Gabriel clears his throat. "She told us to wait out here."

"You wait out here. We're going in." She takes my hand and turns, tugging me behind her. I glance back at my brothers, silently conveying the order to monitor the entrance. Finnegan nods and turns to Maddox, speaking in a low voice. They'll keep us covered.

I lace my fingers through Harlow's and keep pace with her. "Pissing off Chinh is a bad idea."

"What did you promise him?"

Of course she would realize he didn't do it for free. "A boon of his choosing."

Harlow flinches. "Okay." She faces the front door to the Phan place. It's made of glass and has their name on it in stylish gold print. "I'll take care of this."

"Harlow, if he—"

"Eli will be fine," she says firmly, the faintest tremor in her voice. "Cam is the best fucking surgeon in this city. She will save him. I'll do the rest."

Before I can ask her what the fuck she's talking about, she steps through the door, leaving me to follow in her footsteps. I could haul her back onto the street and demand the details of whatever is going on in her head, but the truth is that I trust her to be thinking clearly while my head is all fucked up with worry over Eli. No matter what Harlow's feeling, she's more than proven she can still function under pressure. I trust her, full stop.

So I keep my mouth shut and follow her into the building. It's nearly identical to how they had things set up when my father still ruled this faction. Soothing green walls, a fountain in the corner that's a piece of art on its own, and a seating area filled with tasteful brown furniture.

Behind the receptionist's desk is Cam's mother, Tien. She's a short woman with a rounded figure, a sweet disposition, and a penchant for baking desserts. If rumor is accurate, sometimes those desserts are poisoned. She glances up as we approach and leans over to look at the floor. "You're tracking blood into our place of business."

Harlow seems to morph before my very eyes. Gone is the fear and worry, replaced by cold calm. She gives a sharp smile. "It hasn't been the first time and won't be the last."

Tien sighs. "I suppose you're here to cause further trouble."

"Hardly. We'd like an update on Eli." She pauses. "And I would like a word with your father."

"He's busy."

"No, he's not." She sounds so damn cold. Dangerous. That's my girl. "Now, Tien."

Tien's gaze flicks to me. "This woman speaks for you?"

I slide my hands into my pockets to mask their shaking. When I speak, I almost sound normal. "She's my Bride and my partner. She does."

Finally, Tien shrugs. "Come along. I can't have you sitting out here and smearing blood all over the place."

We follow her into the back and through a series of hallways. She finally leads us into a waiting room that's damn near identical to the first, right down to the fancy fountain. "Please wait here."

It takes fewer than five minutes before Chinh appears. He's as unflappable as ever, as if his sons didn't cart him away from the violence the way parents would haul a child. He smiles at Harlow. I've seen that same smile a thousand times in the past. It's warm and cheerful and as much a lie as anything else in Sabine Valley is. "Hello, dear."

"Hello." Her smile is tight and comes nowhere near thawing her eyes. "How is Eli?"

"My Cam will take perfect care of him. From what I hear, she's removed the bullet and is patching him up as we speak."

I want to breathe a sigh of relief, but his words just make Harlow tenser. Her hands fist at her side before she seems to make a conscious effort to relax them. "We will honor the bargain...as long as he survives."

Chinh tsks. "The bargain was struck, the terms set."

"Chinh, that bargain was a shit one, and you know it. If Abel had been thinking clearly, he would have included the caveat of Eli surviving." She leans forward, not quite close enough to get in the old man's face, but close. "You're a savvy man, and a savvy man might instruct his granddaughter to ensure Eli doesn't make it through. Looking at it from your perspective, your life would be simpler if he didn't. Civil war isn't good for business, whether it's within an individual faction or between one faction and another."

Chinh folds his hands in front of him, dark eyes shrewd. "I am a businessman."

"Yes, you are." She motions at me without looking away from him. "Eli is valued to both of us. If he dies by your granddaughter's hand, we will dig out every last root of the Phan family tree and burn it to ash and then salt the ground. Your legacy will vanish overnight."

I tense, but Chinh smiles. "I'm delighted to see that you've finally found your feet, dear." He transfers that smile to me. "And that you recognize a valuable asset when you see it."

"What she promised stands," I say roughly.

"That's all well and good, but I told the truth when I said Eli is doing well enough. You should be able to see him soon." He turns and walks out of the room.

Harlow slumps, and I have to rush forward to catch her before she hits the ground. I guide her to a chair and sink down into a crouch before her. "That was stunning, sweetheart."

"I feel like I'm going to puke." She rubs her hands over her face. "He must have weighed the odds and decided not to kill Eli before we got here."

I agree. "Even so, it drew a very clear line in the sand. I suspect the Phan family will think twice before they fuck with us."

"Hopefully." Her lower lip trembles. "I'm really worried about Eli."

"Me, too."

"I'm terrible at waiting."

I rise and sink into the chair next to her. "So am I. But we're together. That counts for something." I take her hand, letting her presence anchor me, and settle in to wait for as long as it takes.

33

We wait in that room for two hours and thirty-six minutes. Abel manages to sit still for about ten minutes, and then he's up and pacing for the rest of the time. I might be doing the same, but I'm not sure my legs will hold me. Sheer determination got me from the compound to Old Town and through the conversation with Chinh, but I have nothing left right now except fear.

Eli can't die.

Not when we have so much left to figure out. Not when I finally, *finally* have settled into the idea of a real future where the three of us are together and happy. It seems cruel that just last night he and Abel were reassuring me that this was real, that I had nothing to worry about, and now I'm sitting here, waiting for news on if Eli will survive.

"Abel."

He turns on his heel, in the middle of another circuit around the room with his phone in his hand. It's been buzzing regularly, no doubt with updates from his brothers. "Yeah?"

"I love you."

His expression goes soft and then hardens. "Save it."

I blink. "What?"

"That sounds a whole lot of goodbye or some kind of final words before everything goes to shit. Tell me again after Cam shows up to let us know that Eli's fine and awake and already making himself a pain in the ass." He crosses to me and takes my hands, pulling me to my feet and into his arms. "I love you, too, Harlow. And I'm not just saying that because I'm scared shitless right now."

"I know." Abel's never lied to me. It seems too soon to feel this way, but despite the rocky start, we've eased into each other's lives with barely a ripple. We just *fit*.

We fit better with Eli in the mix.

The door opens, and Cam steps in. She looks exhausted, sweat dampening the hair at her temples and lines imprinted on her cheeks from some kind of mask. She gives us a tired smile. "He's pulled through. He's a lucky son of a bitch, because if that bullet was a few inches lower, it would have fucked up his internal organs instead of just lodging in muscle and bone. He's not awake, but you can see him now."

Abel and I cling to each other's hands as we walk through the door and down yet another series of halls into a room that would be at home in any hospital in the city. I give Cam a long look, and she shrugs. "Sometimes the family business gets complicated."

"I understand." Honestly, this is something we should have in the compound, too. I add it to my mental list, but most of my focus is on the man in the hospital bed.

Eli is several shades paler than normal and has a series of tubes hooked up to one arm. Bandages wrap around his torso, seeming to wash him out even more.

Cam stops next to the bed. "Once he wakes up, we can arrange to have him transported to the compound, but after that, his health is on you. He'll need to see another doctor to be monitored, and if he tries to do something noble and bullheaded, he's going to rip open his wound and probably bleed out all over again. I highly suggest you prevent him from doing that."

"We will." Even if I have to tie Eli to a bed to make it happen. I can't stop myself from reaching out and pressing my hand lightly to his back, measuring his slow breathing for several long moments. He's alive.

He's alive.

Cam leaves at some point, and Abel drags two chairs over to the side of the bed. And then we wait, and wait, and wait.

I'm not sure how long it's been when Eli stirs and opens his eyes, but it's the happiest sight I've ever laid eyes on. I squeeze Abel's arm, and he jumps to his feet. "You fucking *fool!*" He plants his hands on either side of Eli's hips and leans over him. "What the fuck were you thinking, jumping in front of that bullet?"

Eli blinks up at him, looking a little lost. Cam must have him pumped up on a boatload of drugs, because he simply says, "I love you. I couldn't lose you."

Abel opens his mouth, no doubt to deliver a blistering lecture, but then curses and closes the distance between them and kisses Eli. It's quick and thorough and when he lifts his head, he growls. "Don't you ever do some bull-headed shit like that again."

"I make no promises," Eli says faintly. He looks at me and holds out his hand. "The compound?"

Trust him to gather his wits about him faster than anyone I've ever met. "Broderick took care of it. Half the team tried to infiltrate the walls—I think they were headed for the supplies—but they didn't have a chance to harm anything." From the contents of their packs, they planned to poison us. Which means there will be questions for the Mystics at some time in the future; if there's a poison in Sabine Valley, it's sourced back to their faction. I'm sure Fallon will have some thoughts on that as well, which is an unexpected boon. Shifting the Mystic Brides' allegiance in our direction would have been impossible yesterday, but today, one of their own decided that they were expendable. Dropping that information...

I shake my head. We'll figure it out later, once we're home and have had a chance to get Eli looked over. "We need a doctor on staff."

"We need a lot of people on staff." Abel sinks onto the edge of the bed next to Eli. "But yeah, doctor takes precedent."

"I have someone I can call," I finally say. "I don't know if they'll do it, but I can ask."

Abel passes me his phone. "Go for it."

It takes two minutes to make the call, and Rae surprises me by agreeing to come check Eli out and consider the position, which means they're between jobs again. Not surprising given their attitude—every surgeon I've met has a god complex, but Rae is on another level. It doesn't help that they're something of a prodigy. Or they were when they were a teenager.

It takes a few more hours before Cam announces Eli fit to travel the short distance back to the compound. Abel gets things arranged with his brothers, and there's a convoy waiting for us as we help Eli into a wheel chair and get him out the back door to the street that runs parallel to Old Town. Abel lifts him into the middle truck despite his protests, carefully setting him on the bench seat. I climb up after him while Abel goes around to the driver's seat.

I lace my fingers through Eli's. I can't stop touching him, can't stop trying to reassure myself that he's real. "I was really worried about you," I say quietly.

"I know." He squeezes my hand. "I'm sorry." He waits for Abel to put the truck in drive before continuing. "I promise to loop you both in on any meetings or plots in the future."

It's the best offer we're going to get. I squeeze his hand again. "Good."

"I've half a mind to whoop your ass once you're healed." Abel follows the lead truck around the corner and toward the compound. "But I guess your promise will suffice."

Up ahead, the compound comes into view. Something in my chest eases. I used to feel like this place was a cage, but for the first time in years, it feels like a physical representation of safety and security.

It feels like home.

That feeling has nothing to do with the place and everything to do with the two men in the truck with me. I twist to look at them. "I love you. Both of you."

Eli gives a faint smile. "We love you, too."

Abel grunts. "Look, it's a three-way of love and all that shit. Can we talk about this once we have the doors shut and locked behind us in the compound?"

"I want to make the compound home. A real home." I reach over Eli and brush my fingers over Abel's knuckles where they're whitened on the steering wheel. "Someplace that's really safe for us and your brothers and their Brides and your people. I also want to expand that home to the entire faction in a way we've never tried to do it before. So that everyone is safe."

"Why stop there?" Abel replies. The shadow of the top of the compound moves over us as we drive through the doors. "Why not make all of Sabine Valley home?"

I give him a look. "Isn't that what you've been planning from the beginning? Sabine Valley under Paine rule?"

He opens his mouth and then huffs out a laugh. "Yeah. It is."

Eli shakes his head. "I knew it."

It would be smart to tell him no, to redirect that ambition to peace. But you know what? Fuck it. Abel's already put his plan in motion, and we have a year to lay down the foundation to enact it. Not a lot of time in the grand scheme of things, but with the three of us putting things into motion? It's possible.

It's more than possible.

"We start with the compound."

"Deal. We start with the compound." His gaze flicks to Eli. "But first we get Eli on bedrest until your doctor shows up."

"Yes."

"Stop talking about me like I'm not here," Eli grumbles, but it's half-hearted at best. He's already looking a little green around the edges from the car ride. The faster we get him somewhere stable, the better.

I wait until Abel puts the truck in park to say, "So we're doing this. Together."

"Together," Eli echoes.

Abel gives us both a fierce grin. "Fuck yeah. With the three of us working together, Sabine Valley doesn't stand a chance."

Not a conventional happily ever after. Not really. But it's one I trust with two men that I love. And I couldn't be happier.

～

THANK you so much for reading Abel! I hope you enjoyed Abel, Harlow, and Eli's wild ride! If you did, please consider leaving a review.

Need more of these three in your life? Sign up for my newsletter to receive a bonus short!

The Paine brothers' story continues with BRODERICK. Broderick never wanted a Bride, let alone one as volatile and dangerous as Monroe. He's loved his best friend, Shiloh, for years. *She's* the woman he'd choose if he had a choice. Unfortunately for him, Monroe picks up on that love *very quickly* and sets about tormenting him by seducing Shiloh...

JOIN my Patreon if you'd like to get early copies of my indie titles, as well as a unique short story every month featuring a couple that YOU get to nominate and vote on!

CHECK out this sneak peek of BRODERICK!

I ALWAYS KNEW it would come to this. Handfasted, not to the woman I want, but to the heir to the Amazon faction. Monroe Rhodius stands next to me, her silence doing nothing to detract from the danger rolling off her in waves. She's gorgeous, of course; all the ruling Amazon family is. Long blond hair, pretty green eyes, and a mouth painted blood red. She only comes up to my shoulder, which is the most surprising thing about her. Given her reputation, I thought she'd be bigger.

It feels like the ceremony occurs between one blink and

the next. The Herald says the appropriate words, binds my hand and forearm to Monroe's with pretty silk.

There's no going back now.

My older brother, Abel, leads our group through the crowd to the waiting trucks. My six brothers, our seven Brides—eight Brides now that Abel has had his way. No one stops us, but we still rush out of there as if someone will sink a dagger between our shoulder blades at any moment. Old habits die hard.

It's only when we've piled into the back of one of the trucks that Monroe breaks her silence. She gives me a slow smile that feels more like a threat than an expression of joy. "Bold move, Broderick Paine. You're going to live just long enough to regret it."

I already regret it.

Not the necessity of these theatrics. They *were* necessary. Arriving back in Sabine Valley during the feast of Lammas, one of the four times when the city's three factions come together in ritual designs to maintain peace. Abel stepping into the ring and issuing his challenge—seven fights, a Bride the reward for each victory. By taking Brides from each faction, we forged a forced peace. They can't move against us for the year we're hand fasted. Technically, we can't move against them, either, but it's more than enough time to get our roots in deep and prepare for the coming confrontation.

If we survive this year.

The problem with taking Brides from the enemy factions? It means we're essentially married to that enemy, that we've invited them into our beds and our lives and close enough to harm.

I stare at Monroe. I'm not as hard as some of my brothers, nowhere near as cold as others, but I've survived eight years of exile and that's put scars on my soul that will be there until the day I die. "Cross me, and I won't be the one who regrets it."

Monroe gives a throaty laugh, a sound so full of the promise of sin that it sends a bolt of desire straight to my cock. Damn it, I don't want to react to her. It doesn't matter that she's mine for the year, that she's beautiful. None of that changes the truth.

She's not the one I want.

Not the one I love.

Monroe lets the jostle of the truck bounce her nearly into my lap. She leans against me, her breasts pressing to my upper arm. "I'm a Bride. That means this handfasting isn't official until it's consummated."

I clench my jaw and stare at the buildings we pass. We cross the bridge into Raider territory—territory that used to be ours, at least until we were betrayed and exiled. It doesn't look like home. I don't know if I'll ever consider it home again. "I'm aware."

She drags her finger down the center of my chest and over my stomach. I catch her wrist before she reaches the band of my jeans. "No."

Monroe gives another of those throaty laughs. "I was going to do my duty—no oathbreaker, after all—but this is going to be *fun*."

"What?" I finally drag my gaze to her face. She's got features too perfect to be real. It almost hurts to look at her.

She tugs her wrist out of my grip. "You have to do your duty, too, Broderick." She draws out my name as if tasting it for weakness. "Even if you hate every moment of it."

"I'm aware." My voice is too hard, giving away how much I don't want to do this. Damn it, I have to get myself in line.

She's been in my presence less than thirty minutes and she's already digging around beneath my skin.

"Like I said—fun."

We pull into the warehouse that we've been secretly staying in while we got everything lined up for the feast. It's as secure as we could make it, which is why it's where we'll spend tonight. Where we'll consummate the handfasting with our respective Brides.

We climb out of the trucks, piling into the open space around Abel and his two Brides. Harlow, we planned on, an extra little revenge against the faction that used to be ours. But Abel's second Bride? I study Eli Walsh, the man I used to consider a friend who was nearly a brother. The man who stood by while our father and people were killed in a coup eight years ago. *He's* running the Raiders now, which more than speaks for itself.

I hope Abel knows what he's doing.

My brother looks at each of us in turn, his expression hard. "Consummate the handfasting tonight. No exceptions. Get it done."

There's nothing to do but exactly what he said; get it done. I turn and head for the bedroom I've been using, and I'm relieved when Monroe keeps pace with me. I don't want to have to drag her behind me. No matter what we want, this has to be done tonight or the handfasting won't hold. It's not necessary for normal handfasting, but Brides are different. It's an old tradition in Sabine Valley, a way to ensure peace for a period of time. But it only works if the rules are followed to the letter.

We're nearly to the door when the person I dreaded seeing appears. Shiloh. She's flushed as if she's been running, her dark hair pulled back in a ponytail. Her gaze skates over Monroe and lands on me, and the relief on her face has guilt worming through me.

Shiloh.

My best friend.

The woman I've been in love with for years.

"You're okay." She doesn't touch me, doesn't close the last bit of distance between us, but she gives me a trembling smile. "I was worried."

"I'm okay." I speak softly, just like I always do around Shiloh. She's a capable fighter and scrappy as hell—she has to be to run with our group—but there's something soft about her that even years of violence hasn't hardened. It's something I cherish.

Her smile goes a little strained. "I, uh, I guess I'll see you tomorrow."

"Yeah." I can't look at Monroe, but I *feel* her watching us. She's gone still, a predator scenting weakness. I clear my throat. "Tomorrow."

Shiloh searches my face, gives me one last faint smile, and then she's gone, weaving her way through the trucks and disappearing from sight. I turn toward the door, but Monroe is there, pressing herself to my chest and staring up into my eyes with a devious smile on her red, red lips. "Broderick Paine, you've been holding out on me. Who was *that* delicate little creature? She looks tasty."

Alarm blares, and it's everything I can do to keep it out of my tone. "She's no one." Better that Monroe believe that than literally anything else. *Especially* the actual truth.

Her smile widens and her green eyes light up. She's never looked more beautiful than she does in this moment. She's never looked more dangerous, either. "We both know that's not the truth. It looks to me like she's *everyone* to you." She presses her nails to my chest, a cat toying with its prey.

"I changed my mind. This isn't going to be a drag. This is going to be fun."

Gods alone know what Monroe considers *fun*.

I'm suddenly sure that I'm going to find out...and that Shiloh is going to bear the cost.

PURCHASE BRODERICK NOW!

ACKNOWLEDGMENTS

Huge thank you to my readers for taking the journey to Sabine Valley with me. This series promises to be one of the most challenging and rewarding I've ever worked on, and I'm really excited to share the Paine brothers' stories with you!

Endless thanks to my developmental editor Manuela Velasco for helping me make this book the best version of itself. Thank you to Lynda M Ryba for copy editing the hell out of this book! Much love!

Special thanks to Sabra's Bun Tschi for coming up with the name Sabine Valley for this city, and also to Melody of the Heaving Bosoms for all the Amazon inspiration. You, my friend, are an honorary Amazon forever!

Writing can be a very solitary experience, so I cannot thank my friends enough for being support squad, brainstormers, and just endlessly being there for me and my increasingly worrisome "what if" questions. Asa Maria Bradley, Piper J

Drake, Andie J Christopher, Nisha Sharma, and Jenny Norbak, THANK YOU. I'd be lost without you. Biggest of thanks to Tasha L Harrison and everyone in the Word-makers group for keeping me company while drafting this book! I appreciate those word sprints more than I can say!

Always at the bottom of the acknowledgements list, but at the top of MY list: Tim. Thank you, babe. I love you. Your faith in me never fails to motivate the hell out of me. Love you forever and always.

ABOUT THE AUTHOR

Katee Robert is a *New York Times* and USA Today bestselling author of contemporary romance and romantic suspense. *Entertainment Weekly* calls her writing "unspeakably hot." Her books have sold over a million copies. She lives in the Pacific Northwest with her husband, children, a cat who thinks he's a dog, and two Great Danes who think they're lap dogs.

www.kateerobert.com

Keep up to date on all new release and sale info by joining Katee's NEWSLETTER!

CPSIA information can be obtained
at www.ICGtesting.com
Printed in the USA
BVHW031818250623
666343BV00030B/368